CROSSCURRENTS
Stories of People in Conflict

Richard V. Barry

Winterlight Books
Shelbyville, KY USA

CROSSCURRENTS: Stories of People in Conflict
by Richard V. Barry

First Printing – December 2007
ISBN: 978-1-60047-165-0

Printed in the USA

Table of Contents

Introduction

Whenever I begin reading a collection of short stories – and I do read a lot of them because that's the genre I've been writing in for the past few years – I always think of the famous line from the movie "Forest Gump": "Life is like a box of chocolates: You never know what you're going to get."

It's strictly a matter of personal taste which stories will, or will not, appeal to me. So, like Forest sampling the chocolates, rejecting the nougat while searching for the raspberry cream, I dive into a short story collection, free to skim, sample and taste, and then skip those stories that don't satisfy my literary sweet tooth. I honestly cannot say what I'm looking for or what will speak to me from the first paragraph and hold my interest. I know I'm a sucker for intelligent writing: an original phrase; dexterity with sentence structure; compelling choice of words; above all, stylistic clarity and an interesting voice. But that's ***how*** a writer tells a story, and sometimes beautiful writing can be hollow, like a chocolate shell with no filling.

When it comes to the ***what***, I can never predict what character will grab my interest, what plot will engage my curiosity, what situation or outcome will capture my imagination, or what theme will linger in my memory. I recognize that to be both intellectually and emotionally involved with a story brings me the greatest satisfaction.

I don't analyze a story when I'm reading it, if it's a good one. I go with it, enter its world, live in it, and savor it. After I've read a good story, of course, as a writer I want to know what makes the story moving or arresting or impressive. But often the results of my reflective analysis vary widely, and I'm forced to some vague, general conclusion that those stories that show the human heart in conflict – angry, sad, confused, resentful, longing or defeated – and that shine a novel beam of understanding on a character's condition, thereby giving me a sharper insight into our human condition, these are the raspberry creams I'm looking for. But I also love the chocolate covered cherries: the stories that tickle my funny bone and hold a mirror up to our human family for us to see how silly or vain or narrow-minded or superficial we can be, and that gently poke fun at us for taking ourselves, and everything, too seriously.

To you, dear reader, I offer the following samples. My attempted range is wide: humorous, nostalgic, solemn, satiric and possibly discomforting. The scope encompasses small character studies to big-themed dramas. A writer uses material from everyday life: personalities observed, a casual remark, a scene witnessed, stories told, a lingering image, a newspaper item, a haunting theme, all filtered through one's own current and past experiences. But that is only the starting point, the basic scaffolding. Writing fiction is, for me, engaging in a mysterious, magical process, for I never know where my characters, once they come alive on the page, will take me, or how my story will tell me where it wants to go.

Wander and browse and sample, and, with any luck, you'll find, I hope, some stories that match your taste. Don't like the caramels? Try the chocolate peanut clusters. Enjoy!

Word Made Flesh

The mystery has continued for a long time and has never been solved. Years later, across the country, people would say that the singing voice was unlike any other they had ever heard. But when pressed to particularize its unique qualities, they became frustrated. They'd stumble about in their memories, mentioning one thing or another, and then acknowledge their inability to share the full impact of their listening experience without resorting to trite expressions like "the voice of an angel," or "sent shivers down my spine." The impression they conveyed to any listener was vague and rambling: a voice that was felt more than heard; that magically resurrected dormant longings and disquieting passions while also being intimate and comforting.

Everyone agreed that the tone was startlingly clear and full, and that the vocal range was remarkably broad. Some people found other nuances to share. It was a naturally warm, rich voice, they said, resonant with complex shadings and expressiveness. It was pure and sweeping, they said, unadorned of all pretense, hesitancies or tricks. It was enhanced, they said, by a joyful exuberance that sounded guileless and soulful. Above all, they said, it communicated a pathos that was haunting.

From the aggregate responses one thing seemed clear: The secret behind the ensuing public frenzy, the initial adulation (and the subsequent horror and mass deception) seemed to lie in striking some primitive emotional chord, evoking within each hearer a personal response that caused the voice to soar beyond the physical senses and, in some inexplicable way, to speak directly and profoundly to individual hearts. The young, the old, the ambitious, the indolent, the privileged and the forlorn: all were drawn centripetally into the chorus of praise and wonderment, the emotional catharsis, and the compelling need to hear more.

Journalists, politicians and clergy were quick to point out that it wasn't just the voice but also the message. The singer, a female of indeterminate age – for her voice mingled the freshness of youth with the smokiness of maturity – and unrecognizable regional origin, sang a new song, never heard before. From the day the unsolicited tape arrived at a small broadcasting station in Texas and a young intern, appeasing boredom on an idle afternoon, listened to it, the singer was thereafter coupled with the one song the tape contained, like Kate Smith's "God Bless America," or Bob Hope's "Thanks For The Memories." As circumstances unfolded, to the distress of the public and endless speculations by commentators, this would be the only song forever associated with the singer, an indelible imprint on the collective American psyche.

With only a piano playing softly as background, the long song told a saga of broad sweep and unlimited possibilities, for while it dealt with particulars, it seemed to capture universal truths, to symbolize the essence of human experience. The lyrics spoke of love and loss, adversity and triumph, fear and hope, betrayal, courage, sacrifice and renewal. The soft, lilting melody lodged instantly in the brain and the refrain, plaintive and resolute, soared in semi-military cadence to galvanic effect.

From the bored intern to the local disk jockey to the station manager and engineer, to those hearing it across the county and then across the state and the nation for the first time, people felt moved, startled, charged, uplifted. And the remarkable voice and the new song lingered on their minds like wisps of smoke curling inside their heads, replaying itself hypnotically, as everyone continued with daily routines but, somehow, inexplicably, considered themselves transformed, ennobled, comforted. The station's phones lit up under an avalanche of calls that first day, inquiring about the singer and her song, requesting that it be played again and again, and asking where it could be bought. People telephoned and e-mailed their friends and relatives who tuned in to that station for the first time. And the number of listeners swelled and the calls kept coming and the song kept being played and the word went out and the buzz kept spreading and other stations picked it up and, like some internet virus, the song raced along the intersecting network of airwaves until the entire country seemed wired together in one gigantic party line, joyful, giddy, dizzy with speculation about this mysterious, transcendent phenomenon. Who was this singer – this singer with the marvelous new song that made us feel so alive, so connected, so patriotic, so much better off than we were before we heard it? The nation was entranced and the mystery deepened and the song played on, as questions increased, rumors multiplied and demands exploded.

There seemed to be no clues for identifying the singer. The envelope in which the tape had been sent to the radio station had been discarded. The tape itself had a paste-on label with the printed message, LISTEN TO THIS! While it was assumed that the singer was from the area that the local station reached, no one could be sure. Still, day after day, the station's announcers made a plea for information about the singer or for the singer to come forward and identify herself. No response. The local newspaper took up the call and each day featured on its front page an update on the quest to learn the singer's identity. Since no information was forthcoming, the paper's writers creatively developed articles on rumors, speculations or incidental human interest angles – anything to keep the story going and the paper's circulation rising.

When the song gained national attention, the media frenzy was unrelenting. Television crews from all the major networks descended on the little radio station where it all started and interviewed every employee including the station's custodian who nervously explained that all paper refuse was automatically shredded before being carted off to the town dump. The station's young intern received the lion's share of the attention at first, for having discovered the tape. Nineteen years old, painfully shy, afflicted with both severe acne and a bad stutter, he froze whenever anyone tried to interview him. No degree of professional journalistic charm could coax anything more than three-word answers from him, with each word laboriously elongated or repeated, as sweat poured from his forehead and his shoulders jerked forward in a defensive hunch. His acute discomfit was magnified on television, causing empathic audiences to feel intensely uncomfortable. One enterprising reporter tried to interview the intern's parents but discovered that they belonged to a religious fundamentalist group that considered all communication media the devil's workshop. They slammed the door in the reporter's face after threatening to let their dogs, heard snarling and barking in the background, loose on the next person who came on their property. The hoards of reporters quickly lost interest in the intern and searched for more congenial, charismatic players in this red-hot unfolding drama.

The station's one secretary, Mrs. Eugenia Baker, received much media attention. This lady, whose sole connection to the celebrated event had been to take the incoming mail containing the tape from the postman and deposit it in an in-basket, seemed to welcome the national focus on her. Fifty-eight years old, the mother of four grown children and grandmother of seven toddlers-to-teenagers, Mrs. Baker had taken the secretarial job at the station three years ago, which was two years after her husband had died and his insurance money had subsequently run out. A woman of kind disposition and secret romantic yearnings, she had been delighted to leave her full-time role as housewife and babysitter for grandchildren and enter the work force. Her typing skills, picked up in high school before dropping out to marry Mr. Baker when she found herself pregnant by him, were rusty; her Gregg steno, completely forgotten and her filing, erratic. She had only a basic knowledge of computers thanks to the tutelage of her oldest granddaughter. But she was warm, dependable and jolly, and people immediately liked her. Her other asset was a pleasant speaking voice that soothed callers when she answered incoming calls.

The first time Mrs. Baker had a television camera pointed in her direction, accompanied by a question from an out-of-town reporter, she fled to the bathroom. After calming her nerves, combing her gray hair and applying some lipstick, she returned to her desk, ready to take the spotlight. For all the years that she had adored celebrities, admiring their nonchalance as they navigated serenely in front of cameras, flashbulbs and clamoring reporters, she was amazed to find that she was now, momentarily, the cynosure of all eyes. As more and more media people competed to interview her, so enthralled was Mrs. Baker with her new, but long fantasized, celebrity status that the workings of her mind took strange twists. Casually and innocently, while speaking to a group of reporters surrounding her desk, she let it be known that on the day of the tape's arrival she had felt an odd rush of excitement, a presentiment of unusual things to come, as she walked from desk to desk, the magical package held firmly against her ample bosom. Given the extraordinary nature of what followed, the public embraced Mrs. Baker's professed intuition as part of the growing myths surrounding the song.

The nation took this gregarious and chatty lady to its heart. An archetypal American grandmother of sweet disposition, plain language, direct gaze and innately shrewd perceptions, Mrs. Baker found herself catapulted into a national orbit along with the hysterical response to the unknown singer and her energizing song. Some of the words Mrs. Baker uttered to a reporter in the morning, she was thrilled to note, were being heard on television that very evening, as her image was sent across the country. She loved it; she courted it greedily. And the press kept coming.

Mrs. Baker, or Ginny as the press now intimately referred to her, after learning that this was her lifetime nickname, had been interviewed at her desk, in front of the building housing the radio station, in her home, beside the church that she attended and even at the local diner where she and other station employees went for lunch. Eventually, as she watched herself repeatedly on television, surrounded by excited relatives and friends, she noticed that not only did the camera make her look heavier, more jowly, but also that her comments had a repetitive pattern, a limited focus and were quickly growing stale.. She pondered this predicament, fearful of exhausting her time in the spotlight. During the next interview conducted by a national female reporter of such prominence that she, herself, was regarded as a major celebrity, the same questions had been asked. Every ounce of human interest had been extracted from the few prosaic facts surrounding the secretary's marginal role in an ordinary-turned-extraordinary occurrence. Mrs. Baker, sensing the tension in the celebrity reporter's body language and feeling the arc of interest sliding down, suddenly found herself saying, "I think I know who the mystery singer might be." The reporter's head jerked up, her eyes grew large and her voice was raised to underscore the exciting revelation that might be unfolding.

"Who do you think it is?" the reporter asked, giving dramatic pause between each word, picturing millions of viewers leaning forward expectantly, eyes riveted on Mrs. Baker for her response as the television camera zoomed in for a tight close-up.

Mrs. Baker smiled sweetly and waved her hand in a dismissive motion.

"Well, of course, I can't be sure so I really shouldn't say, but I have my suspicions and I just have to follow up before I know for certain."

She seemed on the verge of saying more but then checked herself and smiled sweetly again at her interrogator. She had been startled to hear herself claim to know the identity of the singer and had been equally startled by her nimbleness in devising an equivocal response to the reporter's direct question. In rapid-fire succession the reporter now hurled a series of questions probing Mrs. Baker's titillating assertions, but Mrs. Baker, hands folded demurely on her lap and eyes fixed firmly on the ceiling as if in deep thought, heeded the cautionary bell that was ringing in her head and dexterously deflected this barrage. The reporter's mood changed from excitement to annoyance.

Hopeful that she had dangled just the right lure to keep everyone interested in her, Mrs. Baker calmly assured the reporter that she would be the first to know, once Mrs. Baker was certain. After the cameras stopped recording, the reporter continued her probing but to no avail. Then she tried to persuade Mrs. Baker to sign an agreement, making formal what the grandmother had promised during the interview in terms of an exclusive disclosure. Again, the cautionary bell was sounding and Mrs. Baker sweetly demurred.

On returning home, Mrs. Baker went immediately to bed, not to sleep but to wrestle with her conscience. Was she deliberately deceiving the entire nation? Was she a liar? Her new addiction to the public spotlight was being weighed against a life of simple, straightforward values and sound ethics, leaving little room for self-deception. Yet her inner longings and unabashed pleasure with her new status prompted her to explore her discomfort with a subtlety that she had never summoned before. Lying in her bed, clutching the covers around her chin, she found herself acting as her own lawyer in exploring a defense for her actions. It occurred to her that she could think of at least a half-dozen people who could, possibly, perhaps, maybe, in a long shot, be the mystery singer. With this thought lodged foremost in her mind, she smiled and turned over on her side. A course of action was taking shape: She would investigate those people more and she would tell that ferocious reporter first if any of her suspicions proved true. With this resolution formed, reconciliation between her words and actions seemed possible, and Mrs. Baker suddenly felt sleepy. She had pitted her conscience against her desires and found a novel position that allowed both sides to claim victory. Soon she was sleeping soundly.

* * * *

Forces beyond Mrs. Baker's control were soon turning the national spotlight away from her. First one person, then several people, followed soon after by several dozen more people, came forward claiming to be the singer. Even a three-hundred-pound man from Hawaii swore that he had sung the song in falsetto. Female rockers, rappers, choir members, trained opera singers and those who heretofore had only sung in the shower but dreamed of stardom, now moved onto the national stage for a fleeting second, and the more outrageous the claimant, the more attention she received. The public was temporarily amused by this sideshow and the media, recognizing the entertainment value of all these pretenders, went along with the joke. But, like too many Elvis impersonators, the novelty quickly became stale while the curiosity about the real singer deepened.

Across the country radio stations received thousands of unsolicited tapes from people claiming either to be the singer or to be as good as the singer. Disk jockeys in the sophisticated metropolitan areas played the worst tapes for comic contrast. The very few singers with exceptional voices also got their tapes aired and one or two minor careers were launched. But no voice came close to the unique sound and electrifying effect of the original. All the attendant publicity served to intensify the public's interest in the singer whose song, no matter how many times heard, continued to inspire and thrill.

* * * *

The next event thrust Mrs. Baker back into the spotlight but in the same peripheral context as her original whirl. A man whom she would later describe as having a "strange aura" appeared at her desk and asked to see the station manager. In the weeks since the famous tape had been discovered, the radio station had become a very busy place, with reporters, television crews, pretenders and local citizens buzzing in and out. Mrs. Baker considered herself the guardian at the gate, which added professional heft to her emerging celebrity status. Although still pleasant, she was becoming more discriminating about who passed her desk. The man standing before her appeared to be in his late thirties, tall and lanky, with a sallow complexion and flaxen hair that fell limply across his forehead. He wore jeans and a wrinkled suit jacket and held an old fashioned gray fedora in his hands, nervously playing with the brim. His clothes and his posture were both crumpled. His shoulders sloped and his head hung forward and his arms seemed too long for his body. Then Mrs. Baker looked directly at his face and was startled to see that his eyes were different colors: one pale blue and one deep brown. She had seen this distinctive feature in dogs but never in a person. It was unnerving.

"What is this in reference to, please?" Mrs. Baker politely inquired. She was speaking more formally these days and imitating office protocols that had been demonstrated in the classic movies of the 30's and 40's, which she loved. The man shifted his weight from one foot to the other while his body realigned itself in asymmetrical patterns.

"It's about the song," the man said in a low, reedy voice, without smiling. His thin lips barely moved when he spoke. Mrs. Baker knew what song he was referring to, since all visitors seemed to come about that song. During this exchange she was in the process of alphabetizing some files on her desk and she decided that she would protect the station manager from this man with the crumpled clothes, ungainly posture and alarming eyes. Yet always polite, she asked, "What about the song?

"I wrote it," he said quietly, staring down at his fedora.

Startled, Mrs. Baker stopped her file arranging and stared at the man. Of all the people who had come to her desk in the past weeks, no one had made this claim. There was something so unusual, so quietly intense about this man that she found herself believing him. She asked him to wait and quickly moved across the office to the station manager's door, opened it and stuck her head in. The manager was finishing a phone conversation and waved her in. She stood in front of his desk as he said the formal pleasantries expected at the end of a business call, and when he had hung up she told him about the claim of the man in the main office.

"Ray, there's just something about this guy that makes me believe him. Almost," she added, revealing her own confusion.

Ray Anderson listened and said nothing but his temples throbbed. He was sixty-three years old with a full head of white, closely cropped hair matched by great tufts of unruly, arching white eyebrows that pulled the top half of his face upwards, while the heavy creases descending from the corners of his nose and mouth to his heavy jowls pulled the lower half down, giving him the appearance of a deeply conflicted man. But Ray Anderson was not conflicted; he was resigned, most of the time. He had been this small station's manager for over ten years and had come to this position from a much larger, more important station after a drinking problem had ruined his career aspirations. As a younger man brimming with ambition he had discovered that his eagerness for advancement was not matched by his ability to handle the pressures of increasing responsibilities unless bolstered with alcohol. The more responsibilities he assumed, the more alcohol he consumed, until the scales had tipped against him and the alcohol far outweighed the responsibilities and he was fired. After a successful stay at a rehabilitation clinic, he and his long-suffering wife had returned to the area where they both had grown up and he grabbed the first job that was offered to him. In coming to this rural station in a backwater Texas area at the age of fifty-two, he knew that this was the end of the line. But he also felt a sense of relief that he was no longer anxious, self-doubting and discontented, and he no longer had the recurring dreams about walking a high wire without a net or flying above the clouds only to suddenly start plummeting to earth. Now he didn't have to prove anything or build his resume. He just had to do his job and stay sober. His newly acquired maturity and low-key manner blended well with small town life. The years passed and he found himself resigned to his fate, not really fulfilled but not unhappy, and with resignation came a sense of ease and contentment. He was two years away from retirement when his life turned upside down and that damn song pushed him back into a world that was relentlessly intrusive and messy. His peaceful cave was being invaded by all the carnivores. He increased his attendance at AA meetings, refused to answer frivolous questions from out-of-town reporters and was consequently characterized as grumpy and taciturn. Reporters played him up as a real-life version of Lou Grant from the Mary Tyler Moore show, which increased the nation's interest in him. He prayed that all the attention would pass quickly and when it did not, he was grateful that Mrs. Baker, whom he had always liked, was shielding him from it whenever possible. Yet now she was urging him to see this man. Begrudgingly, he nodded his agreement.

Mrs. Baker returned to her desk where the man was still standing silently in a lopsided contour and she led him to Ray Anderson's office. Following the usual station protocol, once the man was inside Ray's office, she closed the door and returned to her desk. Her curiosity and excitement mounted as the minutes ticked by and the door remained closed. What was happening in there? Why were they in there so long? Was he really the writer of the song? Was the mystery of the singer about to be solved? What about her hints to the lady reporter that she might know the singer's identity? Had she ever seen this man before? Would this be the end of all the attention she had received? Or, would she again be caught up in a headlong rush of frenzied reporting on the singer's identity and all the details and people involved in this drama? Nearly breathless with anticipation, Mrs. Baker didn't pretend to be doing any work but sat in perfect stillness, her eyes riveted on her boss's door.

Thirty minutes passed. When the door finally opened, the lanky man had donned his gray fedora and with long, jagged strides, scurried out of the office, looking straight ahead, intent on escape. Before Mrs. Baker could leave her seat, Ray was at her side.

"Ginny, I've got to make some calls. No interruptions, please," he said in a weary voice and disappeared into his office, with the door again closed.

Mrs. Baker was too polite to run after her boss, barge into his office and unleash a fusillade of questions. In frustration, she sat at her desk and monitored the light on Ray's private extension while pretending to continue her alphabetizing of files. The light stayed on for a long while and then went off for only a few seconds before lighting up again. Her excitement mounted as this pattern continued for over an hour. When the light finally went off and stayed off, Mrs. Baker could restrain her curiosity no longer. She tapped on Ray's door and peeked in. She saw her boss with his elbows on his desk, his hands holding his head, his eyes staring straight ahead. The slight rise of his shoulders with each breath was the only discernable movement.

"Excuse me, Ray," she said in a near whisper, "Do you need anything?"

For what seemed like a very long, awkward time to Mrs. Baker, he remained both motionless and silent. Then without lifting his head from his hands or shifting his eyes, he spoke. His voice was calm but flat.

"Ginny, I think we'll soon know who the singer is."

Bringing his head up and staring past his secretary, he added, "The whirlwind has just begun. God help us all!" Then dropping his hands in a helpless gesture, he announced that he was going home.

Mrs. Baker was bursting with questions but she saw the defeated look in her boss's eyes and her gentle, grandmotherly nature overcame her eager curiosity and she said nothing. She patted him on the back after he had put on his coat and she watched him walk, dejectedly, out of the office.

* * * *

Ray Anderson never revealed the details of his conversation with the strange looking man to the press or the public. The day after the closed-door meeting, he was grumpy and terse and Mrs. Baker knew when to leave him alone. He left the office in the early afternoon and told her that he was taking a short trip and would return to the office sometime the following day. She asked no questions but she felt sure that this sudden trip was connected to the man and the singer. She was tempted to drop some hints to the reporters still buzzing around the station, picturing how eagerly they would hang on her every word and how this revelation, no matter how unspecific at present, would renew their attention on her. But this temptation was overcome by her fierce loyalty to her boss who, she knew, expected her to keep his confidences. So she said nothing and nervously awaited his return. When he did return the following morning, he had the same weary, dejected look that he had worn two days earlier when he had left.

Mrs. Baker followed Ray into his office with his phone messages. She also carried a Diet Sprite, his habitual mid-morning drink. Settling into his leather chair, he asked her to stay but first to close the door. He then told her, in his typically plain, laconic style and in the strictest confidence, the broad outline of everything that had taken place in the last twenty-four hours. Mrs. Baker leaned her elbows on her boss's desk, her eyes never leaving his face as she absorbed the exciting, bizarre details of recent events.

The man's name was Noah Cantrell. During his meeting in Ray's office he had convinced the station manager that he was the writer of the now-famous song and that he could arrange a meeting with the singer, who was his sister, Rachel. Noah explained that Rachel was a recluse who had not ventured out into the world since she was a child. Her link to everything was through the radio and television. She loved to sing and he liked to compose songs for her. He had sent in the tape of Rachel's singing his latest composition as a lark, thinking how thrilled she'd be to hear her voice on the radio if the nearest local station played it, but he had never expected the reaction it received. Even the President of the United States said it was now his favorite song after The Star Spangled Banner and Rock of Ages. So overwhelmed was his sister by the outpouring of admiration and acclaim that she, anonymously, was receiving, as reported on all the television and radio stations, that she told her brother it might be nice to sing the song for a live audience and meet some of the people who lavishly praised and admired her singing. He had grave reservations about this, but her whimsical notion grew as each day increased the enormous popularity of the song and the endless speculation about the extraordinary singer. So he had come to the station where the song had first been heard.

Knowing his sister's extreme shyness, her total unfamiliarity with the world, her intense sensitivity and her fragile nature, Noah was torn between protecting her and fulfilling her wish. And there were other complications. He didn't elaborate. Could Mr. Anderson meet her and talk to her and give them the benefit of his advice? Reluctantly, Ray Anderson agreed, for he understood that any role he played in revealing the singer's identity also meant the loss of his secure, anonymous little world. But the unique gifts that this singer could bring to the public far outweighed, in Ray's mind, his nervous reluctance to be thrust into a national spotlight, however fleetingly, as her discoverer

* * * *

The next day, following Noah's directions, Ray had driven west about eighty miles into a barren, desolate area that had prospered long ago but was now nearly deserted. Passing only a few ramshackle houses and dilapidated trailers, he came to the broken gates of a former estate. In the distance on a high knoll he could see a huge, crumbling mansion. Several pillars on the front porch had collapsed; all the windows were broken and the roof had gaping holes. As instructed, Ray turned left at a fork in the long driveway and came quickly to a much smaller house that, while shabby and paint-starved, seemed still intact. Noah was waiting for him at the door.

Ray paused in his story, took a drink of his Diet Sprite, then continued but in a heavier voice. Mrs. Baker let her lively imagination soar and filled in any blanks with vivid details.

The inside of the house was dark, musty and worn. Noah, clearly awkward in the role of host, ushered Ray into a small, cluttered living room filled with frayed, oversized furniture and dominated by a grand piano. He offered Ray a choice of tea, coffee or cola. Ray asked if he had a Diet Sprite. Noah flushed and said no. Ray chose tea. Rachel was nowhere in sight as the two men settled into dusty leather armchairs and Noah, obviously nervous, spoke rapidly, sharing a bit of his family's history.

He and Rachel had lived in the big house on the knoll as children, but the family money, squandered through three generations of speculators, gamblers and wastrels, had run out, and after the deaths of their parents Noah, then twenty, and Rachel, fourteen, had moved to this house, formerly the groundskeeper's home. The county seized the estate for back taxes but it was such a white elephant in an area in steep decline that the county never did anything with it, and the Cantrell brother and sister were left alone in their small house in the woods, hidden from the world and forgotten. Noah worked as an attendant and part-time mechanic at the only gas station for miles around, but Rachel, who had never attended any formal school, retreated to a hermetic life, living vicariously through her radio and television programs. She loved to sing and during the day she would vocalize for hours. At night, after supper, they would sit together at their old piano and Rachel would sing the songs that Noah had written for her. When they felt that a song had been thoroughly mastered, Noah would tape Rachel's singing it, on a battered old recorder that he had bought from a man who stopped for gas but seemed desperate for money. Noah pointed to a crowded bookcase in the corner of the room and identified the center shelf as containing over twenty tapes of his songs, all sung by Rachel.

"The one I sent to the station just seemed special," he said, turning pink with self-consciousness. "It was the best we'd ever done."

The late afternoon sun was casting long, slanting shadows across the room as Noah finished speaking, and the two men sat in awkward silence, sipping their tea as dust motes danced all around them. Ray asked if he could meet Rachel. Noah cleared his throat and began talking slowly, pausing frequently before plunging on.

"Well, the thing is…you see…Rachel is very shy. She knew you were coming and she was looking forward to your visit…and she wants to sing for you…but she's not used to visitors and…if you don't mind…I thought it might be best…that is, she thought…she's just so nervous…she would like you not to look at her while she sings."

Ray Anderson, a man who had battled the demon of insecurity all his adult life, was empathetic to Rachel's sudden stage fright and offered an understanding nod.

"So if you don't mind," Noah continued, "she'll sing from the top of the stairs."

Ray again nodded his agreement, and Noah left the room and climbed the stairs in the hallway adjacent to the living room. From his chair Ray could see him ascend nearly to the second floor landing but then he was lost in the gathering dark. Ray heard a knock on a door and a brief, muffled exchange between two voices. Noah descended and went to the piano, opened the lid and adjusted the piano stool. He turned on a small light illuminating the keys but leaving the rest of the room in shadows.

"Ready when you are, Rachel" he called out, encouragingly. Ray tried to pierce the gloom at the top of the stairs but could make nothing out. Then he heard a voice speaking; a voice that was soft and warm and intimate.

"Hello, Mr. Anderson. Thank you for coming. I hope you don't mind my performing for you in this manner, but I've never sung for anyone except my brother and…well…this just seemed the best way. I'm ready, Noah."

Noah laid his fingers gently on the piano keys and played a brief introduction. The voice that had captivated America, singing the song that had enthralled so many millions, came floating down the stairwell and across the living room. Ray recognized the voice but now it had extra dimensions, even greater impact, because it was live and not filtered by machines. The voice swept over Ray Anderson and he surrendered to its power and its pathos. Every note was pitch-perfect yet inflected in dramatic variety with ease. It seemed to be many voices, soprano, alto, contralto, as it effortlessly glided across vocal ranges. At times it reminded him more of a musical instrument than a human voice: a flute, a clarinet, an oboe. Light one second, sonorous the next, it kept the listener surprised and attentive. Ray was transfixed with its beauty. He had never experienced a more thrilling moment. His mind played tricks on him and now he thought he could see the figure singing at the top of the stairs: young, slim, tall, graceful, delicate, and smiling.

Rachel sang all seven stanzas just as she had on the tape. At the end of the last refrain her voice swelled in volume and rose to a stratospheric note of perfect pitch and indescribable sweetness. She held it long and effortlessly before it seemed to drift away. Noah ended with a few more quiet notes, followed by silence. It took time for Ray to recover from his total immersion in Rachel's singing and the emotional journeys she had sent him on. Finally he broke the silence.

"That was truly beautiful, Rachel" he called out to the darkened hallway.

"Thank you, Mr. Anderson" the disembodied voice replied in a tremulous tone. Now she sounded like a little girl, tired after an all-day outing.

Noah left the living room and bounded up the stairs. Ray rose from his chair in polite preparation for meeting Rachel. Muffled voices again came from the landing and then seemed to recede. Ray heard an upstairs door close. Noah came down the stairs and returned to the living room.

"I'm sorry," he said, raising his arms in a helpless gesture. "She's just so shy. And the excitement about singing for you and practicing all day has worn her out. She asks to be excused. I hope you don't mind." Then he added in a brighter tone, "But your reassurance means a lot!"

"Her voice is even more remarkable in person," Ray said, "but can she overcome her shyness to sing in front of an audience of strangers?"

"I know, I know," Noah said quickly. "I've asked myself the same question over and over, and I've discussed it with Rachel. She says she wants to do it as a way of thanking everyone for all the praise they've given her."

Noah paused and looked toward the stairwell.

"You see, Ray," he said quietly, "she really feels they love her, and she just wants to give back, to return their love."

Ray was startled by Noah's statement. Love, that most intensely personal and intimate emotion, was not a word he would ever use to describe the interest that the public currently had in Rachel. In the broadest, most casual sense, yes, they loved her singing voice; perhaps, in a truer application of the word, they really did love the song, for many had a deeply emotional response to it; and in a total misuse of the word, yes, they would love to know the singer's identity. But beyond their emotional response to the song and their appreciation of the singing voice and their innate curiosity and possibly their desire for more singing and more songs, Ray recognized that there was no personal bond between the singer and her millions of listeners that reflected any emotion that could be mistaken for love.

Noah interrupted Ray's thoughts.

"I've never seen her so happy," he said. "This is all she talks about. She's never been this excited, this hopeful or so determined."

Public applause and adulation is a strong, addictive drug, Ray thought, smiling as he rose from his chair.

Promising to call Noah soon, Ray left the darkened house in the woods. On his way home he drove slowly, pondering the best course of action for Rachel's debut, but still doubting that she could face any live audience. Yet that voice! That remarkable voice! So much more impressive in person than he could ever imagine! She should be heard live, but where? Then he realized that if it was announced in advance that the mystery singer had been found and was performing, the world would descend on her, and no stadium would be big enough to hold the crowds who might want to hear and see her. This would overwhelm anyone not use to the public spotlight, much less a young woman who lived in isolation and was unbearably shy and apparently fragile. No, an announced performance would not be the way to introduce Rachel to the public eye. Better to arrange for her to sing at some local venue with no advance notice, and without all the extravagant hoopla that would surely overwhelm her. Her introductory exposure had to be carefully planned. His mind evaluated possible settings until he settled on the right one. Having decided on the place and the circumstances to best protect her, he picked up speed, anxious to reach home, still filled with unclear forebodings.

* * * *

Two weeks later, on a sunny and warm Saturday afternoon, the bleachers of the local ballpark overflowed with more than three hundred people. All had come to celebrate the great American sport: baseball. A ragtag league of teams from several neighboring towns had been informally formed many years ago, and the strong support for each town's team and the spirit of competitiveness, with both the players and the spectators, raged as much in these local contests as at any major league game.

The current game being played had drawn a large and enthusiastic crowd of supporters for both the home team and the visitors because they were tied for first place in the unofficial league. The teams seemed evenly matched, for whenever one team would surge ahead with runs, the other team would soon even the score. The players, all heroes only on weekends, were performing at the top of their game, spurred on by the cheering, shouting, whistling, hooting, stomping, jumping, jeering, booing and clapping crowd.

Without ever articulating it, the spectators sensed that they were part of a quintessential American tradition, like Thanksgiving or the Fourth of July, which was being played out in sandlots and ball fields and stadiums across the country, as everyone enjoyed an afternoon of leisure, fully engaged with their all-American sport. Nothing seemed to capture their ideals of democracy as readily as baseball. The fame of the players, at any level of professional or amateur standing, depended exclusively on performance: the talent and timing and stamina and agility and accuracy and focus and grit. Regardless of any social, political, cultural or racial distinctions that Americans might observe in everyday life, at the ballpark all members of the audience were equal. Baseball was the great leveler that could pack the stands in big cities, sprawling suburbs, small towns and rural junctions with the rich, the well-to-do, the blue-collar strugglers and the hardscrabble poor. The plumber and farmer and construction worker and hairdresser and postman and housewife and sales clerk sat side by side with the auto dealership owner, the real estate developer, the town lawyer, the local doctor, the school principal and the prosperous merchant: all united in a zestful spirit of team support and genial comradeship.

As the innings passed and the air grew hotter, the concession stand ran out of soda and beer, but many people had brought their own. Since neither team was being badly beaten, all the people in the stands were still hopeful of victory for their team and in a raucously festive mood by the seventh inning stretch. Lines formed by the restrooms and people laughed and waved to friends spotted in other sections of the stands.

A small flatbed truck, with three people barely discernible in the cabin, slowly moved across the outfield until it was midway between home plate and the pitcher's mound and stopped.

Ray Anderson got out from the driver's side and climbed onto the flatbed. Looking gray and haggard, he waved his arms in wide arching motions over his head and yelled:

"Folks, can I have your attention, please."

He repeated his request several times before the restless, charged crowd focused on him and grew quiet. Most of the local townspeople recognized the radio station manager and wondered what he was going to say.

High in the stands, Mrs. Baker smiled down on her boss. She knew what was coming and was nervous with anticipation. Ray spoke in a loud voice and she could hear him clearly.

"Folks, we have a special surprise for you now. We all know that there's been a lot of talk and commotion lately about a song that was first played on our own radio station and now has become hugely popular across the country."

Ray stopped for a moment as the crowd started murmuring its reaction to his remark. Then he continued.

"And there's been a great deal of speculation about the unknown singer of that song."

Mrs. Baker could feel a tension starting to build in the crowd.

Ray continued.

"Well, it turns out that the singer comes from around these parts and for the first time in public she's going to sing for you today."

There was a momentary silence throughout the stands while each and every spectator processed this last statement, hardly believing what had just been said. Then as they individually realized that by a spectacular stroke of luck they were about to witness a momentous event, a unique happening of national interest, in their little town, in this very ballpark, their excitement and joy exploded. No home run by any local hero had ever sparked, in volume or intensity, the frenzied response that now erupted across the stands. Shouts and screams of jubilation attacked the afternoon sky, as arms waved wildly and punched the air. This singer who had touched each of them in a special, deeply personal way, who had cast a spell each time her song was heard, who had become the most talked about person in America, was now about to become a living presence before their eyes.

No matter how many times Ray Anderson raised his arms in pleading gestures for silence, the crowd's roaring could not be stopped. Finally, recognizing that their tumultuous response was delaying the appearance of this idolized singer, they quieted down, and Ray continued.

"First, I'd like you to meet the man who wrote that marvelous song, Mr. Noah Cantrell."

The crowd watched intently as the door on the passenger side of the truck slowly opened and out stepped a tall, thin, gangly man with white-gold hair. He stood by the door in an awkward stance, not quite erect, not smiling, not indicating any response to the applause, cheers and clapping that greeted him.

"And now," Ray yelled, with mounting strain in his voice, "Here's Noah's sister, Rachel, the nation's favorite singer!"

Waiting to react until she appeared, the crowd watched in frozen silence as Noah leaned into the cabin of the truck. When his upper body reappeared, he was holding an object that was not, at first, recognizable. As he moved toward the back of the truck and mounted the flatbed, he appeared to be carrying a child, but it was difficult to see her because she was enveloped by Noah's arms and hunched shoulders. Everyone in the stands leaned forward, straining to see the figure in the blond man's embrace.

Noah knelt down, opened his arms and released his sister but kept his large hands planted at her sides, steadying her from behind. Now, after what seemed an interminable time, the crowd had its first full view of Rachel Cantrell and responded as one living organism with an audible intake of breath, followed by confused, disorientated silence. All eyes focused intently on the diminutive figure on the platform of the flatbed truck, as every brain worked feverishly to make a sensible pattern of the images and impressions being sent to it.

To those who were not present, when those who were, tried to convey what they saw, their attempts seemed as imprecise, as over-ripe and as emotionally laden as when they had described their initial reaction to first hearing her sing on the radio. It was difficult to look upon Rachel Cantrell and not immediately turn away, as all decent people avert their eyes when beholding any person who violates the normal, expected patterns of humanness and whose defects and deformities are both repugnant and fascinating; the way we recoil in anguish when suddenly coming upon any scene of suffering, mutilation or carnage, be it human or animal, but then seem irresistibly drawn to witness the horrific, the haunting. Otherwise, our most celebrated and honored journalistic pictures would not preserve the searing images of victims of car crashes, gangland clashes, natural disasters, wars, the Holocaust, and the circus side shows of another era.

In her torso, limbs and face, Rachel Cantrell's misalignments and distortions raised her appearance to a state of pure theatrical imagination or cartoonist sketchiness. She resembled an abstract painting of a female whose parts must be mentally reassembled to perceive a recognizable form, but some parts are still missing. Her comic grotesqueness was accentuated by the way she was dressed: a garish gown with a sequined bodice and a multi-layered tulle skirt, befitting any beauty queen's triumphal parade down Main Street, USA.

Shocked into protracted silence and embarrassment, the crowd stared mutely. Then Rachel Cantrell began to sing. Her voice soared through, around and over the crowd, stunning each listener once again with its sheer beauty and emotional depth. Many spectators closed their eyes and disconnected the image of the amorphous, unsettling creature standing before them from the ravishing voice that carried them away to realms of fantasy and delight. But their enthrallment, eventually, could not be disassociated from the hard reality of the singer, and harsh, uninvited thoughts were taking shape as strong emotional conflicts bubbled to the surface.

The increasing heat of the late afternoon sun; the beer and liquor that had been consumed throughout the day; the carefree joy of watching a well matched game; the stunning surprise of Ray Anderson's announcement followed by the shock and revulsion at Rachel Cantrell's appearance: all were contributing to a hazy disquietude, a nervous unrest. As Rachel's magnificent voice and inspiring song continued to fill the ballpark, discomfit could be seen clearly etched on many faces. The incongruity of so much beauty emanating from a source so ludicrous and repellant was too much for the average spectator to grapple with and reconcile. The shattering of idealized visions of what the singer with such a marvelous voice, of such an inspiring song, would look like, unexpectedly took on added weight and broader significance. In only vaguely perceived and inarticulate ways, this current disillusionment seemed to symbolize, to evoke in vivid contrast, the gross discrepancies of other, more universal, shattered visions, until it became the touchstone of an illusory house of cards, all falling at once: visions of happy marriages and respectful children, and a secure job for life, and one's assured standing on the economic ladder, and a reliable bedrock of community values, and America's unchallenged supremacy in the world and religious leaders who practiced what they preached, and elected officials who kept their promises and looked out for the average guy, and equal justice under the law, and equal opportunity for everyone, and a country that represented the highest values and was a beacon of freedom, honor and fulfilled dreams to people everywhere.

The more the beautiful notes filled the air, the more they seemed to mock the inspirational words of the song and the aspirations of the people in the stands. In the abstract, the singer and her words had inspired hope; in the flesh, she prompted despair, which led to rage. Deep, primal rage. This creature simply could not be the singer they had come to cherish.

From her seat high in the stands Mrs. Baker could sense the negative energy charging through the crowd. Then she heard what sounded like a low, moaning noise all around her. It grew in volume until it was clearly a hissing sound, as more and more people gave vent to their angry frustrations. The hissing turned to audible boos that now erupted across the stands, as people rose to their feet and flailed their arms in indignation. Then, from somewhere far down below her in the stands, Mrs. Baker saw an object fly over the infield and land a short distance from the flatbed truck. This was quickly followed by a volley of objects coming from every section of the stands. Through this steady barrage of makeshift missiles, mostly empty beer cans and soda bottles, Mrs. Baker could see that a few were landing on the flatbed and one hit the pitiful creature in the fancy dress who had stopped singing but whose mouth remained open in total puzzlement, as tears wet the corners of her distorted mouth. More missiles were now landing with accuracy on the flatbed as Noah and Ray Anderson used their bodies to shield the creature from them, and Mrs. Baker sat in terrified paralysis, worried for her boss's safety and that of the singer and her brother. She felt that this storm of rage was still intensifying and could, at any moment, lead to the spectators' leaping onto the field and attacking the three of them. She clutched her throat and wept openly.

Quickly, Noah lifted his sister, jumped from the flatbed with Rachel in his arms and disappeared into the truck's cabin, while Ray was equally fast in reaching the driver's seat. The truck started to move, heading for the exit by the left outfield fence, just as the first person jumped onto the field. In seconds the infield was a swarm of rioters hurling objects at the speeding truck and chasing after it. When it disappeared behind the fence and all that could be heard over the shouting on the field was the increasing roar of the engine as it sped away, the unified mob's anger did not abate, and, in unfocused frustration, they randomly destroyed the playing field, ripping up the bases and tearing out the sod and breaking the floodlights and pelting the people remaining in the stands with dirt. A few young men spilled out into the parking lot where they attacked the first few cars they came upon.

The police arrived, and their presence seemed to break the ferocious spell that had possessed the crowd. Meekly, in dazed confusion about what had just taken place but recognizing their guilty participation in an egregious betrayal of principles and decency, they dispersed to their homes, forgetting that their cherished baseball game had not been finished.

* * * *

A reporter for the local paper who had attended the unfinished ballgame was quick to write a lead story about the unforeseen and unforgivable events at the ballpark. In defense of his hometown and his neighbors, however, he gave the story a bogus twist, attributing the ensuing riot when the mystery singer appeared to her wildly enthusiastic reception from the crowd. In his published version, as the singer began her song, the spectators down front were still standing and cheering and refused requests from those higher up in the stands to sit down and stop blocking the view. Spirits being so keyed up, the journalist reported, words were exchanged, someone shoved someone, a punch was thrown and reciprocated and fights broke out. For anyone who had not witnessed the Saturday event first-hand, it seemed as though the resulting melee was between people in different sections of the stands and not directed at the singer who, it was noted, left the ballpark abruptly when the fighting spilled over onto the field and jeopardized her safety.

While the journalist discreetly drew a veil over Rachel's appearance, describing her only as small and oddly shaped, he could not supply her name because in the excitement and hubbub generated by Ray Anderson's surprise introduction, he forgot it. Candidly he admitted that no one present that afternoon with whom he had checked, could remember it either. Ray Anderson, of course, knew her name but he had his own story about that, which he was currently giving to another reporter from the same paper.

Upon reading the newspaper article, all the townspeople gave a collective sigh of relief, accepted the Big Lie as bedrock truth and adjusted their consciences to suit the revised facts. Their town had been saved from the disgrace and national derision that had seemed inevitable and their role was officially regarded as mere excess of spirits, like city people who run amuck when their team wins the pennant.

When the article was picked up by syndicated news agencies and repeated in the national press, a second wave of reporters descended on the little Texas town. No matter whom they interviewed, singly or in groups, and no matter how hard they probed and questioned, badgered or cajoled for more facts, more details and possible new slants, all the townspeople stuck to the same story.

Mrs. Baker was once again besieged by hordes of reporters who now found her strangely subdued and tight-lipped. This time around, she offered no juicy tidbits, no nuances of details, no local gossip and no sharing of presentiments or imagined auras. The well-honed instincts of certain senior reporters suggested that she was not telling all, but, like the rest of the folk, her story never departed from the universal version. A short time later she quit her job and resumed her role as full-time grandmother.

The lion's share of attention by the national media centered on Ray Anderson who was responsible for bringing the singer to town and who knew her identity. But here, too, the press was thwarted. Despite his direct, laconic style and low-key manner, Ray proved to have a crafty, inventive side. Staring media reporters straight in the eye and smiling sheepishly, he explained that this had all been a staged joke, not unusual in the seventh inning stretch at local ballgames. The singer was not, of course, the true mystery singer but an impersonator, like an Elvis or Cher or Streisand impersonator. Since nobody knew what the real singer looked like, it was easy to trick the audience, and the impersonator's unusual appearance was part of the joke. The harmless ruse was going to be revealed after she finished her song, but before that, things got out of hand and all hell broke loose. He was very sorry for the resulting brawl and notoriety, and, no, he would not identify the impersonator, at her request.

"For the brief time she sang," Ray said matter-of-factly, trying not to betray how long he had studied his lines, "there was such noisy excitement that nobody even realized how inferior her voice was – in comparison to the singer on the tape – or noticed how she kept forgetting the lyrics."

Thus another chapter was added to the official story that circulated among the cities and towns of America, but faded quickly because people were not interested in impersonators or the antics of a local station manager.

No one ever came close to discovering the identity of the mystery singer, so she moved into the realm of myth, to be discussed and speculated about and enlarged. Her enormously popular song soon was elevated to the category of "a classic" and, while played intermittently, would never fade from memory. On every Fourth of July, every singer appearing at a state fair, local beauty pageant, charity bazaar or patriotic assembly sang it to the delight of every audience.

* * * *

A few weeks after that fateful Saturday, Ray Anderson drove west again to the lonely house in the woods. He had brought flowers for Rachel and had written her a long note of apology and encouragement, for he had spoken to Noah on the phone and learned that she was not well. Stepping out of his car in front of the house on that warm summer afternoon, he once again heard her beautiful voice pouring out from the open windows. This time it was not live but one of Noah's tapes, and the song was a different one. But the remarkable power and clarity of the singer produced the same awed response that he had felt before, on another afternoon, sitting in the musty parlor of this old house when he had heard that thrilling voice sweep down the stairs and caress his soul.

He thought of what the world had lost through its vanity and false dreams, its rigid, narrow views and self-deceptions. He decided not to knock on the door, but left the flowers and the note on the doorstep. The strains of Rachel's voice followed him down the driveway, into the future.

A Clearer Picture

My father sits by the window, the sun highlighting his deflated profile and haloing the wisps of white hair that cling to the sides of his head. He holds an open book in his lap but his glasses have slipped down his nose, his head is bowed, his eyes closed. The metal rim of his glasses and the metal spokes.in his wheelchair are glinting in the sun when I enter his room. I lay the magazines I've brought on his bed and quietly sit in the chair next to him, observing his shallow breathing and the slight twitching of his craggy face. Mindful of his age – he'll be eighty nine in two months – I know these catnaps don't last long. Soon he rouses from his mid-morning doze and looks puzzled to see me.

"Hi Dad," I say, bending over and kissing the top of his head. He says nothing, just smiles, and laboriously readjusts his glasses.

I know he finds my displays of affection, even at his age, awkward, something beyond his fixed concept of manly relationships, something we never practiced in our family, but I don't care. With Mom and my brother Georgie gone, we just have each other now and who knows for how long, so I need to show him how much I cherish him. How I cherish his strength, surviving two strokes and still struggling to live. How I cherish the very nature of this man who gave me my existence and committed his life, a most ordinary life, to taking care of his wife for forty-seven years and seeing that his two sons were fed and clothed and sheltered and given a decent start in life. So now, when I visit him in the nursing home on Saturday, I kiss him hello and goodbye and often hold his hand while I talk. When I first started these gestures of love, I could feel his body stiffen and could hear a quick intake of breath, but now he seems to tolerate them, even expect them.

"How are you feeling?" I ask, and he moves his head and smiles. "Fiiiiiiiiiii", he replies, his face contorted with the enormous effort he makes to speak.

"The nurses taking good care of you?"

He shakes his head slowly, the crooked smile, half pleasant, half grotesque, never leaving his face.

"I brought you some more magazines," I say, pointing to the small pile I placed on the bed, and his eyes follow my hand. Then he lifts his right hand – his right side is still functioning – and reaches for the glass of water on the table next to his wheelchair. His movement is slow and jerky, and I want to reach across him and get the glass and bring it to his lips but I know this would make him angry, so I sit passively and watch the slow, jagged process. Only after he's taken several small sips, may I assist by taking the glass from his knolled, blotchy hand, the veins transparent though the paper-thin skin, and returning it to the table, then filing it again from the adjacent water pitcher. His eyes watch all my actions, betraying no signs of frustration, and I return to my chair by the other side of his wheelchair.

After his second stroke, more severe than his first, our time together was mostly spent in silence, but this was frustrating to me for I felt an urgent need to communicate with him, to understand him better, and for him to know how much I had come to respect and love him, especially now as I struggled to be a father to my own three kids after my divorce. I couldn't just express these feelings over and over, so I began to fill the long silences of my visits with my telling him the scenes I remembered from my childhood. He seemed genuinely pleased to hear what I remembered about him when I was a boy, and in some instances he even attempted to provide an additional detail. Mostly, though, he would close his eyes while I talked and from the movement of his lips and his right hand I knew he was listening. So our ritual began.

* * * *

Dad, I remember the time we moved to Cleveland when you got that bigger sales territory. I was ten and starting the sixth grade at St. Cecilia's. And there was one kid in the class – I'll never forget his name – Henry Quigly – and he decided he didn't like me. He was a huge kid, a head taller than most of the boys in the class, including me, and he must have outweighed us by at least fifty pounds. Now Henry was the leader of a bunch of the toughest kids in the class. I think they followed him out of fear that he'd turn on them if they weren't loyal. Anyway, every day when school let out and I'd start walking home – remember, Dad, we lived in that white colonial with the nice yard, only about six blocks away from school? – there would be Henry, surrounded by his gang, waiting for me around the corner from the school. Then the torture would begin. Henry didn't like anything about me: my Boston accent, my size, my glasses, my clothes, the book bag I carried and the fact that I was smart.

"Hey, shrimp," was how he usually started, as he stood blocking my way while his friends formed a circle around me. "Where dja get that stupid shirt?" He'd laugh and pull the shirt out of my pants. "Are there any more fruits like you in Boston, four-eyes?" Then he'd get very close to me, his black eyes looking disdainfully down on me and his face a huge mocking smirk. "Why don tcha go back where you came from? Fruitland!"

On each occasion, I was gripped with fear, unable to speak or move. Then one of his cronies would quietly come behind me and kneel down on all fours. Henry would give me a quick shove and over I'd go, my book bag and glasses flying, while Henry and crew laughed.

"See you tomorrow, four-eyes," he'd say menacingly before strolling off with his henchmen.

Fearful that if I got up too quickly, he'd return to do more damage, I'd lay there in abject defeat until my attackers had all disappeared. Only then would I get up, straighten my clothes, collect my books and check to see if my glasses were broken.

True to his word, Henry waited for me each day, just outside of school range so the nuns couldn't see anything. I tried taking a different route home but he always found me and treated me to the usual forms of verbal abuse and physical aggression, always leaving me disheveled, defeated and demoralized.

Henry Quigly was haunting my life, and at home I went from being a sunny kid to being cranky and withdrawn. Mom noticed this dramatic change and asked me if anything was troubling me, but you know how it is, Dad: I couldn't tell her about Henry for fear she'd go to school and complain to the nuns and then I'd be labeled a snitch and a mama's boy and all the kids would despise me. So I said nothing but started pretending to be sick so I could stay home. You remember, Dad, how I was a very healthy kid who hardly ever missed school, so now Mom knew for sure that something was wrong, but no amount of coaxing could get me to open up. You were on the road most of the time during the week and Mom didn't like to bother you with problems when you got home.

One Friday, after I had won the class spelling contest by defeating Patricia McBride who, before my arrival, always won the spelling contests, Henry was especially angry. During our after-school encounter he ripped my shirt and gave me a punch in the stomach that left me doubled over and gasping for air.

"Think you're so smart, four-eyes?" he asked derisively, grabbing my glasses from off my face and tossing them in a nearby shrub. "I bet you can't even spell your name right"

Still trying to catch my breath, I remained doubled over, hoping to be a smaller target. Henry grabbed me by my hair and yanked me upright.

"Let's hear ya spell your name," he demanded, still holding me by my hair.

In abject misery I began "W…A…L," but Henry yanked my head back further.

"That's not how ya spell it. Start again!"

My confusion and panic grew. "W…A…"

Another yank at my hair. "Fellas, is this kid stupid or what?" and the surrounding gang snickered in unison. "He don't even know how to spell his name," Henry said triumphantly. "Try again!" he commanded.

Totally defeated, the tears spurting from my eyes, I knew I had to follow his command and spell something other than my first name, Walter, so, barely able to make any sound other than a sob, my mouth puckered as I tried to spell my last name. "M…O…R…"

Henry gave my hair another yank until my head was tilted back parallel to the sky and his black eyes loomed above me.

"No, idiot. Wrong again!"

His grip on my hair tightened as he made me turn in a circle, the tears and sweat and snot streaking my face, so everyone could see my miserable, craven condition.

"I guess I'll just have to spell it for you, so you'll remember it."

Raising his voice to a louder pitch he began. "F…R…U…I…T! That's how you spell your name! Now you spell it!"

Wishing with all my heart that the earth would open and swallow me, my voice hoarse with choking sobs, I said the word 'FRUIT.'

Henry laughed and his laughter was imitated by the entire circle of boys. "No, idiot! Don't say it! Spell it!" My humiliation and desperation were total. I felt I would crumple to the ground if Henry was not holding me up by my hair. I was now his puppet, willing to do anything at his command.

"F…R…U…I…T," I mumbled, but Henry shouted "Louder!" and I forced what seemed like the last remaining breath from my sagging body and spelled FRUIT in one long , agonized screech..

"That's better," Henry said, "And don't forget it! That's all the spelling lessons for today."

The gang let out a cheer when Henry let go of my hair and I slumped to the ground. I closed my eyes and wrapped my arms around my chest, trying to make myself as small a target as possible, fearing more blows and humiliation, but Henry and his cronies were satisfied with the blood sport for the day. I heard their shouts and jeers and laughter receding into the distance but I was too afraid to open my eyes for fear that if I even moved, they might return for another round. Finally, when all was silence except for my labored, shallow breathing, I dared to look around and my tormentors had disappeared. Still, I stayed in my crumpled huddle, filled with anger and self-loathing, my brain teeming with smart put-downs and caustic insults that I wished I had been defiantly brave enough to hurl at Henry Quigly and his gang, but knowing that only in some other universe or through some fantastical transformation would that have been possible. No, everything seemed hopeless and I was condemned to endure Henry's tortures for eternity. I wished I were dead.

How long I sat there, reflecting on my hopeless condition, I couldn't tell, but finally I roused myself and went searching for my glasses. When I found them, the left stem was badly bent, probably from when Henry had yanked them off my face. I tucked my shirt in but several buttons were missing. Exhausted, I dragged myself home. Of course, my disheveled appearance didn't escape Mom who was always there to greet me when I returned from school. One quick appraisal and she was bombarding me with questions, her face a mask of alarm and concern.

"What happened to you? Where have you been? Where are your glasses?" (They were in my pocket which, or course, Dad, was a clear signal of something very wrong since, as you know, my eyesight was so bad that they never left my face except when I took a shower or went to bed.)

I felt trapped. I tried to avoid giving any answers but my mother placed her hands on my shoulders and insisted on knowing what was wrong, all the while speaking to me in a soft, soothing voice. Well, Dad, you know how strong and persuasive Mom could be when she set her mind to anything. As she stared into my eyes and I saw the deep concern registered on her face, all my defenses crumbled and I burst into tears, flinging myself against her body. She encircled me in her arms and held me tightly, rocking gently back and forth, saying nothing, just letting me cry until all my hurt was spent in the comfort of her embrace. As my racking sobs subsided, she stroked my hair and made soothing sounds.

"There, now. There, now," was all she said over and over again, and, Dad, I remember her words as if it were yesterday and I can still remember the warm, fragrant odor of her dress and the vague smell of the lavender soap she always used. You used to buy her boxes of it for Christmas and her birthday – it came from France – and she'd laugh and say it was her one extravagance and thank you for being so indulgent. I guess it was pretty expensive, huh, Dad? Anyway, when I finally finished crying, she led me into the kitchen and gently rinsed my face with cold water. Then, still with her arm around my shoulder, she guided me to the sofa in the living room and sat very close to me. I took comfort from her warm body next to mine. She spoke softly.

"You know, Walter, whatever has happened, you can always tell me, son, and I'm here to listen and help in any way I can."

There was a long silence and I struggled with my fear of "snitching," and my great desire to unburden myself of this heavy weight of fear and frustration. Finally, as she squeezed my shoulder, I could resist her no longer, and, with my lower lip still trembling and tears again welling up in my eyes, the entire story of Henry Quigly's persecution of me since the first week of school, culminating in today's major assault, came spilling out of me in a torrential, cathartic confession. When my rush of words finally came to an end, we sat together silently in the gathering gloom of a late fall afternoon. I was conscious again of her comforting smells and felt at peace, almost drowsy. Then the chimes of the grandfather clock rang from the hall, disturbing the stillness. Mom squeezed my shoulder.

"Go upstairs and wash up and change your shirt and get ready for dinner," she said. "Your father will be home soon. He'll know what to do."

I headed up the stairs, barely conscious of where I was or what I was doing, as old fears gripped me. I was afraid, Dad, that when you heard about Henry Quigly, you'd be mad at me for not standing up to him, but honestly, Dad, he was so much bigger and stronger than me and he had all those kids surrounding me. And I certainly didn't want you going to the school and telling the nuns what happened, but I told myself, No, you wouldn't do that. You had never gone to any of my schools about anything; it was always Mom. And I thought I could talk her out of going if that was her plan. Still, I couldn't take much more of Quigly's abuse. There had to be some way to escape him. I thought that maybe you'd decide to send me to a different school. That seemed to me to be the only answer, and if you didn't think of it, I was going to suggest it to you.

I heard you come in while I was upstairs, and I heard you and Mom talking in the kitchen but I couldn't hear what you were saying. Then I heard Georgie coming in from basketball practice and, in an excited, loud voice, telling you he had just been made captain of the high school varsity team. When I came downstairs, you and Mom were in the living room having a cocktail and you said "Hi Walter," and then continued your conversation with Mom as though there was nothing wrong. That made me think that maybe Mom hadn't said anything to you about Quigly, but I couldn't be sure. While we were having dinner and Georgie was rambling on about basketball, you looked at me – you really had an intimidating look, Dad, when I had done something wrong, but this was not one of those looks – and you said, "I understand you're having some problems at school."

I remember, Dad, how my face turned red, and all I could do was nod my head, yes, and stare down at my plate. You said nothing else and I was grateful that Georgie filled the awkward silence with his rambling on about how much he loved his new high school, compounding my misery and filling me with jealousy.

On Saturday, you and Georgie were working on your car and the weekend passed with no further mention of my trouble until Sunday dinner. Georgie was talking about a fight that had broken out at a basketball game the previous week between two players from opposing teams. You interrupted him, Dad, and, looking directly at me, said, "You should never fight if you don't have to, but if you have to fight, then you should always throw the first punch and make it a good one, as hard as you can."

Georgie continued his story about the basketball players' fight until Mom objected to all the talk about fighting and said she hoped her boys never had to engage in fighting. Then, Dad, you said quietly, "Sometimes, Mary, it's unavoidable," before changing the subject.

On Monday, when I left for school, you were still home, which was unusual because you normally got on the road before I was up, but I figured you were getting a late start. Mom handed me my lunch at the door, gave me a hug and said, "Be sure to come straight home from school, Walter." Of course, that reminded me of what I usually encountered while trying to come straight home from school, and I left the house in a totally dejected mood, feeling that Mom and you had decided to let me handle my own problems, but I knew that that I couldn't handle this problem.

My school day followed the normal pattern. Because Sister Margaret arranged us by size in the classroom and I was the shortest boy, I sat in a front desk, and Henry, being the biggest kid, sat in the back. I liked Sister Margaret. She was lively and cheerful and made lessons interesting, especially history. I had become absorbed in that day's class work and forgot about Henry looming in the back of the room. At lunchtime, I never strayed far from the nun supervising the playground and didn't take part in the roughhouse games that Henry organized with his buddies, fearing more torture. Occasionally, one of the members of his gang would run past me and, in a stage whisper so the nun couldn't hear him, hurl some taunting remark like "Hey, four-eyes!" or "Hi ya, fruit."

Returning to the classroom after lunch, I tried to concentrate on the lesson Sister Margaret was giving us, but my fears were mounting as I watched the big clock on the front wall of the room, dreading the approaching time when we would be dismissed and the assaults would begin. On that day, Dad, about fifteen minutes before dismissal time, a note was surreptitiously passed along the row of desks until it reached me. I opened it and read, "Hi, four-eyes. Are you ready for another spelling leson?" (I noted his misspelling of the word, lesson) "This will be a good one."

My mind wandered away from the homework assignment Sister Margaret was giving the class for that night. In desperation I resorted to the last hope of salvation: prayer. Quickly I sought the intercession of Jesus, then of Mary, and finally of the Infant of Prague, known for his miracles. "Please, please," I silently begged, "help me in my hour of need." I bargained with the heavenly assemblage, promising a life of good deeds and greater charity toward others and stricter obedience to my parents' directions and greater reverence and attentiveness at Mass – anything in exchange for escaping from this constant torture. But all my emergency prayers didn't bolster my sinking spirits, and by the time we were dismissed I was nearly paralyzed with apprehension and was the last to shuffle out the schoolhouse door. Like a condemned man whose appeals have all been exhausted, and cursing my fate, the heavenly host and you and Mom, I dragged my trembling body toward home.

After turning the first corner I peered down the street, and although I couldn't see too clearly because I had taken off my glasses to prevent them from being broken in the inevitable confrontation, I saw that Henry and his gang were not visible. This street, like the other streets I had to travel, had only a few houses set far back from the road, some enclosed with high walls of shrubbery, and a number of empty lots. There was hardly any traffic at this time of day, which made it the perfect spot for an ambush. Of course there were other kids usually walking home in my direction, but as soon as they spotted Henry and his gang, they scurried away, happy, I'm sure, not to be the target of Henry's bullying. Henry liked to surprise me by emerging from behind some thick bushes or lying in wait around a corner with his followers, so seeing this street empty did nothing to relieve my spiking nerves as I waited for the surprise attack.

Looking back up the street to be sure the gang wasn't coming up behind me, I saw a car slowly moving in my direction. My imagination ran wild as I thought that maybe Henry had an older brother who was joining in this game of torture and was now driving Henry and some of his cronies to a spot where they would jump out and attack me. I stood in a frozen stare, my heart racing. The car stopped about a hundred feet away. Without my glasses I couldn't see who was inside or how many. I could see that it was a big black car, like the one you drove or like the ones gangsters in the movies drove when they'd drive by and the doors would open and men would pile out with machine guns and open fire and bodies would be falling everywhere, and then they'd tumble back into the car and speed away.

I started walking again and could see over my shoulder that the car was moving very slowly, keeping the same distance behind me. Maybe it's a kidnapper, I thought, compounding my panic. As I approached the end of that block, Henry and his gang appeared from around the corner.

"Hi, four-eyes," he said cheerfully and then added, "Wait a minute! Four-eyes is missing two of his eyes!"

This word play was seen as being very clever by the eight or ten kids in Henry's wake. They snickered and guffawed and then started to chant, "Four-eyes lost two eyes," as they made their usual circle around me, blocking any chance of escape. Henry loomed over me with a mocking grin. I dropped my book bag to the ground and stood frozen in abject misery, waiting for the oncoming assault. Then, from the corner of my eye I saw a blurred movement. The car had pulled up alongside the gang and a man jumped out and rushed up to the circle, pushing his way through the blockade. It all happened so quickly that not until the man was standing by my side did I realize it was you, Dad. You reached out for Henry's shoulder and pulled him toward you until your faces were inches apart and his eyes were bulging – with surprise or fear, I couldn't tell.

"I hear you've got some issues with my son," you said in a low, menacing voice I had never heard before. Henry said nothing, but his whole body seemed to sag, looking like it was propped up only by your grip on his shoulder. I glanced around the circle, which was totally silent, and I saw only sullen looks of confusion and shock.

"Now my son has issues with you," you said, staring directly into Henry's eyes. Henry looked like a deer caught in the headlights. "And since you're such a big man, I think the best way to handle this isn't ten to one, the way you've been doing it, but one to one."

You stopped speaking, letting your words sink in, and I was the one who was the most surprised. Once again fear gripped me as I considered your intention. Surely you didn't mean that I was going to fight Henry. Maybe you were going to pick out a kid from the circle who was more my size and weight and challenge him to fight me. I wasn't a fighter. I didn't like fighting. I had no desire to fight. I just wanted to be left alone, but it was dawning on me that a fight with someone now seemed inevitable. Then, Dad, you said what I feared most.

"Let's keep this little circle," you said, letting go of Henry's shoulder and turning to stare disdainfully at each kid present, "and you and Walter will settle your differences here and now. What do you say to that?"

Henry looked at me and then looked back at you, Dad.

"Sure," he said, regaining some of his swagger, probably not believing his good luck in being offered such an easy challenge.

My heart was beating so fast and so loud that I really thought I could hear the beats screaming out of my ears like a bugle call. You stepped between us, Dad, and extended your arms, pushing us away to arms' length.

"When I say three, begin!" you said, moving off to the side, still within the circle of silent boys, holding my book bag.

With a pause between each number that you said, Dad, you looked at me and I knew you were trying to convey encouragement, trying to reassure me. But truthfully, Dad, I felt betrayed, like a lamb being fed to a lion. I thought about turning and breaking through the circle of boys and running home, knowing that with you there, Henry and his gang would never chase me. Then I realized that I could never disgrace myself like that in your presence. I dreaded disappointing you almost as much as I dreaded the beating I was about to get from Henry.

"Three!" rang in my ears and seemed to hang in the air, echoing through my brain. My doom was now at hand and I was resigned to my fate. I looked at Henry who was standing in a nonchalant pose, his hands hanging loosely down his sides, a challenging smirk on his face. He was daring me to make the first move. A light went off in my head, and flashing across my brain were your words from Sunday dinner about if you had to fight, always be the one to throw the first punch and make it as hard as you could.

Dad, that whole scene is so vividly imprinted on me that I can see it as clearly as if it were happening now. Henry standing about five feet in front of me, looking huge, and you off to the side, the other kids all silently watching, as everyone waited to see what would happen next. I remember stepping forward and then taking further steps – honestly, Dad, it seemed like I was crossing a wide desert – and then I was directly in front of Henry, looking up into his mocking face, his hands still hanging at his sides, and I knew instantly what his strategy was. As long as you were present, he wasn't going to be the first one to start the fight, and I guess his ego told him that, given the great difference in our size and weight, I wouldn't dare attack him.

Dad, I swear I can still hear his breathing, and I can see the white in his eyes as I stared up at him. I don't know to this day how I summoned the courage to follow your rule, Dad, and everything seemed to be in slow motion as I drew my right arm back behind me, made a fist and swung it around with all my might to land on the side of Henry's nose.

Now time was completely suspended. I'll never forget the look of total surprise on Henry's face. Then I heard a collective shout from the kids forming the circle, and, transfixed, I watched a small trickle of blood coming from Henry's nose, heading toward his mouth. His tongue shot out and tasted the blood; his face turned first a bright red, almost matching the color of his blood, and then a dark gray as rage replaced shock.

Then time speeded up and nothing was distinct, really just a continuous blur, as Henry swung into action to the cheers of his followers, and blows rained down on me from every direction. You said later, Dad, that he wasn't really a good fighter and mostly used his weight and arm length to get to me, and you said I put up a good defense. All I remember is that I kept flailing my arms as fast as I could but nothing seemed to be landing on Henry, while all his punches seemed to be hitting the mark. My body was registering increasing pain with each blow it received, but I kept telling myself over and over, "You can't cry! You mustn't cry! You can't let them see you crying!"

After what seemed like a battle longer than an entire war, you parted us, saying, "That's enough! I think you've settled your differences. Now why don't you shake hands?"

I was sniveling uncontrollably and taking huge gulps of air. I looked at Henry for the first time since I had landed that lucky first punch. Blood was still visible beneath his nose and he looked embarrassed. I stepped up to him and extended my hand. He took it limply and quickly released it. There was not even a glimmer of triumph on his face; just a drooping hound dog look. Then, Dad, you addressed the circle of kids. "Now if any of you boys have any issues with my son, he'll be happy to settle them with you, one-on-one, here and now. Just step up."

On hearing your words, Dad, I swear I nearly fainted, and everything around me – you, Henry, the kids – started spinning before my eyes. When I was finally able to focus on the kids, I saw closed faces, downcast eyes, no one moving or making a sound.

"Okay, then. Walter will see you all tomorrow in school."

You swung your arm over my shoulder and led me out of the silent circle and into your car. We pulled away and I glanced back at Henry and the boys who had not moved. They seemed frozen in some tableaux depicting shocked and anxious children. I was still sniveling and you handed me your handkerchief and said, "I'm very proud of you, Walter." Such a straightforward compliment from you, Dad, was so rare – we didn't really talk much back in those days, remember? – and now the shock of the entire afternoon's episode caught up with me, and in one second I relived it all and the floodgates opened. Tears spilled down my checks. I ached all over. I remember you drove with one hand and kept patting my knee, saying, "That's okay, son. Let it all out. You did fine."

I don't know how long I cried but when I finally stopped, I looked out the car window and saw that we weren't heading home.

"Where are we going, Dad?" I asked in a still-weepy voice, and you said "We're going to celebrate your victory with an ice cream sundae. Would you like that?"

My mood brightened at the prospect of a sundae, a rare treat to share with you, but mostly because you had declared me the victor in a battle where I felt I had been vanquished. I handed you your handkerchief and said, "But he whipped me."

You lifted the handkerchief in front of my face. "You see that, Walter? You see that?"

I looked at your handkerchief and thought maybe you were angry for my making such a mess of it. I said nothing and you continued.

"There's not a drop of blood on this handkerchief! Not one drop! You drew blood, Walter. That's what those kids will remember and that's what Henry will remember. You threw the first punch and you made him bleed. That's all that matters."

We rode in silence for about five minutes until we came to the ice cream parlor. I remember how I headed for the counter but you steered me into a booth. When a girl came to take our order, she was staring at me with a concerned look on her face, but you smiled at her and said, "Miss, my son and I are celebrating today. We want the biggest size sundae you make. No, wait a minute…" You turned to me. "How about a banana split, Walter?"

My eyes must have lit up at this extravagant offer, and I remember shaking my head vigorously. A dialogue ensued between you, me and the waitress as we chose the ice cream flavors – they gave you three scoops back then – and the assorted toppings. I went for hot fudge, pineapple and marshmallow.

"Make mine the same," you said, "and don't forget lots of whipped cream and the cherries," you called after her as she left our table. Then you turned your attention to the small juke box at our booth, flipping through metal framed pages of song titles.

"Let's have some music," you said and drew a quarter from your pocket, placed it in the slot and then pressed the buttons for the five songs you had chosen. Frank Sinatra's soothing baritone voice filled the air.

Dad, I have to tell you that I remember all of this – every detail – because I think it was the first time I had ever been alone with you; not alone like our being alone together at home on a Saturday while Mom was out shopping and Georgie was away at camp and I was upstairs in my room working on an airplane model and you were outside mowing the lawn. You know what I mean: alone together, face to face, sharing the moment, talking to each other man-to-man. Remember, Dad, you were in the army for three years and I was nine when you returned home from the war. And I know we did a lot of things together as a family like camping trips and going to county fairs and a few vacations at Lake Lorimar, but that afternoon in that ice cream parlor was different and very special, and even though I was just a kid, I realized then how special it was and I was thrilled that I had earned your approval and you were proud of me and had said so for the first time.

The waitress brought us the banana splits in boat-shaped glass dishes and we both waded joyfully through mounds of whipped cream, sauces and ice cream. Halfway into my second scoop, I summoned the courage to challenge you on one issue. I asked you why you made me fight Henry Quigly and why couldn't you have picked some kid who was my size. You put down your spoon – you had whipped cream on your upper lip – and you smiled.

"Because, Walter, you had to challenge the leader or else Quigly would not stop bothering you. You saw how they reacted when I invited them to fight you. They were all scared little rabbits."

At the mere mention of your challenge to all those boys my heart began again to race.

"Believe, me, son, nobody's going to bother you any more. That's something I learned in the Army."

I briefly thought that you might be suggesting that you had had some similar experience. Dad, you're shaking your head. You did? Yes. Well, back then I didn't have the sense to follow up on what you said, so we finished our banana splits and listened to the songs from the juke box. As I was scooping up the last bit of ice cream and scraping the dish for any remnants of whipped cream, you handed me your comb.

"Go to the wash room and splash some water on your face and comb your hair and tuck your shirt in," you said. "We don't want your mother seeing you like this."

When I got to the sink in the wash room and looked in the mirror and saw myself for the first time, I was shocked. No wonder the waitress had been staring at me! I had two red welts, one on my forehead and one at my temple, and my left cheek was puffy and red. But, as you had said, Dad, and now I saw for myself, there was no blood. I rinsed my face with cold water and it hurt. I wet your comb under the faucet and slicked down my hair and tucked in my shirt. As I walked back to the booth and saw you smiling at me, I had never felt closer to you. Actually, I felt quite grown up.

Upon our arrival home, Mom took one look at me and let out a yell.

"Oh my god," she said, rushing toward me. "Bob, what happened?"

You answered in a mild tone, 'Now, Mary, it's all right. Walter handled his problem the only way he could."

Mom was holding me by my shoulders, examining my face, her eyes misty with tears. You stepped up behind me and placed your hands over hers.

"You would have been very proud of our son," you said, but the tears were now racing down Mom's cheeks.

"He needs ice on those welts." she said, assessing my ravaged face.

I was smiling like some returning war hero – like you, Dad, when we met you at the train station when you came home from the war. For the next half-hour Mom fussed over me and I tolerated her attention with good humor, proud of my badges of courage. Then you suggested that I should probably have a rest before dinner because it had been a long, eventful day. I did feel unusually tired after all the excitement and I went upstairs to my room. I didn't doze off right away because I was reliving the great event in all its no-longer-blurred details, enhancing my bravery, my fighting skills, my audacity until I felt like some mythic hero they write songs about. Meanwhile, downstairs, I could hear Mom's voice raised in anger, hurling accusations at you for allowing me to "be so brutally beaten." Your voice, Dad, was steady and calm.

"I'm sorry, Mary, but you just don't understand. There was no other choice. Walter had to stand up to the leader of the bullies and show all of them that he could fight back. You asked me to handle this and I did – in the only way that would settle the problem for good."

There were more recriminations from Mom and more patient explanations from you, but I suddenly felt very tired and drifted off to sleep. When I awoke, my room was dark but I could see Mom's silhouette on the chair next to my bed. Still groggy but immediately conscious of feeling sore all over, I let out a few, small groans. Mom turned on the light.

"You've been asleep for a long time, Walter," she said. "We didn't want to wake you. Would you like some dinner? We've already had ours."

I nodded yes and tried to get up but the aches just got worse and I sucked in my breath. Mom pushed me gently down on the pillow.

"You stay there and rest. I'll bring you up your dinner on a tray."

And, Dad, I can even remember what that dinner was: meatloaf and gravy, mashed potatoes and corn and chocolate pudding for dessert. I suddenly felt very hungry and ate everything quickly, with Mom sitting in the chair and, for once, not telling me to eat my food more slowly. She brought me a second glass of milk and some homemade ginger cookies. We never spoke about what happened that afternoon. I sensed, somehow, that she didn't want to know; that it was a man's thing, shared and appreciated only by you and me, Dad. After I finished everything, I said something about doing my homework, but Mom told me it was very late and I should go back to sleep and I should probably stay home from school the next day. I lay back down and she bent over and touched my still swollen cheek, and then she kissed me on my forehead, put out the light and before closing my door said, "Goodnight, son."

Dad, you were gone the next morning when I awoke and I stayed home that day while Mom applied more ice packs and some homemade remedies to my welts and bruises, including new ones we discovered on my torso. They were nearly gone the following day when I returned to school. And, Dad, you were right: Nobody ever bothered me again.

At lunchtime my first day back, two of the kids from Quigly's gang came up to me and, in a friendly way, much different from their usual manner, invited me to join their group in a game of touch football. Henry Quigly was the captain for our side and he even passed the ball to me in a couple of plays. I was always better at running than I was at fighting and I caught Henry's pass and scored a touchdown. Several kids clapped me on the back and then Henry came up to me and said "Good job!"

Henry and I never became friends, but we now had respectful boundaries within which to operate peacefully.

* * * *

"I've been so immersed in the details of my story that now, when I focus more on my father's face, I see the right side of his mouth raised in a smile. He's trying to say something.

"I….I….I….ummmmmmm…..ummmmmmm"

He struggles to form a word, and I watch his face contort in concentrated agony, then frustration and finally defeat.

"Try to write it, Dad," I suggest and put a small pad on his lap and a pencil in his knolled hand. He grips the pencil tightly, bends his head toward the paper – I gently push his glasses back up his nose – and with fierce concentration he slowly scribbles some letters. He pursues this writing for several minutes, struggling to form each letter, while I watch helplessly. Finally, he lets the pencil drop and his head sinks back in exhaustion against his wheelchair, but his eyes are now focused clearly on me. I reach down and pick up the pad. The letters, jagged and rambling, deeply imprinted on the paper, I can, after a few minutes of studying, decode, and then see the words that form his thought. Silently, I read, "Very proud of you," and turn away from him to catch my breath and settle the tightness in my throat. But when I turn back, his eyes are closed and I see his twisted lips forming a half-smile.

"Thanks, Dad," I say awkwardly, knowing that we are sharing another special moment between just the two of us.

Slow Exits

Sarah Boyd sat at her kitchen table, the late morning sun pouring in from the windows behind her, flooding the room with sharp, white light. Sarah liked to work at this spot, paying bills, writing letters, doing crossword puzzles, in the late morning hours when the light fully illuminated her workspace but glanced off the other side of the table from where she was sitting without giving off a strong reflection. At seventy-three, her eyesight, even with glasses, was poor and she needed lots of light to read or write, but also had to be careful of too much glare that could bring on severe headaches.

On the table in front of Sarah, side by side, were two address books: one with a worn and battered cover, its pages extruding at odd angles, competing with different colored Post-its for attention; the other book new and sleek and promising, its gold embossed "addresses" gleaming from its cover. Next to the two books were a black ballpoint pen, a blue ballpoint pen and a red ballpoint pen. The red pen was for crossing out numbers in the old book that shc no longer needed; the black pen was for writing names and addresses in her new book and the blue pen was for listing the corresponding telephone number. She approached this task as she approached life: methodically and deliberately.

Sarah reviewed her arranged materials and made an audible sigh, determined to complete a task that she had put off for many years, blaming the rush of life and all her responsibilities in caring for Charlie and their six children as her primary excuse.

"This address book is probably more than forty years old," she said aloud, having recently developed the habit of speaking her thoughts as a defense against the oppressive silence surrounding her now that she was living alone. "It's really a shorthand history of my married life, crammed with names of people I've known through the decades. Some made quick exits, others lingered, and a few stayed at the center."

After turning seventy, Sarah had felt a strong need, a compulsion, really, for simplifying her life – clearing out, streamlining, disencumbering – so that with her reduced energies and limited patience, she could focus on essentials.

She had started this process two years ago when she sold the house where she had lived for over forty years and moved into her current condo in an over-fifty-five gated community. The move had been far more wrenching than she had expected but still, as she told herself repeatedly, it was necessary. The house, over sixty years old, with its four bedrooms and a huge family room, was too large and too demanding of upkeep for one widow whose five children, not counting Johnny who had died from leukemia at age four, were grown and all established in homes of their own, with only Ruthie, her unmarried, gay daughter, living close by and the rest scattered across the country. After her husband Charlie died, she stayed on for two more years, struggling to adjust to a solitary life following forty-six years of marriage and a household filled with the tumult and clamor, first of children, then teenagers and finally young adults, before their permanent departure and the ensuing eerie silence.

By the time of Charlie's death from a massive coronary, she and Charlie had been adjusting to life as a couple again, and they had talked about selling the house but only halfheartedly, for she knew that he was very sentimental about his home, the only house they had ever owned, and he could not bear to be parted from it. So they closed off three of the bedrooms, except on the rare occasion of visits from children and grandchildren, and confined their living pretty much to the kitchen and adjoining family room. Yet every week Sarah would thoroughly clean the entire house, including the living and dining rooms that were now museums of past lives.

The house seemed to be in perpetual need of maintenance or repairs, but Charlie had met these challenges eagerly, and she was grateful that these demands filled up his days in those brief years of retirement before his death. Sarah had struggled on alone, with only Mr. Rebus, her cat, for company, paying people to do all the chores that Charlie had done and rambling about the nine rooms, seeing only visions of the past and cares of the future. As she turned seventy and then seventy-one, she felt her energy draining out from her like air from a days-old birthday balloon. Arthritis and macular degeneration were her recently new afflictions and she felt herself slipping into a "slough of despair." Then she took hold of herself, exorcised all self-pity and resolved to rid herself of unnecessary burdens, the greatest of which was her home.

She knew of a new condominium complex just opening in her community where several senior members of her church were moving. She called the realtor, inspected the model units, toured the amenities on the premises and, in an act of desperate but inexplicable impulse, made a deposit on a two bedroom, two bath, single level, corner unit with a one-car garage and a lovely view of an adjacent nature preserve. All work on the outside of the condo and on the grounds would automatically be taken care of and, best of all, house cats and small dogs were allowed, so she wouldn't have to part with Mr. Rebus.

Stunned by her own audaciousness, she hurried home to call her children and joyfully announce this major leap forward. Her children, however, with the exception of Ruthie, did not respond positively to the news. Her two sons expressed first surprise and then disappointment at no longer being able to return to their childhood home at any time in the future.

"You live more than a thousand miles away and are always urging me to visit you," Sarah reminded both her boys.

Her two other daughters expressed interest in, or concern for, all the family mementos and familiar objects of past decades that they had no room for in their homes but wanted their mother to be sure to cart to her new condo, only one-third the size of the family house. Sarah heard long streams of meandering monologues, recognizing that her adult children were still her children and, like children, were mainly focused on their needs and memories. She listened impatiently to each child's objections.

"I'm sorry, dear," she calmly replied to each in turn, "but my mind is made up, and I'll be discarding most of the house's contents, so if there's anything special that you might want, you'd better come quickly and get it. If it's something small, I could send it to you. I know this must be difficult for all of you," she said in even tones tinged with tiredness, as she ended each of her phone conferences, "but I can't shoulder the responsibilities of this big house any longer, and I have to move on."

Fortunately for her plans, Sarah knew that her house was located in a good neighborhood where older homes had been kept up and often completely refurbished or expanded, and new, larger houses had been erected on the few empty lots. Consequently, the entire area reflected solid middle-class stability, comfort and pride of ownership and, as the realtors said, it had "cachet."

Sarah had called a realtor who was the son of a former neighbor. She felt comfortable with him since she had known him all his life. His name was Bud Tanger and he had come right over to meet with her and inspect the house from attic to basement. He then informed her that while her home was both spacious and sunny and had lots of "curb appeal," the kitchen and bathrooms needed updating.

"Everything is granite and marble these days, and stainless steel appliances are an important selling point, and a Jacuzzi bath and walk-in closets, all of which your home doesn't have," Bud said in his best professional manner, rattling off these details with impressive authority.

Sarah couldn't help but think of him as the little boy who had raced in and out of this house several times a day, the constant companion of her oldest son. Now he stood beside her, assessing what had been like a second home to him with total objectivity and candor. She felt somehow personally affronted by his catalogue of imperfections about the house, but then his face brightened and he spoke with enthusiasm.

"The good news is that the housing market is on the upswing right now and this is such a desirable neighborhood and there are few available houses in the area and your house has good bones and could easily accommodate a large family, so it's likely to go fast if it's priced right."

He then suggested a selling price and she unconsciously took a few steps back, her face registering genuine shock at the tremendous sum he said. So shocked was she, in fact, that she repeated the quoted sum back to him, her voice rising in the form of a question, and he shook his head affirmatively and added.

"That's for a quick sale. If you weren't in any hurry, we could add another fifty thousand and wait to see what happens."

"Oh, no," she quickly responded, happily recognizing that the price was many, many times more than the price that Charlie and she had paid for the house and it would easily cover the cost of her condo, with a great deal left over.

Sensing her eagerness, Bud suggested they draw up a contract immediately so he could arrange an open house as quickly as possible, to which, in an excited daze, she readily agreed. He then returned to applying his critical eye to the premises and suggested that in order to emphasize the spaciousness of the family room, several pieces of furniture should be removed and stored in the basement. He also suggested that she should begin right away to clean out the attic.

"Just in case any potential buyers might be interested in further expansion," he added.

He sat at the kitchen table where he had eaten so many meals with her family, and she had trouble seeing the competent businessman for the rambunctious boy. Without thinking, she asked him if he'd like some milk and cookies and he broke out in a wide grin, acknowledging this long past ritual.

"No thanks, Mrs. B," – what all the neighborhood children had called her – "but I'll take a soda if you have one."

She took a can of Sprite from the refrigerator, poured it into a tall glass, added some ice cubes and presented it to him.

"Thank you," he said with the same politeness he had exhibited as a boy, which always made her feel that he was a good influence on her own boys whose manners, no matter how much home instruction and drill, went awry when the family was out together in public.

After signing the contract – seeing the selling price in print brought a new surge of wonderment and joy – and agreeing on an open house date just ten days away, Sarah inquired about Bud's mother and father who had moved to Arizona, and his wife and twin boys. He jovially responded with brief descriptions and small anecdotes, all tinged with a nervous edge that suggested he was eager to be on his way. Glancing at his watch he uttered that long honored cliché, "Look at the time!" and said he had another appointment back at his office that he'd have to hurry to keep. She walked him to the front door and he turned and gave her a brief, awkward hug.

"Good to see you, Mrs. B," he said softly. Looking back across the hall, his face fell into a pensive pattern for a fleeting moment. "So many memories! Wonderful memories!" Then the big smile returned as he cheerfully said, "I'm sure this house will sell very quickly," and he was out the door and gone.

* * * *

In the ten days remaining before the Open House, Sarah hired a neighbor's son to carry some of the furniture from the family room down to the basement. Then she tackled the attic. Standing in the thick, sour air, surrounded by trunks and boxes and assorted artifacts of four decades, she suddenly felt pangs of guilt at disturbing these settled mementos of so many lives, so much family history, so much elapsed time. Her first impulse, a terribly selfish one, she admitted, was to have the whole place cleaned out, without looking through things and deciding what to save and what to discard, without investing time and emotional capital in what was sure to be a long, compelling journey into the past. She was fearful of this task, of the possibilities it presented for subverting her resolve to move on, to simplify, to live more fully in the present without ignoring her family's story but not being submerged in it.

"It would be so easy," she said aloud, "to turn around, walk down the stairs, turn off the light and leave all the ghosts in peace. I could call Bud Tanger and cancel the sale and call the condo agent and cancel that."

She felt tired and conflicted and then angry that this massive and daunting task had been left to her alone to undertake, to discriminate between what was trash and what were treasures.

"This job should rightly belong to my children," she protested to the crowded attic. Then she realized that the vast geographic distances and the hectic patterns of their lives and the shortness of time before the Open House precluded any sharing of this burden except with Ruthie, who was curiously lacking in all sentimentality – was this because she was gay? – and who, she knew, would advise her to "chuck the whole mess in a dumpster and be done with it." Anticipating that response brought her back to reality and, recognizing her burden as head of the family, she resolved that she would somehow get through this task and then get on with her plan.

For the next several days, she rose early each morning, had a quick breakfast and climbed the stairs to the attic. Under bare, hundred-watt overhead bulbs that made cobwebs dazzling in their opalescence, and with the humid air so thick and heavy that she felt she could almost see her breath, she tore through boxes and wardrobes and chests and suitcases and garment bags and mounds of assorted athletic equipment. This daylong effort, repeated over and over again for five days, left her in a surprisingly curious mood as she progressed from one end of the attic to the other. Perhaps it was the growing fatigue that reduced her reflection on individual items and their associations with past events, happy and sad, but the more she worked, the angrier she found herself becoming and the more uncompromising she became in her split-second decisions to save or discard.

"You ought to hold a yard sale, Mrs. B," Bud Tanger had suggested in a phone call to see how she was progressing. "You know what they say: 'One man's trash is another man's treasures.' You'd be amazed how much money a yard sale can bring in." But halfway through her prolonged work, she decided that she didn't have the strength to undertake the pricing and arranging and setting up for display that a yard sale required. Ruthie had offered to help her with the yard sale on the weekend, the only time she was free from her busy law practice, but Sarah declined.

By the second day she had rehired her neighbor's son, Ted, and together they had carted down endless armfuls of prom dresses, shoes, outdated overcoats, athletic equipment for nearly every sport known to man, Halloween costumes, ballet tutus, and dresses from every fashion era of the last half century, and had loaded them in a borrowed van and taken everything to the Salvation Army. There, the lady in charge instantly rejected more than half the offerings, which Sarah immediately deposited in the dumpster behind the building. After that experience, Sarah decided to follow Ruthie's advice, at least partially, and chucked almost everything, leaving a large record collection, a rickety rocker, an unpainted chest of drawers and several boxes of toys at the curb which, in her community, signified that they were free to anyone for the taking, provided that they were taken before the scheduled date for pickup of large items by the local sanitation trucks.

Sarah had been amused to observe expensive new cars from her neighborhood cruising by the discarded items at the curb, then returning and stopping while someone got out and inspected the things more closely. Within two days there was hardly anything left for the sanitation trucks to haul away. Bud was certainly right, she thought, about discards and treasures.

What she kept, besides family heirlooms like her grandmother's two handmade quilts and her mother's Christmas china, that had been hauled down every year for family dinners between Thanksgiving and Christmas, then carted back up after New Year's Day, were mostly documents of her children's lives: a box filled with old report cards, diplomas and cards they had given her and Charlie on birthdays, Mothers Day and Fathers Day, and letters from camp and college and the letters of Charlie Jr. from army boot camp. She kept some of Charlie's fishing gear in case either of her two boys, or their boys, might like to use it, although when they were little, she reflected, the boys only went begrudgingly with their father on fishing expeditions and came home complaining about everything. Still, she thought, some grandchild might become interested in fishing and be delighted to have his grandfather's gear, carrying on a tradition, so to speak. A box filled with disheveled photograph albums documenting family outings, birthday celebrations, school performances and assorted graduations was put aside, along with a box of christening gowns and baby blankets and the first favorite stuffed toy that each of her six children had adopted as an inseparable companion: two bears, a rabbit, two ducks, and an elephant, all worn and bedraggled and sad, with missing eyes or, in the case of the rabbit, an ear. This was her only concession to sentimentality.

Ted, who was fifteen and big and strong, had been a tremendous help. After the first two days and for the remaining four days, he had insisted that she stay in the attic and sort things and he would haul everything down the two flights of stairs. By the evening of the sixth day – "Just like God," she said, "I have to rest on the seventh day." – she was numb from exhaustion, but now the attic was almost bare. She had given Ted two hundred dollars and a box of baseball mitts that he wanted. She had told him to take anything from among the discards, but he expressed an interest only in the mitts and a pair of ice hockey skates that were one size too big for him.

There was one remaining chore that she had put off until she had rested for a day. Now, for what she hoped would be the last time, she climbed the attic stairs, her leg joints protesting at every step, and stood at the top of the stairs surveying the empty space. The roof beams slanting on either side elongated the attic so that it seemed to her like a long tunnel with the bare light bulbs marking progressive distances. Ted had swept the floor and the large empty room had a blank and barren look, with no imprint of its having been a repository for the flotsam and jetsam of so many lives, embracing so many years.

She had gone through the history of her family, she thought, and had removed most of the tangible objects pointing to that history so that the burden would now rest entirely on her memories: of things, of places, of events, of personality quirks and endearing traits, of sadness and joy, of conflicts and accommodations, mostly shaped by those inconsequential events that, for some reason that no one can explain, remain vividly stored in one's memory bank for life. Then she felt the tears on her cheeks and she realized that she had been standing there, lost in memories and reflections, for what now seemed like a long time.

"Pull yourself together, old girl," she said, and wiping her eyes with her hands, she headed down the tunnel to the far corner of the attic and its last remaining item: a four-drawer filing cabinet that Charlie had brought home from his office when he retired from the accounting firm where he had worked for thirty-two years. She knew it would be full of client files and other business ephemera, and her first instinct was to throw all the contents out without even a brief inspection. But her fastidious conscience told her that this would be a betrayal of Charlie's memory and what he had valued, so she resolved to give the contents of the four drawers at least a cursory once-over.

At her instructions, and as his final task, Ted had dragged the metal cabinet from its original space to where the nearest light could illuminate it. She instinctively dusted the top and front of the cabinet with a rag she had brought with her and then opened the top drawer. A long procession of neatly labeled files met her eye, all, she noted, in alphabetical order by the last name of what she assumed were clients. She took out the first folder, marked "Andersen," and quickly saw that the contents were an informal history of this man's business dealings with Charlie's company, as recorded by Charlie in numerous handwritten notes of phone conversations, visits and drafts of tax proposals Charlie had made to this gentleman.

She skipped to "Davis," and then to "Longworth," and each file contained the same type of material.

"Now why on earth would Charlie want to haul these records home when his last several years with the company had not been happy ones?" she protested. Then she remembered that he had always enjoyed excellent relations with his company's clients, just not the company's bosses, and probably these files evoked happy memories of those relationships.

The last folder in the top drawer bore the name Maddox, so she assumed the remaining alphabetized folders occupied the next three drawers, but on opening the third drawer from the top she saw that the folders ended with Zajohn. Tired and achy from leaning over, her eyes straining under the bare hundred-watt bulb, she sat on the newly swept floor and opened the bottom drawer where she found a few more folders randomly arranged. One contained numerous receipts from business trips that Charlie had taken: hotel bills, restaurant checks, airline tickets and convention admission passes. When clients had moved their businesses to other locations, she remembered, Charlie's firm made every effort to keep them as clients and had sent Charlie on these trips for that purpose. There was a time when she had five children under twelve and Charlie would be away a lot and she found it very hard, not only to cope with the children alone but because she herself was experiencing a period of feeling overwhelmed, incompetent and lonely. Yet she tried to conceal these feelings when he was home, and after several years Charlie finally insisted that the road trips be delegated to the junior accountants with the firm, which was rapidly expanding, and his traveling was over.

Sarah closed the folder and glanced at the labels on the others. One last folder in the rear was marked KR and she pulled it out and opened it. The first thing she saw was a note, handwritten in what she thought was rather fussy penmanship, saying, "Thanks for lunch and your thoughtful gift. I sure smell pretty! See you next Tuesday. Kay." Next she saw a Valentine card, one of those inexpensive, funny ones with cartoon characters on the front and a greeting, "Hey, Fella, Will You Be My Valentine?" She opened the card where the drawing showed the same cartoon character behind bars, with the message, "Oops! I Forgot! You're Already Taken!" The card was signed "Your secret admirer," and the handwriting was identical to the previous note. She picked up another note that, in the same handwriting, said, "CB, Thanks for the lovely blouse. I'll wear it to the Christmas party. 'Till next time, KR."

Sarah had read these messages in some neutral state of curiosity and suspended judgment, but then her focus became sharper and her thoughts raced in confusing speculation. Who was this Kay, with a last name that began with R? Charlie had had several secretaries during his business career but she was pretty sure she remembered all their names and no one had been named Kay or had those KR initials. And Charlie had never bought any gifts for a secretary for either a birthday or for Christmas; he had always delegated that task to her. She had stuck to the impersonal items like a box of good soaps, scarves and pocketbooks, certainly never a blouse and never perfume. Her confusion mounted and was now tinged with alarm. She read a fourth note: "CB, Just a quickie to let you know how great your presentation was yesterday. You looked calm and totally in command. You sure impressed the hell of me, but then I'm prejudiced and you know why. Congrats, KR."

Sarah was still sitting on the floor and she could feel the perspiration forming on her forehead. She picked up the next piece of paper and read: "Hi, good lookin, Glad you like my cookin. Too bad you're already 'tookin.' Happy Birthday again and again, Kay." She felt like she was suddenly peering through a microscope, seeing startling, ugly details of ordinary things around her that she had never conceived of before. She was fearful to read more but fascination demanded it.

She quickly skimmed the remaining assortment of notes and cards. They all had a breezy familiarity bending into intimacy, with details and expressions that could, she supposed, be either innocently explained or provocatively explored. Her mind was a jumble of conflicting emotions: astonishment that some other woman had had such an apparently very personal relationship with her husband, her Charlie, that she had known nothing about; suspicion, because to her recollection, he had never mentioned this person, suggesting a clandestine connection; anger at being blindsided with such a stunning, disconcerting discovery when all her energies were depleted because of this move, and the course of her life was undergoing radical change as she tried with fierce determination to put the past in perspective and focus on the future; guilt, as the swirling, confusing speculations played havoc with her concentration and stirred memories of betrayal long hidden in her heart.

Her head was throbbing. The light from the overhead bulb seemed to be growing dimmer and the air around her felt almost too thick to breathe. She threw the folder back into the drawer and slammed it shut. Gripping the hand pull on the top drawer, she struggled to rise from her sitting position, feeling sharp aches rampaging across her body. Once erect, she hurried across the attic until she reached the stairs and descended those in haste, without gripping the handrail. Only when she had switched off the lights and closed the attic door did she lean against the door and finally take one long, deep breath.

Later that day, after doing her marketing and then taking a long, hot bath and making herself an early supper, she felt ready for the next step she knew she had to take. She fixed herself a gin and tonic, a drink she enjoyed no matter what the season, and went to Charlie's desk in the far corner of the family room. Mr. Rebus jumped up on the top of the desk and was meowing for attention but she was too focused to respond to him. She knew exactly what she was looking for and where to find it. Opening the bottom left-side drawer, she pushed aside some papers and withdrew a black, faux leather-bound booklet with Charlie's company's name emblazoned in large gold lettering across the cover and the year printed underneath. Every year the company distributed this booklet in early December, containing all the names and addresses of its employees, who numbered over a hundred. The founders of this firm had, from its inception, encouraged a family feeling and this tradition, attenuated and erratic over the sixty-five years of the company's existence, sprung to life during the holidays with much office decorating, a lavish party and the updating of the expanding company roster so that holiday greetings could be exchanged. This was another task that Charlie had left to Sarah, after he had gone through the roster of names and placed a check next to those he wanted, or thought prudent, to send a card to. She bought the cards, signed each with "Best wishes for a successful New Year, Charles, Sarah and children," addressed them, stamped them and mailed them, usually about fifty in all.

She sat in the high-back leather desk chair that she had given Charlie for some birthday and switched on the ersatz colonial desk lamp. Then, taking another sip of her drink, she opened the booklet and began scanning the names that, in a democratic spirit, were all listed alphabetically, from partners to custodians, so she skipped to the last names beginning with R. While she found one Kitty, there was no Kay. The trail had ended.

She sat there drinking her gin and tonic, searching her memory for some vague recollection of any reference by Charlie, or anyone else in his company whom she had interacted with over the years, to a woman named Kay. She was concentrating intently when the phone rang, startling in its loudness. It was Ted's mother, Wilma, who thanked Sarah for her generous gift to Ted for helping in cleaning out the attic. Wilma inquired if there was anything she could do to help, and when Sarah, still distracted by her search for Kay, thanked her but politely declined, Wilma invited her to dinner the following Saturday. Sarah knew that that day was the Open House day but, eager to end the conversation, she accepted.

While listening to Wilma's commiserating with all the work involved in cleaning out a house and moving to a smaller home, Sarah idly turned the pages of the company directory and came to the last page labeled "Our Consulting Law Firm," with a list of a dozen names. Then she saw it: the third name down was Kay Rollins. When she had said goodbye to Wilma and replaced the phone on the receiver, she sat motionless for several minutes, staring at the name, working images of what Kay Rollins might look like, sound like; how tall she was and the color of her hair and did she wear it long or short – Charlie liked long hair – and what perfume she wore and how she dressed – probably in tailored business suits since she was a lawyer. This last thought disturbed her, bringing an invidious comparison since she had dropped out of college after her sophomore year to care for her ailing widowed mother and then shortly after her mother died, ending a long and painful illness, Sarah had met and married Charlie and never returned to college.

Charlie had wanted a large family, and as an only child, she did too. When their children arrived in rapid succession, there was never any thought of her being anything but a stay-at-home mother. But as more and more women pursued professional careers and balanced this pursuit with being a wife, mother and part-time homemaker and, according to the magazine articles Sarah occasionally read, you could do all of this and find fulfillment, she began to feel inadequate in some vague, uneasy way. Now she sat there picturing this Kay Rollins as a woman of style and wit and sophistication and breezy charm, possessed of all manner of worldly allure that she herself lacked and Charlie might find diverting. Then she remembered something important. The booklet was arranged with the names of employees' spouses in brackets after the employee's name. No name in brackets signified that the employee was not married. Next to Kay Rollins' name there was no bracketed name.

So there it was, laid out before her: her husband of forty-six years, her Charlie, her best friend and life partner, had had an affair. To her this fact now seemed irrefutable, knowing him as she did, yet obviously not knowing him as well as she thought. Her Charlie was a highly sexed man, which had been the one difficult area for most of her marriage when at the end of any day, no matter how long and hard he had worked at the office and she had worked in the house and handled the children, when she was exhausted and just wanted sleep, he was usually eager for sex. Her responses were so perfunctory, so listless, but even this passivity curiously seemed to challenge and excite him, or, in her darkest moments of doubt, possibly he didn't care how she felt or responded and she was simply a vessel for his private satisfaction. One conclusion she drew was that Charlie could never just be a friend with any attractive, unattached lady who had shown an interest in him.

Raw anger at Kay Rollins, at Charlie, at herself, was churning inside her and she felt on the verge of some physical explosion. So intense were her feelings and so furious her thoughts that she had gone back to the kitchen and made another gin and tonic before realizing where she was. She was standing by the sink, holding her drink, seeing nothing. Her legs felt weak and she sat down at the kitchen table and gazed absently ahead, remaining motionless while the evening shadows crept across the room and darkness enveloped her, matching the darkness within. The flight of her weary, disturbing thoughts careered between Charlie and Kay Rollins whom, strangely, she felt she knew intimately, and finally came to rest on herself. Sharp, intermittent pinpoints of light flickered beneath her half-closed eyelids as she journeyed deeper into the past, dragging forth thoughts and new associations that paralyzed her with dread and fueled her anger.

Her son Johnny had been her fourth child and, contrary to Charlie's desires, she had hoped he would be her last. He had been an easy delivery, unlike his two older brothers and sister, and from the beginning he had been a sweet, happy baby, curious, responsive and content. Everyone in the family was ensnared by his mild, sunny disposition and incurable smile, resulting in his really having five parents who cooed, cuddled and attended him. Then, when he was diagnosed with leukemia at two, and the next two years were one constant, prolonged, passionate focus to save him, she had been like a deranged woman, teetering between exhaustion and despair, incapable of functioning satisfactorily in any other area of her life and only going through the motions, guiltily.

Although she knew that Charlie was affected deeply by Johnny's illness, she felt that he was able to carry on and just add this burden to the package of burdens he carried. It was during those agonizing two years that a seismic shift took place in their relationship, especially in the bedroom. She wanted to talk and he wanted sex. She wanted to share her heartbreak, her fears, her fury. He would have none of that. His answer to her agonies and frenzied states was greater physical intimacy and more sex. Her frustration, anger and spitefulness grew in direct proportion to his physical overtures until she aggressively, heatedly resisted him at all turns. In rare moments of any state bordering on lucidity, she recognized that they were fundamentally and unalterably at odds in communicating their distress and succoring the other, but in the painful, emotionally charged battlefield of their bed, her disappointment and rage were revivified each night. Sullen, alienated, self-righteous, both Charlie and she had withdrawn from the battle, lying side by side in heart-pounding silence and frozen unease, separated unfathomably by hurt, confusion and resentment.

When Johnny died, her despair knew no bounds. She would have given into it and let herself slip into a total shutdown had it not been for her primordial sense of duty to her three living children. She went through the motions, returning to the routines of daily life with seeming equilibrium, but raging and shattered within, and the intimate rift between Charlie and her seemed unbearably set as she withdrew into herself, and, she admitted now, took his role in the family and all his good qualities for granted.

During this nearly two-year period of estrangement, little attempt was made by either Charlie or Sarah to resolve their charged issues, once initial overtures had been clumsily rebuffed on both sides. Sarah knew that her marriage had become a hollow shell but was incapable of changing it. To the world, and to their children, they were still a solid couple, adeptly performing all the rituals of parents and gregarious community members. Charlie went to work, earned bonuses, played golf with business clients, coached his sons' soccer team, helped around the house, amiably acted as host at dinner parties they gave and was an attentive husband at any social gathering they attended. On Valentines Day he had given her a dozen roses but unlike previous years, there was no Hallmark card expressing shallow sentiments, only a blank card with the flowers saying "Love, Charlie." She had given him a tie, boxed but unwrapped, and another blank card on which she had written, "Happy Valentines Day! Your loving family."

One night shortly after the first anniversary of Johnny's death, she awoke from a deep sleep to feel dull vibrations of the bed. Rapidly rising to full consciousness, she heard Charlie sobbing convulsively. Turning to face his back, she softly asked him what was wrong. Not turning to face her, his voice came in short spurts, high pitched and struggling for air amidst the pulsating sobs.

"It's too much," he cried. "I can't bear it any more."

She was stunned by this admission because up to that moment she thought he had been bearing up very well while she, on the other hand, had been slowly sinking in quicksand with no one in sight to rescue her. In an instinctive gesture, she placed a hand on his shoulder and he immediately rolled over and faced her, his face contorted in a welter of tears, snot and saliva, his body shaking with deep sobs.

"I'm losing you and my life is falling apart and I've made mistakes and I'm sorry," he blurted in one long stream of breath, then the sobbing continued.

Again, without thinking she drew closer to him and stroked his hair, saying nothing but recognizing with electric clarity that he was as miserable as she was, and that their mutual misery somehow suggested the hope of salvation. Then he wrapped his arms around her and clung to her as though he were drowning. They continued to lie in silence, broken only by his subsiding sobs, and when morning light glanced off the bedroom blinds they were sleeping in each other's arms.

That evening after dinner, when the children had left the table, she tentatively suggested that they see a marriage counselor. This idea, so alien to her sense of privacy, had come from both her desperation and her determination to take some dramatic step to get her marriage back on course. To her surprise and relief, Charlie, who seemed startled at first and asked a few questions, weighed her suggestion for only a few moments before agreeing. For the next five months they met with a counselor once a week, mostly together but sometimes, at the counselor's direction, separately. They were both strongly motivated to regain the loving bond they had enjoyed before Johnny's protracted illness and death, and, gradually, under the counselor's expert, gentle guidance, and much unburdening of sorrowful guilt and misperceived actions surrounding their responses to Johnny, they came to a new appreciation of each other and a new acceptance of meeting the needs of the partner through effort and open communication. When the counselor ended their sessions, both Sarah and Charlie felt that the marriage was back on an even, solid keel, and the ensuing years and two more children proved their notion to be correct.

Still sitting motionless in the intensifying darkness of her kitchen, Sarah had reviewed this sad chapter of their marital life from a new, provocative perspective. The cause of her sorrow at that time was specific, centering on her unbearable sense of loss and her withdrawing into herself, nurturing her pain like a miser with gold and refusing to acknowledge the pain of Charlie or her children. Charlie's sorrow, as he expressed it, was more generic and while focusing on Johnny, it included broad assessments of "mistakes" as he floundered about, seeking escape from his profound unhappiness and despairing of how to rectify his deteriorating marriage. These "mistakes," while generally alluded to, remained unspecified. Now she viewed them in a sharper light and, having made a judgment of guilt, weighed a sentence from her heart.

If you subtracted the three years of our growing estrangement, she thought, against the forty-three years of contented married life, the temporal balance would be heavily on the positive side. Then she pondered the debilitating nature of emotional pain and acknowledged that when the partners in any relationship are fully immersed in their individual problems, harnessing all emotional and intellectual assets to deal with them, they have little or nothing to give to their partner, leaving him or her adrift in silent, confusing isolation. She now saw that while she was nursing her pain, she had severed all meaningful connections with Charlie, literally casting him off. He was a man who, she knew, needed support, bolstering and confirmation through physical intimacy, all of which she had denied him. In a bizarre twist of reasoning, she now reflected that if Kay Rollins had stepped in and been a surrogate wife during their troubled time, thereby saving Charlie from total collapse, and facilitating his return to Sarah as a contrite, wiser and committed husband, with his ego and generosity of spirit intact, then Kay Rollins had actually done both Charlie and Sarah a favor.

In exploring the gray areas of the black and white facts, Sarah found forgiveness but not peace, for the scenario she had conceived, especially the time frame, was her construction of events which, she reminded herself, could have been very different. Still, in light of the remaining decades of happiness she had with Charlie after their estrangement, she felt willing, for her own sanity, to accept a truce with all lingering doubts and to relegate Kay Rollins to a distant, if occasionally nagging, past.

* * * *

As Sarah worked through the pages of her old address book, making a big X through most of the names and recording a few in her new book, she was mindful that she was making slow progress, primarily because she had lingered over names associated with significant events in her family's life: her obstetrician who had delivered all her children; the contractor who had built the family room addition to their house and all the frustrating delays and unforeseen problems and headaches associated with him; their former good friends, Sally and Joe Bendick, neighbors with whom she and Charlie had interacted nearly every day for fifteen years until Joe was convicted of embezzling funds from his company and sentenced to ten years in prison and Sally sold their house and with her two kids moved to her mother's home in another state; the local elementary, junior high and senior high schools her children had attended; relatives who had died; Mr. Johnson, the local florist who, in her younger years, was persistently flirtatious with her, and this secretly amused her until he left his wife and three little children and ran off with the widow of the former alderman; some business associates of Charlie's who had spilled over into their personal lives.

After several hours she had gotten to the S's and here she came upon the name of Martha Skelly, Charlie's last secretary, who had been with him for over twenty years. Martha was not only a good secretary; according to Charlie, Martha was completely loyal to him. Sarah never felt any tinge of jealousy in this office relationship since she and Martha had enjoyed a warm, friendly interaction and they were often co-conspirators. When Charlie had a cold or was feeling under the weather, Sarah would alert Martha to see that he didn't work too hard; or when Charlie undertook another diet and Martha, having been told by Sarah, would be as vigilant about Charlie's snacking at work as Sarah was at home. Although several years younger than Charlie, Martha retired from the company when he did, saying that after so many years with the same boss, she just couldn't see herself working for anyone else. Sarah and Martha continued to exchange Christmas cards but had had no other contact since Charlie's death.

A dangerous thought crossed Sarah's mind. She dismissed it but it kept flickering before her. As if dictated by sheer impulse, one minute she was at the kitchen table and the next minute she was standing at the kitchen wall phone, dialing Martha Skelly's home number. After four rings, she heard a voice that she instantly recognized as Martha's. Sarah had no idea what she was going to say but she stumbled forward.

"Martha, dear, hello. This is Sarah Boyd."

There was a slight pause. "Oh my goodness! Sarah!" Then another awkward pause.

Sarah spoke rapidly. "I was going through my old address book and when I came upon your name, I decided to give you a call and see how you are."

"Well, isn't that nice!" Martha said, in a surprised and sweet tone that Sarah knew was genuine. "I'm very well, thank you. What about you, Sarah?"

"Oh, the usual aches and pains of an old lady, but nothing major to complain about." Sarah said. "How is your husband?"

"He's fine," Martha replied, and Sarah remembered that Martha and Jim were a devoted couple who had never had children. "Are you still enjoying your condo?" Martha asked since on Sarah's previous Christmas card she had included a note assuring everyone that she loved her new life style.

"Yes, I am. It's so much less responsibility, you know. How is your father?"

Martha's voice took on a deeper tone. "He's as good as can be expected for ninety-one. He broke his hip this past spring, but he's on the mend and as chipper as ever."

These few pleasantries had given Sarah time to formulate a plan.

"Martha, do you remember Kay Rollins?" she asked in the most innocent, casual tone she could muster.

"Of course I do," came Martha's immediate reply with no elaboration but also, Sarah noted, no alarm or reluctant hesitancy in her voice.

Sarah forged ahead, trying to sound casual and relaxed

"Well, I've been cleaning out some files – you know how you accumulate more stuff than you know what to do with – and I discovered a lovely note and a Mass card that Kay had sent me when Charlie died," – a lie – "and somehow I overlooked thanking her, but, as they say, it's never too late, and I just thought I'd drop her a note apologizing for my monumental tardiness and explaining that in all the hubbub at the time of Charlie's death, it just slipped past me."

She was talking too much and too fast, in such a light and airy tone that she felt like she was performing in a British drawing room comedy, but once started, she couldn't stop.

"Anyway, I'd like to make it a little personal, you know, refer to some little anecdote about Charlie and her in their work together, but for the life of me, I can't remember anything that Charlie might have mentioned. So then I thought maybe you could help jar my memory."

Sarah finished her monologue, depleted and ashamed, but the die had been cast and now she nervously awaited an answer. After what seemed like an eternity of time, and the silence, itself, seemed to crackle with energy and flying thoughts, Martha spoke.

"Oh, Sarah, I'm so sorry but I thought you knew."

Sarah felt the heart pounding in her chest and she took a great intake of air and held it.

"Knew what?" she asked in a small, constricted voice, feeling she was at the edge of a high precipice, about to plunge down.

"Kay died many years ago. I thought you knew. Didn't Charlie tell you?"

"No." Sarah's voice was barely audible.

"It couldn't have been Kay Rollins who wrote you; it must have been some other Kay," Martha said.

Sarah sensed that Martha had caught her in her lie but the loyal, sweet person that Martha was, she was willing to foster another lie to save Sarah embarrassment.

"Yes, I guess so," was all Sarah could whisper, and Martha filled the void with a nervous monologue.

"It was really so sad," Martha said, "but then you know, of course, that she suffered from muscular dystrophy and had been confined to a wheelchair for all the time I can remember. Poor thing! She was a brilliant lawyer but with all her debilitating infirmities she needed someone to help her do the simplest daily tasks and was always accompanied by a private nurse. She was so brave, insisting on working for as long as she could, right up to nearly the end. She was the most cheerful, upbeat person I ever met. Nothing got her down. Everybody in the office loved her. She was an outrageous flirt, but it was all very innocent and all the men got a kick out of it. Charlie was especially kind to her and the three of us always celebrated our birthdays with a nice lunch, or I should say the four of us, since her private nurse was always present. Kay always baked cupcakes for our birthdays and we'd make a big fuss over them, which pleased her so much. I remember one year when Charlie and I gave her a blouse for her birthday and she cried. She was really a very special person. At the end she was quite alone, no family, and we went to see her in the hospital and she still put on a front and was joking and laughing and flirting. We all missed her when she died."

Martha's voice trailed off and there was more charged silence.

"Yes, very sad, very sad," was all Sarah could think of to say, for her thoughts were so jumbled that she was on automatic pilot. "Well, anyway, Martha, I'm glad to hear that you and Jim and your dad are doing well. You take care, and let's keep in touch."

"Yes, Sarah, you too," came Martha's confused, doubtful response.

Goodbyes were formally exchanged and Sarah slammed the receiver down, thoroughly relieved to escape from her feeble, disingenuous attempt to extract information from a genuinely nice human being. She slumped into the same chair she had arisen from only a few minutes before, now feeling drained and listless. But staring at Martha's name in the old address book brought her back, somewhat, into focus and then she felt lightheaded.

All her convictions now seemed baseless, but she argued in her defense that the circumstantial evidence had been misleadingly strong. Then a whole new thought arose: Why had Charlie never mentioned Kay Rollins? He certainly talked a lot about many people he was connected to through business, yet Sarah was certain she had never heard Kay's name or anything about her.

Clearly, he had a personal relationship, although innocent, with her, but he chose to keep it exclusive, to share none of its details with his wife. Why? It puzzled and perplexed her and she had to find a plausible answer.

For several days her mind worked on this challenge as she went about her daily routines, but she could think of nothing that satisfied her. Then one night while lying in bed and waiting for sleep to overtake her, which was always a long process, a new and not very flattering answer to the puzzle emerged. Sarah had been concentrating on Charlie, his personality quirks and behavioral patterns, but now she shifted her focus to herself.

From the brief sketch of Kay Rollins that Martha had described, Sarah saw Kay as a woman of generous instinct and beguiling warmth. These qualities were, for the most part, Sarah had to admit, not part of her own profile. She considered herself a good wife and mother but not a demonstrative one; it just wasn't in her nature, she reflected, to flatter or pamper or praise excessively or tease lovingly or express herself in gushing tones. She thought of herself as loyal, devoted, dutiful, supportive and strong, but she knew that she lacked that breezy, casual warmth, those quick, easy, small gestures of affection that she had admired in so many women she had observed. As her kids were growing up, they would tease her that she had no sense of humor and she always proved their point by taking self-conscious offense at this characterization. Charlie, on the other hand, loved puns and jokes and high jinks and was known for his bellowing laugh. His was an impish sense of fun that he shared with his children to their great delight, while she observed them from the sidelines, saddened by her incapacity to join in. She had always felt excluded from this inner circle within the family circle where, she consoled herself, she was the rock on which they all stood, the linchpin of their ordered lives. She was fiercely loyal to her husband and her brood and demanded total fealty in return. Charlie's natural gregariousness and zestful personality – so different from what one expected of a tax accountant, people would say – was, in social situations, contrasted by her pleasant but subdued manner, so she never competed with him for the spotlight and most people felt they complemented each other. Yet, if any woman mistook his enthusiasm for interest and became too flirtatious, Sarah was quick to step in with daunting authority.

Sleep still wasn't coming, and in the silence of her darkened bedroom, as Sarah's thoughts raced along this unexplored path, a new understanding was slowly emerging, inexorably and benignly linking Kay Rollins and herself to Charlie.

"Kay Rollins could never be a threat to me!" she cried, sitting up in bed, a broad smile spreading across her face. "She seems to have had all those warm, demonstrative qualities that I know I lack, but with her severe physical disabilities, all she had was her charm and flattery to gain attention. Why wouldn't Charlie enjoy an innocent, ego-boosting flirtation, knowing that this posed no danger to our marriage or his allegiance to me?"

Then she thought back to her own history.

"Look at the innocent flirtation I tolerated with Mr. Johnson, the florist, never dreaming he was serious until he left his wife and family and ran away with the alderman's wife," she reminded herself. "But knowing me as he did, Charlie never mentioned Kay for fear that I might resent her."

Sarah lay back down against her pillow, her mind still racing.

"Yes, I probably would have resented Kay if Charlie had described her the way Martha did. I'm not clever and witty, and I can't be cute or playful, and I envy those women who are. They have such sparkle! People naturally gravitate to them. I've never been like that and Charlie knew this and was being sensitive to my feelings"

Her husband was, she reflected, capable of such sensitivity. In their older years alone together, he had demonstrated this capacity in so many ways. Vivid images of her Charlie flooded her brain:

"Oh, Charlie, I understand. I really do," Sarah said aloud.

In the darkened room she stretched out her arms as if to embrace him, once again keenly feeling his loss. Then, turning on her side, content with the resolution of her nagging doubts, her mind now free to wander peacefully, she quickly drifted toward sleep.

Keeping Faith

HOLIDAY GREETINGS FROM THE BAXTERS

Dear Friends,

It's that time of year again when I look at the calendar and can hardly believe that another year has gone by and it's time for our annual Christmas letter. This year was like many others, filled with a mixture of exciting and sad events, as the Baxter family marches forward, greeting each new day with joyful anticipation, celebrating our happy family occurrences and drawing together as a support team in times of adversity or sadness. And we always remember that everything is God's will.

As many of you know, Mother Baxter passed away last February after a long battle with cancer, surrounded by her loving family. I can honestly say that she was a wonderful mother-in-law. Our relationship always reminded me of the Biblical story of Ruth and Naomi because I lost my own mother when I was only a teenager and then was given the blessing of another mother as an adult when I married Tom and shortly after that, Mother Baxter moved in with us when Tom's father died. I won't deny that we had our difficulties at first, because Mother Baxter was used to bossing people around, but as long as she got her way, she was a great help with the chores and the children. The Lord works in mysterious ways. While we all miss her terribly, we console ourselves that she has put down her bodily burden, been purified through her suffering and is now enjoying her heavenly reward.

You'll remember how a few years back, Mother Baxter sued and won a handsome settlement from the Friendly Trendy Store when their coffee burned her lips and scalded her mouth. We were surprised when her will was read and she had left all her money to the Church of Sanctifying Grace and the Reverend Dixon, especially since she knew that Tom's pension had been eliminated (just seven years before his expected retirement) when his company recently went into bankruptcy. Well, we consoled ourselves with the knowledge that her money was being put to a good cause and the Reverend Dixon could now afford a beautiful big home in which to welcome his flock. He started construction immediately and we will soon enjoy his Christmas hospitality in his wonderful new home. I can't wait to see it and I know that each room I pass through, and all the beautiful things I see, will fill me with thoughts of Mother Baxter and the gift of Christian charity.

The Lord always seems to balance our lives, and the sorrow we felt at Mother Baxter's passing was replaced with joy in April when Stella Rose, our youngest child – at seventeen, really still my baby – was married to John Dooley, a nice young man who she knew since the third grade. Tom and I were hoping that they would finish high school before marrying, but you know how kids are these days, and there was just no holding them back. The Reverend Dixon married them and, yes, I'm now a grandmother for the second time. In September, Stella Rose and John Dooley presented us with a healthy baby boy, Lawrence Thomas Dooley, named after both the baby's grandfathers. It's a good thing we have a double-width trailer now that John Dooley and baby Lawrence have joined our family, for, as you can imagine, with Stella Rose's older brothers, Timothy and Tom Jr., when he's home on leave, still living with us, we're pretty packed in. It would have been nice, of course, if Mother Baxter had left something to her grandchildren but with the Lord's help, we'll get by.

Stella Rose tries to be a good mother and John Dooley is working as an usher at the multiplex cinema over at the shopping mall. It's a challenging time for both of them, adjusting to the demands of a baby when they're still kids themselves and keep thinking about going out and having fun. Tom and I help, but we want them to develop a sense of responsibility and to realize what it means to be parents before they decide to have more babies. It's hard, living in a trailer, not to hear their arguments, and we try to give them their space. They're shocked at how much everything for a baby costs, and John Dooley's paycheck doesn't go far. John Dooley spoke to the Reverend Dixon, but he wasn't much help and now, Stella Rose and John Dooley have stopped going to church. Please remember them in your prayers.

Schooling just doesn't seem to agree with any of my children because they're all so anxious to get on with life. I'm the only one who got through high school, so they must take after their father. Timothy turned nineteen in May and is working at the local super market. He misses his daughter, Rachel, now that she's moved with her mother, Heather, and Heather's husband out of state, and Timothy is saving up to buy a motorcycle so he can visit Rachel.. We understand why Heather wanted a fresh start once she got married, and we pray that Rachel will remain part of our family. Rachel will be two in January and we all miss her.

Tom Jr. is on his third tour of duty in Iraq and we're all so proud of him. He loves the Marines and is planning to make it his career. He calls us whenever he can and from what he tells us, I can report to you that he and his buddies can't always tell who the enemy is, but they are very proud to be fighting for democracy. Last month, he was very sad when his best buddy was killed in a road ambush, but we all know he died a hero for a good cause. He left a wife and two babies and we pray for them and know the Lord will provide.

Our oldest daughter, Margaret Sharon, has inherited all of her father's mechanical skills and is making good money at the Toyota plant just down the road from our trailer park. She likes nothing more than to be in her overalls, covered with grease, fixing a car. She's moved in with an older lady who works as a supervisor at the plant and owns a very nice house, and they seem to be good friends and take long motorcycling trips on the weekends. I'm hoping she'll meet a nice man from the plant but no luck yet. Whenever she visits, I keep telling her that she's twenty-nine and I want more grandchildren, but she just smiles and hops on her Harley and roars off. I'll keep hoping and praying that in the Lord's good time, she'll settle down.

When Tom's factory closed this past June, we had a rough couple of months but my waitressing tips got us by. If Mother Baxter had lived a little longer and saw how rough we had it, I'm sure she would have changed her will, but that's just wishful thinking The Reverend Dixon says that we should be doers, not dreamers, but sometimes I wonder if he ever dreamed about having a big new beautiful home. I know I sure have. Anyway, we kept faith with the Lord and come September, Tom got a job driving a school bus, and Tom Jr. contributes what little he can so we're scraping by, praise the Lord.

I guess you heard about the tornado that touched down in our area last August and even hit part of our trailer park, killing a mother and her young baby. I've never seen such destruction first-hand. Trailers and trucks and cars thrown about in the air like twigs and all twisted and upside down when they landed, and the winds roaring so loud you could hardly hear the folks screaming, and people running about in mad confusion. The Lord in his mercy took pity on the Baxters and spared us, for which we give much thanks, but He did test our faith again in November, just before Thanksgiving. I wasn't feeling well and my doctor found a spot on my lung that the tests say is cancer. I guess that's what comes from smoking two packs a day since I was fifteen.

I'm scheduled for an operation right after the holidays. We don't have any medical coverage since Tom's factory closed, but I'm hoping that the Reverend Dixon might have a little of Mother Baxter's money left over after he finishes furnishing his big new house and he'll help us out. He's always preaching that charity begins at home and I'm sure he'll recall that Baxter money built his home.

I know the Lord will not let us down, and at this holy time of year, I pray that He will bless all of you and abide with you and keep you strong in your faith.

A Blessed Christmas and Love,

Hannah, Tom, Tom Jr., Timothy, Margaret Sharon, Stella Rose, John Dooley, baby Rachel and baby Lawrence.

The Compson Trilogy

It all started as a joke, really. Rebecca and Marty Springer, a couple whom my wife Jenny and I had known since our college days, were visiting us at our condo in St. Croix. We had all been to a big party the previous night, given by our neighbors, the Yorks, and over breakfast we were discussing the people at the party. It was a beautiful day, I remember, and sitting on our terrace we could see the foaming surf and smell the jasmine.

"You have such a nice group of people here," Rebecca said, waving her arm to indicate our condo complex.

"Yes, it's a nice mix," Jenny said, buttering her toast. "We have retired people like the Yorks and Christina Pope, and then we have couples in their thirties, like us, and some in their forties and fifties."

"And we're not all American, as you can see from last night's gathering," I said.

"I enjoyed that couple from France and that funny Russian lady…what's her name?" asked Marty.

"Olga," I said.

"Does anyone live here full time?" Rebecca asked.

"The Barlows – she's the tall pretty blond with the short husband," Jenny said, "and the Lanes – he's the man with the large birthmark on his cheek. And that's about all I can think of"

"Christina Pope," I added, "but she travels a lot so she's not here all the time."

"A good number of people rent, but they come back every year," Jenny said.

"I can see why," Marty said. "This place is paradise." Then, with a broad smile and a wink, he looked at me and said,

"Lucky for you, David, that you married a woman who can keep you in this luxury."

"It's good for his writing," Jenny said matter-of-factly, and I nodded. I was used to our friends' making casual references to the fact that Jenny's inherited money sustained our life style that I, alone, could never have afforded.

Rebecca took a sip of her coffee and then looked hesitantly at Jenny.

"There's only one person I find a little odd," she said, raising one eyebrow.

"You mean difficult!" Jenny said quickly. "And annoying!"

"Yes," Rebecca said, smiling with relief.

"I wonder who that could be," I said in mock confusion, and we all laughed.

"Dianne Addison," Rebecca announced, and our laughter continued.

"She's really something!" Marty said. "Rebecca and I were having a great conversation about Provence with the French couple when Dianne barged in, changed the subject and took over the conversation."

"Let me guess," I said, "Whatever the new topic of conversation was, it was all about her! Right?"

"You got it!" Marty yelled, nearly jumping out of his chair. "She talked about her trip to Norway."

"That's Dianne!" Jenny said, her lips curving down. "Always wants to be the center of attention. If she's not talking about her trips or her damn dogs or her health issues, she's dropping names left and right as though she's on intimate terms with anybody who's somebody. She once mentioned having lunch with a famous designer who my sister Barbara happens to know quite well, and I asked Barbara to find out if he knew Dianne and he had never heard of her. We figured out that it must have been a luncheon for several hundred people at which he spoke, but she made it seem like it was just the two of them. Typical Dianne!"

"Her husband seems quite nice," Marty said. "On the quiet side."

"He'd have to be to live with Dianne," I said.

"Porter's her second husband," Jenny explained. "Her first husband left her, 'childless and destitute' is how she describes it, but she was in her thirties, for god's sake, and she met Porter a short time after and they were married soon after that, and he adores her, the poor soul!"

"Any children with Porter?" Rebecca asked.

"No," I answered. "According to Dianne, her health won't permit her to have children. What these mysterious health issues are, she's never been specific."

"Whatever they are," Jenny said, almost snorting, "they're a blessing to the children she doesn't have."

"What I find pretentious," I said, "is how you can never mention a Broadway play she hasn't seen, although she can't remember any details but can quote some critic. Mention any museum exhibit back in New York and she's either been to it or is planning to see it, even if you know that it's already closed. And you can't name a book that she doesn't have an opinion on, even if she hasn't read it, because some friend of hers has."

"That's like what happened last night." Rebecca said, folding her napkin and placing it on the table. "A group of us were talking about a collection of short stories by Colm Toibin that we had all read, and Dianne came over and listened for about five seconds before announcing that although she had the book, she hadn't read it yet, but then she launched into a monologue on the latest Robert Ludlum book. We all stood there, completely flabbergasted, and then we quickly scattered."

"She sure knows how to clear a room, doesn't she?" Marty said.

"Thank goodness we only have to deal with her for the three months we're here," Jenny said. "She's tried to make contact with us and a few other couples back in New York but we've managed to avoid her." Jenny put a hand on my shoulder and smiled. "David swears that she has a negative effect on his writing and he can't write a sentence for days after he's been with her. Don't you, darling? He says she's affected his productivity and hence his income as a writer."

"Well, all her bragging does get under my skin," I conceded. "The issue for me is that she's a complete phony and everybody knows it but she thinks she's fooling us and we always let her get away with it."

"It's too bad you can't catch her in some outright lie," Marty said. "That might tamp her down a bit."

I laughed along with the rest, but at just that moment the idea came to me and I shared it immediately with the group.

"She's always claiming to have read everything, or at least to have a copy of every book that's currently popular. What if we created a phony book and started discussing it among ourselves. How long could she resist taking the bait and claiming to have read it?" I asked.

And so our innocent prank was born and I never dreamed where it would lead.

* * * *

Since I was the writer in the group – with two published novels and a collection of short stories, well reviewed by most critics but poorly received by the reading public – Rebecca and Marty and my wife looked to me to get our fictitious piece of fiction started. I agreed, but because they were all highly creative people, I insisted that this had to be a collaborative enterprise. That same afternoon, after a lazy day of swimming, snorkeling and sunning, we were back on our terrace enjoying wine and cheese and the late afternoon breezes when all three, in high spirits, urged me to start the process.

"Well, I've been giving it some thought," I confessed cheerfully, "and for starters, I think it should be something monumental, sweeping, the kind of historical drama that isn't popular any more but might be ready for a revival. The kind that places vivid fictional characters in gripping historical settings."

"Like *Gone With The Wind*! Rebecca said excitedly.

"Yes," I said, continuing. "But let's make this so grand that it takes a family we'll call the Compsons and parallels their lives with the history of the country from the Revolutionary War up to the millennium. And it's not just one book; it's three. A huge, sprawling saga! And we'll call it *The Compson Trilogy*."

"I love it!" Jenny yelled, and Marty started to clap.

"What's the name of the author?" Rebecca asked.

"I thought about that, too," I answered. "Let's give it an extra twist by naming the author Thomas Compson, and the author can claim that this is a work of fiction based loosely on facts and stories, handed down through generations, about his forebears."

The broad smiles from my audience encouraged me to continue. "Collectively, the Compsons will be the American Everyman: ordinary folks who, over time, are subjected to all of life's challenges – wars, diseases, crop failures, recessions and depressions, swindles, religious movements, mechanical and technological advances, societal changes and world events – all the things the little guy has no control over – while, on the personal level, they're dealing with love, lust, death, jealousy, estrangement, betrayal, ambition, setbacks and the struggle to survive."

"And through all of this," Jenny interrupted, her eyes dancing with pleasure, "there's a family motto, passed down through the generations and formulated by the patriarch during the Revolutionary War; something very simple that echoes down through the centuries and inspires the clan in all their struggles."

"Nothing grand. Something simple, befitting ordinary people," Rebecca suggested.

"Something about family togetherness," Marty said, "that would have mass appeal to the family-values crowd."

"How about 'Family Always First'?" Rebecca offered.

"Just 'Family First,'" I said. "Keep it simple. Loyalty is implied."

"Agreed!" my three co-conspirators said in unison.

"Now we haven't got much time," I continued, "if we're going to talk about *The Compson Trilogy* at the next party on Saturday at the Devlins'. That only gives us six days to get a broad outline down."

"Ill be recording secretary," Jenny volunteered.

"Nothing too elaborate," I cautioned. "Just a running scenario of major events and central characters we can allude to with Dianne. We can ad-lib the rest, just to rouse her curiosity and see if she claims to know the trilogy."

"Or even better, to have read it!" Jenny said, laughing.

'So think about plot lines that we could connect to events in history and how they might affect some characters," I suggested, "but for every generation we include, it's better to focus on a few central characters."

"We can develop our story over cocktails each day," Rebecca suggested.

"Nothing like a few drinks to get those creative juices flowing," I said. "Give free rein to your imaginations and let's see what we come up with."

We had formulated a plan and were all eager to contribute to the creation of *The Compson Trilogy*. For the next six days our cocktail hour was longer than usual and our imaginations, fueled by wine, Margaritas and pina coladas, were on overdrive. We created Jebediah Compson and made him a foot soldier in the continental Army, crossing the Delaware with George Washington and suffering through the winter encampment. His son, Josiah Compson, we had as part of the Lewis and Clarke expedition to the West while a nephew, Adam Compson, fought at the Battle of New Orleans in the War of 1812, and his grandson, George Compson, was in the Army of the West during the Mexican American War. We had one branch of the Compsons migrating to the West with a wagon train and even had a Compson bachelor joining the rush for gold in California.

For the Civil War we created two Compson cousins: Joseph, who fought for the North with Sherman, and Michael, who worked on a blockade running ship that brought supplies to the South. For the Reconstruction Period we placed Henrietta Compson front and center, as she inherited a small farm after the death of Michael and her two other brothers, all in the war, and struggled to survive on her land. We recognized that we were in a danger zone with Henrietta and, with much alcohol and laughter, struggled to avoid making her a poor man's version of Scarlet O'Hara, so instead of spunk and grit and coquettish beauty and ruthless drive, we made Henrietta plain and unmarried, with only an inarticulate will to survive.

"No speeches like 'As God is my witness, Ill never go hungry again!' for Henrietta," I told my collaborators. "Only a basic instinct to endure."

Switching back to the Northern side of the clan, we came up with Abel and Mary Compson, a young married couple with three children on a small farm in Pennsylvania, who were caught up in one of the religious awakening movements that periodically swept the country throughout the nineteenth century. Abel and Mary came under the spell of an itinerant preacher, the Reverend Elijah Woodstone, a cross between Elmer Gantry and William Jennings Bryan, who bilked them and many of their farming neighbors out of their land and meager assets with a bogus plan for creating a communal utopia. Forced from their land, Abel and Mary migrated to Philadelphia where they struggled to survive and eventually lost two of their children to the dangers of big-city living. A son, George, was killed in a bar brawl. Their daughter, Alice, being forced into prostitution by a manipulative boyfriend, gave birth to an illegitimate child, Henry Compson, before dying from septicemia. Jenny took the lead in this sequence and was carried away with many references to Upton Sinclair, Theodore Dreiser and Hart Crane.

We were all thoroughly enjoying our plot pastiche until we realized that we had only one day left to cover an entire century. Fortunately, there were so many wars or major conflicts in the twentieth century, with the Great Depression thrown in for more fodder, that in one extended cocktail session we consumed two pitchers of Margaritas and quickly sketched successive generations of Compsons engaging in WWI, WWII, Korea, Vietnam and the first Iraq War, with death, dismemberment, divorce and post-traumatic stress dominating this portion of our canvas.

"It's really just the luck of the draw as to when you were born and your eligibility for fighting in any war, isn't it?" observed Marty. "Some poor bastard, like our Peter Compson, is twenty in 1915 and goes off to fight the Huns, then comes home and soon starts a family, and his twin sons, Albert and Steven, are the right age to fight the Huns again in WWII. Then Steven, as a career enlisted man, goes off to Korea. Albert's son, John, gets killed in Vietnam and Steven's son, Steve, Jr., turns eighteen and in some adolescent, patriotic daze wants to continue his family's long military history and enlists in the army just in time to catch the Iraqi Express."

We nodded in gloomy agreement.

"Unless you came from a wealthy family as far back as the Civil War and could pay three hundred dollars to some poor slob to take your place as a soldier," Rebecca said acidly, draining her glass and pouring herself another Margarita before continuing. "And by the twentieth century, the rich and the well-connected had other ways of gaining exemptions and deferments."

"Well," I said, "we wanted to create a history for an American Everyman, and obviously that involves a lot of fighting and dying for whatever cause that our leaders consider worth the shedding of young men's blood."

"But I'll bet," Marty said, "that this fictional scaffolding of a clan we've created could parallel the history of many American families. For every generation since the American Revolution, with few exceptions, there's been a call to arms. Quite a violent history, don't you think?"

Jenny waved her arms excitedly. "That's why we should come up with some quotation about the destructive forces unleashed by wars and place it at the beginning of our book."

"Easy, Jen," I responded. "Let's not get carried away. Remember, this is only a plan to fool Dianne."

"No, I agree with Jenny," Rebecca said. "A good quote that we can all remember, and allude to, just gives greater credence to our story."

"Verisimilitude," I offered with a pedantic flourish, the Margaritas beginning to thicken my tongue.

"I have a good quote," Marty shouted, rising from his chair and waving his arms for attention. 'Older men declare war, but it is youth that must fight and die.'"

"Great!" shouted Jenny.

"Who said that?" asked Rebecca.

"Herbert Hoover," said Marty. "I gave a speech about him in high school."

We all laughed.

"We still haven't said anything about Thomas Compson, the author of this magnum opus," Jenny reminded us.

"That's easy," I said in a rush of alcoholic bravado. "Thomas is the cousin of Steve Jr., and he works his way through Penn State, becomes a high school history teacher and researches his family's genealogy during his summer vacations. Some female cousin had inherited an old trunk from her grandmother, filled with memorabilia from previous Compson generations – diaries, letters, pictures, local newspaper clippings mentioning various Compsons

– and an old family Bible that belonged to Jebediah Compson, whose parents migrated to American from England. This cousin gives the trunk to Thomas and, Voila! a great historical drama is born! Now let's have dinner."

* * * *

The next morning, the day of the Devlins' party, Jenny reviewed with us all the notes she had hastily scribbled during our creative surges, occasionally struggling with deciphering her handwriting when too much exuberance, mixed with too much alcohol, had caused her to falter in her note taking.

"We'll never remember all these names," I conceded, after Jenny had finished reading her notes, "but that doesn't matter. We can ad-lib and fill in the gaps as much as we want. The important thing is to pique Dianne's interest and see where we go from there."

"Or where she goes from there," Jenny corrected me.

Feeling like a college kid about to play an elaborate fraternity prank, I looked forward to the coming party.

* * * *

By seven thirty that night the Devlin party was in full swing and all the guests had gathered. I was making my way back from the makeshift bar holding a drink for Jenny and one for myself when I spotted the always animated Dianne and her ever quiet husband Porter in a tight circle with Marty, Rebecca and Jenny. I handed Jenny her drink and she said with a smile, "We've just started talking about *The Compson Trilogy*."

"Oh, yes," I replied, fully prepared to play my part. "A marvelous read! Really fascinating," I said, probably with overly dramatic enthusiasm as I was warming up.

"I think I've read it, but I'm not sure," Dianne said brightly. "Tell me more about it."

"Well, it's really a history of America as experienced by a large clan, the Compsons, mostly ordinary people, and told by a current family member, Thomas Compson." I spoke as if I were reciting a memorized line from a play.

"Where did the Compsons come from?" Dianne asked, furrowing her brow in concentration.

"Originally from England," Rebecca said, "but they migrated to Pennsylvania before the American Revolution."

Marty entered the conversation. "And you know how all those old families had many children, and they scattered to every part of the country over time."

"Yes," Jenny said, "and this family's history encompasses most of the pivotal events in America's history. I loved the part when George Compson was a soldier with the Army of the West and Kit Carson was a guide and they became friends."

"And they fought the Indians together and Carson saved George's life when he was attacked by a bear," Rebecca added.

"I thought the description of the Battle of New Orleans was extraordinarily vivid," Marty said with gusto. "And in the midst of all the fighting and turmoil, you have the love affair between Adam Compson and the beautiful Creole half-breed, Zanora, who dies in childbirth."

"And the Compson cousins fighting on both sides in the Civil War," Jenny interjected.

"And the horrible descriptions of life in the trenches when Henry Compson is at the front lines in the first World War," I said. "And then the moving scenes when his wife and baby die in the 1918 influenza epidemic."

"And throughout the history of this family, you see how they try to live by the family motto, 'Family First,'" Marty said, "but they're simple, salt-of-the-earth people who get caught up in life-defining events, which is why the author chose a moving quote to characterize their plight. Let's see if I can remember it. Oh, yes. 'Older men declare war, but it is youth that must fight and die.' Very appropriate, I thought." Marty smiled broadly at us, clearly pleased with his segue into the book's motto.

"Is Thomas Compson a professor at Yale?" Dianne asked. Turning to her husband, she continued. "Porter, you remember that charming professor from Yale and his wife – we met then on our trip to China. Wasn't his name Compson?"

Dianne's husband smiled and looked blankly at his wife.

"This Thomas Compson is a high school history teacher on Long Island," I said.

Dianne absorbed this information with obvious disappointment but was undeterred. Turning to her husband again, she asked: "What's the name of that three-volume set you picked up at the bookstall at the fair last summer? It's in your den, right next to your desk, and I've always wanted to read it but I'm just so busy. Is that *The Compson Trilogy*?"

Porter thought for a minute before answering. "No, dear, that's *The Decline and Fall of the Roman Empire* by Gibbons," he said softly.

Dianne fought on. "Perhaps I've only read the first volume," she said tentatively. "It sounds so familiar. Yes, that's probably it: I've only read the first volume."

It was time to spring the trap.

"That's not possible, Dianne," I said, smiling broadly. "It hasn't been published yet. Thomas Compson was my college roommate," I lied, "and he sent me the manuscript for my comments and suggestions."

"And David thought it was so outstanding that he shared it with us," Jenny said quickly, indicating Rebecca and Marty.

For a moment there was total silence within our tight circle of smiling and smirking faces and Dianne's eyes grew larger as she digested my revelation. Then, rather than being crushed by it, she took a new, unexpected tack.

"You say the Compsons originally settled in Pennsylvania?" she asked.

"Originally," I answered matter-of-factly, now bored with the game.

"That's interesting," she said, smiling enigmatically. "My family goes way back too, practically to the Founding Fathers."

She paused, surveying our expressions to gauge the impact of this last statement. I recalled that Jenny had once commented to me that Dianne would like us to believe that her family was standing on the Cape Cod shore to welcome the Mayflower. I had no idea where Dianne was heading but I listened with rapt attention.

"It seems to me that way, way back, I remember a reference to cousins on my mother's line that were from the Philadelphia area."

My mouth drooped. Diane was becoming more animated as we all watched, fascinated.

"I think that their name might have been Compson. I can't be sure because it was such a long time ago that I heard some reference to this branch of the family, but the more I think about it, the more confident I am that it *was* Compson!" she declared triumphantly, and I heard my wife bursting forth with nervous giggles. Dianne was on a roll! "David, where can I contact Thomas Compson? You said he teaches on Long Island, didn't you? He might want to include some of my mother's family's fascinating history." She paused for only a moment. "Or perhaps he has!" she declared, a luminous smile covering her face, her eyes sparkling with anticipation.

Jenny turned to me, still giggling, and in a half-mocking tone said, "Yes, David, tell Dianne how to contact Thomas Compson."

I took a long sip of my gin and tonic as my brain seethed with scenarios. I felt all eyes watching me intently, waiting for my response. This has to be my finest dramatic moment, I thought. I stared directly at Dianne, my voice sinking to a lower register. I took a deep breath, imitating a sigh.

"It's very sad, Dianne. Really tragic! Thomas Compson was killed just two months ago. Only thirty-three years old."

"Oh, my god!" Dianne yelled, her hand clutching her throat. She was never one to shrink from a dramatic gesture. "How did it happen?"

I was prepared.

"Hit by a bus, crossing the main street in his town. The bus driver had had a heart attack and lost control."

"No!" Dianne gasped.

"He was just going for the morning paper and a coffee before heading off to school," Jenny ad-libbed, and I shot her an approving glance.

"How awful!" Dianne exclaimed. Her hand had moved from her throat to her heart. She turned to Porter and in a plaintive voice said, "He could be my relative."

Porter touched her arm sympathetically.

"Was he married?" she asked

"Yes," I answered, "for about a year."

"You must give me his address, David. I must write to his wife," she said resolutely but I knew she probably wouldn't. Still, I cut her off at the pass.

"Sorry, Dianne," I said, my words coming more slowly as if they were waging a battle with my emotions, "but she was with him. Tom was killed instantly and she died the next day. A double tragedy!"

I looked off in the distance as if picturing the scene of the carnage and, affecting a clouded look, imagined the awe my co-conspirators were feeling at my latest inventiveness and stellar performance.

"One of David's college friends sent us a clipping from the local newspaper, detailing the accident," Jenny said, imitating my lugubrious tone.

Dianne stayed in the dramatic mood for a moment longer before turning to practical matters. "What about his trilogy? Is it going to be published?"

"Well," I said, momentarily caught off guard, "it wasn't a final draft…still very rough, actually…"

"But with a good editor," Dianne interrupted me, "surely it could be whipped into shape. I know several editors in New York that might be interested."

"My editor, Jacob Reisman, has already agreed to look at it," I lied, leading her to a dead end.

"Please let me know what's happening with it," she said, adding with a smile, "I've often thought of writing about my family, and I would if my health were better, but the Compsons could be the history of some of my forebears. Promise me you'll keep me informed."

"I will," I said, then drained my gin and tonic and excused myself to get a refill. I told Tom Devlin who was serving as bartender to go heavy on the gin.

* * * *

Dianne was notorious for flitting from one thing to another, for expressing interest in something for five minutes before forgetting about it, and I gave little thought to *The Compson Trilogy* after the Devlin's party. But upon our return to New York,

I received several emails from Diane inquiring about the status of the manuscript, which, by her third email, she was describing as "practically my family history." I kept giving her vague answers about the need for extensive editing and then finding the right publisher, and, when she persisted, even thought about telling her the manuscript had been lost. When she continued to bombard me with questions, I decided to enlist the aid of my editor, Jacob Reisman.

I described my little joke to Jake and told him how we had developed a running outline with a horde of characters and subplots, all interwoven with major historical epochs through the last two centuries. I confessed that because of Dianne's inexplicable persistence, my prank had backfired and suggested that he could help by writing me a letter, on official stationery, of course, stating that after reading *The Compson Trilogy* manuscript, his professional opinion was that it was in too rough a form to do anything with.

"And, Jake, you could add that the market is not currently open to publishing sweeping historical dramas. Than I could send a copy of your letter to Dianne and that should end her pestering me."

Jake, who had been my only editor since my first novel was published, sat behind his desk, the ceiling light bouncing off his steel spectacles and bald head, listening with quiet attentiveness to my plea. When I had finished, we sat in silence for several minutes and he seemed deep in thought. Finally he spoke.

"You know, David, that's not true," he said, leaning forward in his chair and pushing his glasses up to the bridge of his nose.

"What's not true?" I asked, confused. Jake was the last person I'd expect to lecture a writer on creating a fable in formulating an innocent prank.

Jake shook his head.

"It's not true that I wouldn't be receptive to some well-written historical saga. It just might be the right time for a good old-fashioned story with the sweep of history to hit the market."

"But, Jake," I protested, "be that as it may, there is no well-written historical saga."

"But you just said that you and Jenny and your friends had developed an outline and created character sketches," he said.

"Yes, but just as a lark, a running joke, a creative parlor game, fueled with a lot of liquor," I said.

"Do you still have your outline?" he asked

"It wasn't even an outline," I answered, annoyed at the turn in our conversation. "Just some notes that Jenny took on our imaginative ramblings."

"And do you still have them?" Jake asked

"I doubt it," I said, weary of this line of questions.

Jake rose from his chair, stuck his hands in his pocket and starting pacing around his office, circling me as I remained in my chair.

"You haven't published anything in – what's it been – three years?" Jake asked, not pausing for an answer. "You've been working on that mystery novel for the last year and you admit it's not going well and from the first few chapters you shared with me, I honestly don't think this is a genre for you. Except for that, you've told me about four or five short stories you've done, but that hardly makes a publishable collection. And sooner or later, even a wife as wonderful and supportive and rich as Jenny is going to expect some tangible results for all of her support."

Jake stopped pacing and standing behind me, placed his hand on my shoulder.

"Now you tell me about this Compson Trilogy fantasy you dreamed up and I'm thinking that, with your writing skills, you could make this long history come alive. Why don't you try a short draft?"

"But I write contemporary fiction! Not sweeping historical dramas," I said. "Besides, I told you I don't even know if Jenny kept her notes."

"Even without the notes," Jake responded, "You've got the basic idea for a good book. Just try a short draft and let's see how it develops."

That evening I told Jenny what Jake had suggested.

"Oh, David, I think it's a brilliant idea! I never thought about it but Jake is right," she said, her voice crackling with excitement.

"But what about the notes?" I asked, still not enthusiastic.

"I still have them," Jenny exclaimed. "I thought it would be fun when Marty and Rebecca were visiting us in St. Croix next year to do some more creative sculpting of our fantasy trilogy. We had such delightful times with it this year, remember? I never thought about the possibility of turning it into a real novel, but why not?"

Jenny found her notes and the next day she spent the entire morning assembling them on her computer. I suspected that she added a few additional flourishes as she typed but I understood, knowing Jenny's strong creative bent. That evening I called Marty and Rebecca and told them of the latest real-life plans for our imaginary saga. They were wildly enthusiastic and when I asked what credit I should give them, they both said they'd be well satisfied with a dedication.

So, after long hours of research, I began to draft a story about Jebediah Compson and the American Revolution and followed his progeny through assorted trials and adventures. By the time I came to the Civil War and the Compson family's split between North and South, I had amassed over five hundred pages of my draft. Jake read it and felt that I should continue with succeeding generations.

"This really could be a trilogy," he said emphatically, "with each volume published and sold separately."

The rest, as they say, is history, or, more accurately, fictional history. The first volume was published under the title *Freedom's Light* and the following year, the second volume, *The Circle of Fire* was published, followed a year later by *A Triumph of Courage*. Jake had the bright idea to subtitle each volume, *The Compson Trilogy*, so that with the first two volumes, if people liked them, they knew there was more to come and would be a receptive market. I used Marty's quote by Herbert Hoover for the first volume. For the second volume I added a quote by D.H. Lawrence: "War is dreadful. It is the business of the artist to follow it through to the individual soldier." For the third volume, I used a quote by Hemingway: "Never think that war, no matter how justified and how necessary, is not a crime." I concluded the third volume with a quote from Plato: "Only the dead have seen the end of war."

My previous books had been praised by critics and ignored by the public. These books were panned by the critics – "a meretricious mishmash, awash in melodrama," one critic dubbed it – but loved by the public. Jake said it was because the entire work had the upbeat theme of family survival and the Compsons' struggles mirrored America's struggles. He was right, judging from the letters I received from people who claimed to have read nothing since high school but *The Bible* before reading *The Compson Trilogy.* A few claimed to be related to the Compsons, confusing fiction with fact, and I referred them to Dianne who, I understand, began a lively correspondence with them.

As the royalties poured in, I became richer than my wife, which soothed my male ego. Part of my newly realized wealth came from the sale of movie rights, not for the trilogy but for separate sections, from which visionary producers and directors forged small movies focusing on character development with the historical setting only as background. Rebecca and Marty and Jenny and I attended several premiers, and Jenny and I would squeeze each other's arm as the credit, "Adapted from *The Compson Trilogy* by David Stewart" flashed across the screen. Now HBO is preparing a mini-series for which I was hired to co-write the screenplay. I'll finish it in St. Croix.

As for Dianne, the lady who started all this, our little joke brought her much happiness too. As soon as the first volume was published, she ordered Porter to purchase one-hundred copies and then ordered me to inscribe each copy with "Dear Dianne, With Gratitude, David Stewart.," for distribution to friends, acquaintances and new people she met at cocktail parties. She believed that, at her urging, I had undertaken to shape and enhance Thomas Compson's manuscript, and it didn't bother her that the original author's name never appeared and was given no credit, for now she had the best of all possible worlds: a living, successful author whom she could claim as her dear friend. She could also describe herself as being the muse for this trilogy. Best of all, she asserted her conviction that *The Compson Trilogy* was a thinly veiled history of her distant relatives.

When the last volume of *The Compson Trilogy* was published and immediately soared to the top of the New York Time's Best Seller list, I was being interviewed on a national morning show and the host asked me where my idea for the story came from. I smiled broadly and, without further elaboration, replied, "It all started as a joke, really."

Lead Us Not

"To a perfect evening! To a wonderful vacation, shared with good friends," Ed said, raising his wine glass and beaming at the couple sitting opposite him and his wife, Alice.

"Here! Here!" Alice said, smiling broadly at Henry and Karen Jordan and raising her glass in salute.

"Every experience is better when shared with good friends," Henry said.

"So let's have many more," said Karen, as all four glasses clinked in unison.

"To friendship!" Ed said.

"To good times for the Andersons and the Jordans!" Henry said.

"To great memories!" Ed added.

"To future adventures!" Henry responded

"Okay, doctors," Alice cut in, "we get the message. Enough already!"

Both men laughed.

Ed said, "Anyway, I got the deepest tan this year," thrusting his forearm out of his jacket sleeve as evidence.

"But I caught the biggest fish," bragged Henry

"And I beat you at golf," Ed boasted.

"Well, I beat you at cribbage," Henry shot back, still laughing.

"I have more hair," Ed announced in a stage whisper, chuckling contentedly and pointing to his full head of steel-gray hair and then to Henry's thinning blond locks.

"But I have a trimmer waistline," Henry said, affecting smug satisfaction.

Ed was about to respond when Alice thrust her arm across the table. "Stop!" she demanded. Turning to Karen with a mock grimace of disgust, she said, "Even on vacation they can't turn off their competitive instincts. Men!"

The dining room of the Mayaguez Resort Hotel was suffused in a tangerine light as off in the distance the sun leaned into the Caribbean, firing its glancing rays through the open French doors and mirroring the warm glow of friendship that bonded the two couples as they toasted the past, present and future.

"How many years has it been?" Alice asked.

"Let's see," Karen said, after taking a sip of wine and pursing her lips in concentration. "Henry joined the practice in '91, and we took our first vacation together in the summer of '93 – the cruise of the Caribbean islands."

"And the next year we cruised the Greek islands," Alice said, stimulating more memories.

"Then we went to Barbados in '95 and after that, Bermuda," offered Ed.

"But then we fell in love with Puerto Rico," Karen said excitedly.

"At least the western coast of Puerto Rico," Ed corrected her.

"Yes, and we've been coming here now for…gosh, it's been seven years already!" Alice announced, beaming.

"And the best part of it has been that for these two weeks every year we've never included our kids," Henry said with a flourish.

The waiter approached their table and asked if they were ready to order, and all four smiling faces disappeared behind large menus as final decisions on appetizer, entree and salad were made and reported to the attentive waiter.

"And bring us another bottle of this wine," Ed said.

On the last evening of their vacation, the Andersons and Jordans were in high spirits, delighting in the comfortable ease with which the two doctors and their wives had passed the previous weeks. With each passing year and each additional vacation, the two couples seemed to have grown closer. Of course, Ed and Henry were partners in the same busy medical practice, gastroenterology, along with four other doctors. Alice and Karen had both been elementary school teachers before marrying and raising their families: two boys for Ed and Alice and two girls for Henry and Karen, all within a five-year span. They often joked about the girls' marrying the boys to carry their parents beyond close friendship into in-law bonds, but although all four children were now in their mid-twenties, pursuing careers and on their own, none had married. There was no rush, however, and the two couples, in their mid-fifties, brimming with health and blessed with prosperity, were thoroughly enjoying their middle years.

Animated conversation, teasing and joking continued through dinner.

"Ed, our time-share here was the best investment you and I ever made," Henry said as the waiter brought coffee but no desserts since all four of them were weight conscious.

"Especially after the disastrous experience that Ed and I had in Cancun with a time-share in the early 80's," Alice said, wrinkling her brow.

Ed nodded and over coffee told Henry and Karen about the legal entanglements they had unexpectedly encountered with their Cancun time-share. Henry noted that Ed told the story lightly and, from the perspective of distance, made it seem much more humorous than it must have been at the time.

"So beware, my friends," Ed said at the conclusion of his monologue, "Montezuma has more than one way of getting revenge!"

All four friends were still laughing as they left the dining room and headed down the breezy corridor to the front entrance of the hotel.

"Oh, look!" said Karen, pointing to a large sign on a tripod, standing beside double doors, and they all turned toward the sign that read "AUCTION." The doors opened and a couple emerged as an amplified staccato voice was heard, "I have two hundred. Do I hear two-ten?"

"Let's stop in for a few minutes," Alice suggested. "It could be fun."

Karen agreed, adding, "I've never been to an auction; just seen them in movies or on television."

"I don't think this is anything like what's shown on the media," Ed said, chuckling. "No Van Gogh paintings going for forty million."

"It's early,' Henry said. "Let's take a look."

With bemused indulgence, the two men opened the double doors for their wives. Once, inside, they were surprised at the size of the room or, more correctly, auditorium, as well as how crowded it was at the front. An auctioneer was standing on a raised podium, holding a portable microphone. Against the wall behind him, stretching out in jumbled confusion to both ends of the wall, they saw an assortment of pictures, tables, chairs, lamps, boating equipment and assorted household goods of every description. Immediately to the right of where they were standing, just inside the doors, there was a long table with six ladies seated behind it, and in front of it hung a sign reading, "All Proceeds For The Benefit Of The Rosario Safety Home For Abused Women." On the table were paddles, like ping-pong paddles, with large numbers pasted on each. Next to the paddles was a small sign, "$10 Donation For Each Paddle."

"Do we want to bid on any of these treasures?" Henry asked, looking at Karen with amused condescension.

"Well, there might be some small thing we could take home with us, just as a memento of this experience," Karen suggested.

"It might be fun," Alice said.

Ed and Henry walked over to the table and bought two paddles while Alice and Karen surveyed the crowded room for four seats together. They could only spot two seats at the far left in the rear and two seats at the far right in the front, and quickly decided to take them.

"Now don't spend too much," Ed quipped as the couples parted, and Henry shot back, "And don't bid on anything big unless you want to ship it home."

In the best of humor, the couples hurried toward the vacant seats. Ed and Alice settled into the two rear seats, with Ed holding the paddle on his lap. Then they saw Henry and Karen standing against the far wall.

"Someone must have grabbed their seats," Ed said, as Alice and Karen waived to each other.

"I have forty-five, forty-five. Do I hear fifty?" the auctioneer's voice called across the room. "Thank you. I have fifty. Do I hear fifty-five?"

"What are they bidding on?" Alice asked, and just then they heard the auctioneer saying, "Folks, this closet organizer set is valued at over two hundred dollars. Two hundred dollars! And, remember, this all goes to a very worthy cause. Now do I hear fifty-five? Fifty-five?"

A lady a few rows in front of them raised a paddle and the bidding continued until the auctioneer called, "Sold for seventy-five dollars!" and banged his gavel on the wood podium.

The next item for bid was a set of lamps, of modern design, with brightly striped shades.

"They're certainly tropical," Alice observed.

The auctioneer started the bidding at forty dollars and the bid quickly moved to sixty-five. Alice was startled when Ed raised his paddle and the auctioneer announced, 'I have seventy."

"Why did you bid on those ugly lamps?" she asked, her voice mixing surprise and disapproval.

"Just to get in on the action," Ed said, smiling. "Besides, we could use an extra pair of lamps in our time-share."

"But not those! Please!" Alice said.

Another bid was heard and Alice felt relief.

"Henry just outbid me," Ed announced with a half-smile before raising his paddle.

"Eighty. I have eighty," boomed the auctioneer.

Alice glanced over at Henry and Karen just in time to see Henry raise his paddle.

"Eight-five now. The bid is eighty-five," said the auctioneer.

Alice grabbed Ed's arm before he could raise his paddle again.

"Please, Ed," was all she said but she held tightly to his arm.

"Ninety. I have ninety," called the auctioneer as a lady in the front row raised her paddle. "Going once. Going twice…."

Alice saw Karen whispering something to Henry, whose paddle was at his side.

"Sold for ninety dollars!" said the auctioneer, and the sound of the gavel echoed across the room.

A volunteer was now coming toward the podium holding a framed painting.

"Our next item is an original water color painting, capturing the beauty of Boqueron Bay, done by a local professional artist."

The volunteer held the painting up for the audience to view, but Ed and Alice were too far away to see any details – just splashes of vivid colors on a modest-sized canvass.

"The artist has placed a value of four-hundred dollars on this original work of art, but I'm sure that in any gallery this piece would sell for hundreds more. The frame alone is worth another hundred dollars and has been donated by the Archer Gallery, here in Mayaguez," the auctioneer said enthusiastically. "So let's start the bidding at two hundred dollars."

Several paddles were raised, and the bid quickly rose by tens to two hundred and ninety, at which point Ed raised his paddle and the auctioneer announced, "Three hundred dollars."

In support of Ed's bid, Alice said, "It would be nice to have a painting of Puerto Rico back home. We could hang it in the family room."

"Three-ten," said the auctioneer, pointing to the other side of the room, and Alice was pleased when Ed responded.

"Three-twenty," said the auctioneer quickly, acknowledging Ed's raised paddle.

Glancing across the room, Alice saw Henry raise his paddle.

"Three-thirty. I have three-thirty."

Ed raised his paddle again and the bid went to three-forty, then quickly moved to three-fifty as Alice saw Henry's paddle was raised again.

"Henry's bidding against you," Alice whispered, surprise mixed with annoyance.

"I know," Ed said solemnly, raising his paddle.

"Three-sixty."

Henry's paddle was up again.

"Three-seventy."

"Why is he being such a schmuck?" Alice said, her face growing tense with anger.

"Because he can't stand to lose!" Ed answered, his lips tightly composed, his eyebrows furrowed.

The lady in the front row who had bid successfully on the set of lamps raised her paddle.

"Three-eighty. I have three-eighty."

Ed thrust his paddle defiantly in the air.

"Three-ninety," said the auctioneer with a hint of excitement, sensing a competition heating up, followed quickly with "Four hundred," as Henry's paddle was raised high over his head.

Alice saw that Henry and Karen were staring fixedly at the auctioneer. With great clarity Alice also saw from Karen's posture and her hand on Henry's arm that she was urging her husband on. Somewhere deep within her, Alice felt the competitive spark ignite and her eyes narrowed in angry disdain. She turned to Ed and in a horse whisper said, "Don't let them get it!"

Ed's paddle was up. "Don't worry," he said, his face a mask of determination.

"Four hundred. I have four hundred!"

The lady in the front row bid four-ten, followed immediately by Henry's bid and then Ed's.

'Four-thirty. Four-thirty," called the auctioneer, his voice rising to a high pitch.

Then, from across the room, Henry's booming voice was heard, breaking the silent protocol of the auction. "Five hundred," he shouted

Ed's face was turning red, his lips constricted, sweat popping out on his forehead.

"Five-fifty," he yelled defiantly.

Alice could see that the auctioneer was startled by this unexpected procedural change but because the numbers were growing impressive so quickly, he said nothing, only repeating the latest number called out.

Alice leaned into her husband as a gesture of support. She glanced over at Henry and Karen and saw Karen staring back in what seemed, from this distance, like an angry grimace. Alice assumed a cold, haughty stare in return, while calling forth every little thing about Karen that had annoyed her through their years of friendship: Karen's excessive fastidiousness about dress and grooming and etiquette; her endless references to her daughter at Harvard; her pretensions about wine and the way she quizzed waiters about how food was prepared, and always demanded something extra. As for Henry, she knew a lot about him, more than she had ever let on, and he was no prize, she concluded. And she remembered how Ed had been so kind and generous and helpful when Henry first joined the practice, but now that she thought about it, Henry had always exuded an air of superiority, right from the start, always trying to grab the spotlight and outshine everybody else.

"What a show-off!" she said aloud, unintentionally, but then found the remark suitable to share with Ed, who only nodded in agreement.

"Six hundred!" Henry yelled.

"Seven hundred!" Ed boomed

"Eight hundred!" Henry bellowed

"Nine hundred!" Ed shouted, his voice cracking with fury

"One thousand!" Henry screamed.

These figures had flown about the room so fast that the auctioneer hadn't even been able to repeat them, until now, when he said "One thousand," in a voice filled with gleeful wonder.

The room was completely still. People had turned in their seats and were staring at Ed. Alice could see his jaw muscles twitching.

"Twelve hundred!" he shouted, and every head in the room swiveled toward Henry who, Alice noted, had a crazed look on his face.

"Fifteen hundred!" Henry yelled defiantly, as if that figure should finally settle the matter.

Ed stared intently at the auctioneer, who hadn't even bothered to repeat Henry's bid but was looking expectantly in Ed's direction.

"Seventeen hundred!" Ed yelled, his cheeks bright red.

Total silence.

"Two thousand dollars!" Henry said in a deafening roar and the audience let out a collective sigh and a few whistles were heard.

Alice now realized that things had gotten out of hand and that if someone didn't stop, didn't concede, the bidding would keep rising until it reached the stratosphere, as if they were bidding on a Picasso. She saw the intense, almost catatonic, look on Ed's face and she knew she had to take action. Squeezing his arm and leaning into his ear, she said, "Ed, honey, let it go. Henry's never going to stop. You be the bigger man."

Ed tilted his head slightly in Alice's direction and his eyes blinked. She could tell from the involuntary spasms of his jaw muscles that a titanic struggle was taking place inside her husband as his ego battled against the practicality of what she had said.

"Please, honey, show him you're the bigger man," she whispered.

"Two thousand. I have two thousand dollars," the auctioneer finally called, and every one was watching Ed.

Finally, after what seemed like interminable moments of silence, Alice saw Ed's facial muscles relax and a smile spread across his face. Shaking his head No, he called out in a light, bantering tone, "My colleague has just made a most generous contribution to the Shelter for Abused Women," as if this had been his design all along: not to win but to hike the bid.

Through clenched teeth and with a forced smile, Henry hissed, "Gladly!"

Laughter rippled across the room and then people were applauding.

The room now exploded with noise, as people, after concentrating on the electrifying bidding duel for so long, felt the tension subside, and they returned to a casual, chattering state, eager to comment on what had just taken place.

"Let's get out of here!" Alice said, afraid of another mano-a-mano duel with egos and checkbooks. Ed nodded and they quickly made their way out to the hotel corridor where they both headed for the bathrooms.

Alice was at the sink washing her hands when, looking through the mirror, she saw Karen standing a short distance behind her. Alice paused in her hand rubbing, momentarily unsure how this scene should be played. Should the women laugh and make fun of their husbands' antics and agree to effect an immediate reconciliation? Or, did the dueling ego extravaganza extend beyond the two males and, at some heretofore hidden level, ensnare their wives? Alice studied Karen through the mirror for signs. Karen stared coldly back.

"That was some show your husband put on," Karen said scornfully.

Alice straightened up and took a paper towel from the dispenser.

"I think they both put on quite a show," she said in what she hoped was a neutral tone, but she could feel anger rising inside her.

"But Ed was certainly the star!" Karen said in a mocking tone. Alice felt any hope of a reconciliation fading as she instinctively rallied to her husband's defense.

"It was your husband who seemed intent on winning at any cost," Alice said, meeting Karen's stare through the mirror.

"That was quite a dramatic flourish Ed affected at the end, saying he was only trying to inflate the price for the sake of charity," Karen said, moving forward to the sink next to Alice and placing her bag on the counter.

"What makes you think that wasn't his intention and take it as a good joke?" Alice asked in a syrupy style.

Karen had removed a brush from her handbag and had started brushing her short bob vigorously. Then she stopped and turned to face Alice directly. Her voice took on an unmistakably condescending tone.

"Because I know your husband and he hasn't a generous bone in his body. He's always been patronizing to Henry and he's jealous because Henry is a more respected doctor and all of Ed's expressions of friendship are just his way of trying to keep Henry in the practice and not start his own, as I keep urging him to do. Your husband just wants to leech off of mine!"

Alice watched Karen's mouth spit out these words like bullets from a machine gun. Karen replaced the brush in her purse and took out a lipstick. Alice felt a hot rage swelling inside of her until she could barely breathe. She was overwhelmed with an urge to strike out at this woman who had obviously pretended friendship all these years but was contemptuous of Ed and her. She wanted revenge and this desire swept aside all other considerations, all rational thinking.

"You seem to know a lot about my husband," Alice said, depositing the paper towel in a receptacle and walking toward the door.

"You bet I do!" Karen said emphatically, running the lipstick across her bottom lip and staring at Alice through the mirror. "He's very transparent!"

"Oh, I see," said Alice, a frozen smile on her face, masking a blood-hot lust for revenge that overcame all caution. "Well, I happen to know quite a bit about your husband too."

Karen held her lipstick in mid-air. "What's that supposed to mean?"

"Well, you see, my dear," Alice said sweetly, standing by the door, "I've slept with Henry." She opened the door and looked back at Karen, frozen in the mirror, her mouth forming a perfect O. "And I know all of his private anatomical markings to prove it!"

She closed the door and with uncontrollable trembling went to meet her husband.

Teaching Lessons

Bill McGregor sat outside the principal's office and all was quiet. The large clock on the opposite wall read 6:55, thirty-five minutes before the office staff and secretaries were scheduled to arrive and one hour before the official day at Peter Stuber High School began. Slanted rays from the early morning November sun danced through the Venetian blinds and across Bill's face as he busied himself reading student essays from his sophomore English class. Beside him on the bench where he sat lay a brown leather briefcase, bulging at the sides with its contents, and a closed coffee container.

If a snapshot had captured him at that moment, it would have shown a young man of earnest expression in his early twenties, with short, thick brown hair, even features and an overly strong jaw on a tall, lanky body, neatly dressed in dark gray slacks, blue Oxford shirt, striped tie and a blue blazer.

I haven't sat on this bench, Bill reflected, since I first came here for an interview. Now, fifteen months later, I'm still nervous about meeting with the principal, but I've learned so much.

A year ago, Bill had brought eagerness and zeal to his first teaching job at Peter Stuber High School in a small, upscale, suburban community on New York's Long Island, remarkably similar to the town where he had been raised. He had been hired to teach three sections of freshman composition, a course that the more senior members of the high school English department energetically avoided, and two sections of a sophomore American novel survey course. Now in the first term of his second year, Bill had found within himself a love for teaching, a compassion for, and intuitive understanding of, the adolescent psyche, and a gift for communicating his enthusiasm for good literature and the well-written sentence.

At the end of his first year of teaching at PS, as it was called with pride and affection by the townspeople, Bill's department chairperson, Mrs. Baker, had written in her overall review of his first year, "Although Mr. McGregor has much to learn in terms of pedagogy, pacing and lesson planning, it is clear that he is a naturally talented teacher who easily commands both the attention and respect of his students. While he sets high standards for all, he individualizes his teaching strategies to support students at every level of the academic spectrum." Mrs. Baker had concluded her evaluation by stating, "Bill McGregor is a dedicated and exciting, even inspiring, young teacher and a welcome addition to the department and the school."

Bill's principal, Dr. Mathews, had co-signed this evaluation and added his own comments: "Bill McGregor is off to a great start in his chosen profession. He relates well to kids, gives clear directions in the classroom and communicates frequently to parents, keeping them informed of their children's progress and outlining upcoming projects. Many parents have praised Mr. McGregor to me, and, additionally, he's been well received by his colleagues and the students."

Bill's impression of Dr. Mathews was vague, primarily because he interacted with the PS principal very seldom and hardly ever on any individual basis. Dr. Mathews had been principal for only one year prior to Bill's being hired, and he had joked to Bill on welcoming him to PS, "We're both new kids on the block." Not more than mid-thirties and in his first principal's position, Dr. Mathews had come to PS, considered a plum position in an affluent, highly desirable school district, from a three-year stint as assistant principal at a smaller high school in a neighboring community . Cheery, upbeat, jocular, almost perpetually smiling and markedly ebullient, he had dropped in on Bill's classes two or three times during that first year, never staying for more than twenty minutes. In the next day or two, Bill would find in his mailbox a hastily scribbled note under the principal's letterhead, never more than two lines and always encouraging:

"Bill, Nice Job – Good classroom control—Keep it up, Frank Mathews."

From what Bill heard in the faculty lounge, the buzz about the new principal was that he was ambitious and would probably be spending only a short time at PS before moving on to a central office position. A few of the older teachers openly expressed disdain for the principal's title of Doctor, since it was known that his doctorate had been earned from a marginally accredited institution whose program of studies was completed primarily on the internet. Still, Bill found Dr. Mathews pleasant, although distracted, when they infrequently met, and, until his run-in with Mr. and Mrs. Miller, Bill had only the broadest impression of the principal.

From his first days at PS, Bill had been advised by Mrs. Baker to have open and frequent communications with parents.

"Make no mistake about it: In this school it's the parents who run the show," she had tersely stated.

Bill quickly learned that when parents requested it, teachers were expected to hold parent-teacher conferences either before or after school, at the parents' convenience. During the second week of each new school year, a Meet The Teacher night was officially scheduled, at which teachers were expected to give, in a half-hour presentation, an overview of the course curriculum for each class they taught.

With only two weeks of teaching under his belt, Bill had dreaded the open meeting with the parents. Nervously, he had stuck to the official course outlines, conscious of all eyes silently watching him, as rivulets of sweat trickled down his temples and his sides, and he felt his damp shirt clinging to his back. For each of his five presentations, nearly all the seats in his classroom had been filled, mostly with couples but also with some mothers or fathers who had come alone.

Bill's general impression that night of the uniformly well-dressed parents, the men in ties and jackets and the women in well tailored pantsuits, was that they were keenly observing him, assessing him, judging him. Their tight little smiles and tired, penetrating eyes conveyed condescension and a formidable reserve that left him adrift, alone, defenseless in that sea of smugly confident faces.

Bill's colleagues had warned him to leave as little time as possible for a question-and-answer period that was supposed to follow each curricular presentation, but the parents' supercilious reserve had flustered him, adding to his nervousness. He had raced through his presentation, the words tumbling out uncontrollably in a high pitch staccato, arriving at the end in a much shorter time than when he practiced and timed himself at home, and leaving too much time for parental questions.

In smug, weary tones, the questions came: What is your teaching experience? What is your educational background? Do you teach grammar? What is your grading system? How much homework do you expect students to do each night? How are the literary selections made for this course? How closely are you supervised?

The women asked their questions with archly raised eyebrows, like children's slides imprinted on their foreheads; the men, with languid faces and furrowed brows.

Bill stumbled on, sometimes returning to a point two or three times in a frantic effort to make it clearer, more precise, more authoritative. Trying desperately to appear relaxed, he sat on the edge of the teacher's desk, but could not control the rhythmic swinging of his suspended legs. Finally, all questions stopped, and Bill felt that by some silent agreement the parents had taken his measure, found him wanting and disdainfully saw no reason to question him further. He saw from the clock on the rear wall that there were still six minutes left for this first of five presentations.

"Well," he said, jumping off the teacher's desk, his voice already reduced to a thin rasp but hoping to end on a light note, "if there are no further questions, I guess I can give you a few extra minutes of recess before your next class."

What happened next stunned him. While a few people headed for the door in the back of the classroom, most of the parents surged forward toward him until he was completely encircled by them. They jostled one another as each attempted to have a few private words with him, alerting him to some individual need of their child. Some parents, he felt, were trying to intimidate him by pressing their faces to within an inch of his; others were trying to whisper in his ear, while still others were pulling at his jacket sleeves in an insistent effort to get his attention. Against this maelstrom of surging bodies, whispering voices and plucking hands, Bill found it hard to breathe and impossible to think. The air seemed to grow hotter and thicker by the second and so many pairs of eyes staring intimately at him made him feel like a cornered animal. While snatches of individual comments were penetrating his consciousness, his heavy breathing, glazed eyes and frozen smile said clearly that this unanticipated onslaught was challenging him severely.

Ignoring all the other parents, each parent was trying to engage in a personal conference with Bill, alerting him to an individual issue of a son or daughter that was impeding educational progress and needed to be addressed. NOW! Faces floated in close-ups before him, and whispered statements, or snippets of statements, from stern male and plaintive female voices reverberated in the charged air surrounding him.

–All the taxes we pay for our schools and my son still isn't a really good writer;

–Our daughter doesn't know the first thing about grammar;

–I want you to pile on the homework;

–My kid has too much damn homework'

–If Richard gives you any trouble, handle it, but I don't want to be called to school any more;

–If you don't light a fire under him, he's never going to make it into an Ivy League school;

–Sally's very bored with school and needs to be challenged;

–Please be sure to check with the nurse about Angela's little problem;

–My wife and I are separated and I want duplicate communications sent to me;

–I have an order of protection against my ex-husband and he's not allowed near Carl, his stepson, so if that bastard ever shows up at school, call the police.

Not until the hall bell rang, indicating the end of the first visiting period, did some parents start drifting away, while others saw the intervening few minutes between presentations as another chance to snatch a few moments of private conversation. In desperation, Bill excused himself with the need for a bathroom break and hurried out of the classroom and down the long, crowded corridor to the faculty lounge. He went into the men's bathroom where he ran cold water over his sweating face and tried to regain his composure for the next presentation, scheduled to begin, he noted, in three minutes.

Somehow, drawing on unconscious depths of resolve and discipline, he managed to get through the next four presentations, each time quickly escaping to the sanctity of the bathroom. But the details of that evening – the intense faces, the intimidating questions, the phalanx of surrounding bodies and aggressive gestures – were forever seared on his memory.

Given such a devastating experience at the start of the school year, Bill was relieved that the rest of his first year unfolded with surprisingly little parental interaction and no explosive meetings. When he shared his relief with Mrs. Baker during the last month of the school year, she gave him a quick, insightful answer:

"That's because most of the kids genuinely like you. They think you're fair and aren't carrying home negative tales or complaints about you, and your communications to all parents are upbeat and make them feel that their kids are doing well. But," she added ominously, "don't be lulled into complacency. Around here we all know that any minor incident, if taken up by an angry, neurotic parent whose motto is 'win at any cost,' can explode like a bomb in your face."

Bill mentally filed this cautionary advice, but it soon faded as the summer stretched before him and he immersed himself in finishing his master's program at Hofstra University. He returned to PS for his second year in a more relaxed frame of mind and with greater self-confidence. Mrs. Baker assigned him a poetry elective course that a senior department member had driven into the ground over many years before retiring the previous June.

"It was supposed to be an exploration of the poetic imagination through both the reading and writing of poetry," Mrs. Baker explained in an exasperated tone, "but Ken insisted on having students first memorize the definitions of forty or fifty poetic devices before they even got to read a poem, which usually wasn't until the second semester. And even then he insisted they plough through all the Shakespearean sonnets, and they never got to write any poetry until the final exam when they were asked to write an original poem and then identify at least fifteen poetic devices they had used."

She paused, as though weary from disgust, then added, ‘Of course, Ken was an easy marker and that's what usually saved him from the wrath of the students and their parents, but the whole experience was a waste of time, except for the few pedants who delighted in showing off their newly acquired poetic phrases and terms.”

She smiled and in a much cheerier voice said, “See if you can make it come alive.”

Bill was delighted with this new assignment. He had studied a considerable amount of classic poetry in college. He often read poetry for personal pleasure but had made few attempts at writing poetry, except humorous celebratory lyrics for friends. Yet this was perhaps an advantage, he thought, since both his students and he could be exploring their poetic imaginations together as fellow craftsmen, while he could stress sensitivity to language, pattern and thematic content. He was determined, as Mrs. Baker had urged, to make poetry come alive for his students.

His Meet The Teacher night this second year, although causing the usual nervous butterflies in the stomach and little sleep the night before, was not a repeat, he was happy to note, of the first year's hellish experience. He handled his presentations, his timing and his response to questions with greater authority, more poise and humor and much less sweat.

In the sea of people who flowed in and out of his classroom that night, one of the parents from his poetry class stood out. She had arrived late and stood quietly along the rear wall rather than take one of the empty seats, her arms folded across her chest and her face a blank mask throughout his presentation. She was tall and slim, very fair and good looking, with that casually sleek look that careful attention to well-made tailored clothes, expensive accessories and fastidious grooming gave so many of the mothers he observed. Yet there was a quiet intensity, a charged stillness, in her unwavering gaze that drew his attention and caused his eyes to light on her again and again during his twenty-minute presentation, as he visually swept the class in a conscious effort to keep his audience engaged. He never got any hint of a response from her, only the unflinching, unchanging stare from a body that stood frozen in one pose, never shifting its rigid alignment.

After finishing his presentation and having answered the few parental questions – poetry did not seem to be a topic they felt comfortable with – Bill made the request that parents sign an attendance sheet on the desk. The crowd was too small for parents to avoid detection if they did not comply, so they scribbled their names and quickly left the room.

She had waited until the others had signed and then languidly moved toward the desk. Without glancing at Bill who was on the other side of the desk, busily reviewing his notes for the next presentation, she signed the sheet and disappeared immediately into the hallway. He picked up the sheet and read the last name entered: Donna Miller. He mentally shuffled through a quick inventory of the students in his poetry class whom he was just getting to know and came up with the daughter's name, Rachel.

He had formed no hard impression of this student other than she was pretty, a little on the plump side, quiet, and seemed nervous and shy. As much as he was encouraging full student participation in discussing initial conceptions about poetry and in responding to a few selected poems, she sat toward the rear of the classroom in the last row against the wall farthest from the door, observing the other students obliquely. She only spoke when called on by Bill, and then in few words and muffled tones, with awkward pauses and downcast eyes. When seated at her desk and not writing or holding a book, she rubbed her hands obsessively. She entered and left the classroom alone and did not seem to have any friends in the class.

The afternoon following the Meet The Teacher night, Bill found a note in his teacher's mailbox from the department secretary saying that Mrs. Donna Miller had called and wanted to make an appointment with Bill, preferably in the AM before school. She had left three numbers where she might be reached: home, office and cell phone. That same afternoon, after school, Bill dialed the home number and a Latino lady answered and, in heavily accented English, said that Mrs. Miller was at her office. He called the office number. A young, pleasant voice answered, saying "Donna Miller Interior Designs," and informed Bill that Mrs. Miller was out of the office and not expected back for another two hours at least. Finally, he dialed the cell phone number. After five or six rings he heard, “Donna here,” in a throaty, slightly impatient voice.

“Hi, Mrs. Miller. This is Bill McGregor returning your call.”

“Bill who?” she said quickly

“Bill McGregor, Rachel’s English teacher,” Bill said

“Oh, yes, Mr. McGregor,” she said and there was a short silence. “Thanks for getting back to me. My husband and I would like to meet with you at your earliest convenience.” The tone was peremptory and business-like.

“Is there something wrong?” Bill asked.

“Well, no…that is…well, it’s something we’d prefer to discuss with you in person. When can we meet? Tomorrow?”

“I could meet with you and your husband tomorrow morning before school,” Bill said.

“No, that’s no good for my husband. He’s a thoracic surgeon and he’s in surgery tomorrow morning. What about tomorrow afternoon, after school?”

“Sorry, no,” Bill answered. “I’m in surgery myself tomorrow afternoon – that is,” he said with a half chuckle, “dental surgery, as the patient. What about Thursday or Friday afternoon?”

She made no immediate response and when she did speak, her voice had an impatient edge.

“No, the rest of the week is out. Look, Mr. McGregor, we really need to meet with you. Couldn’t you postpone your dental appointment?”

Bill was startled by this imperious request and sensed that she was not asking but demanding and expecting immediate accommodation.

“Well,” he said, trying to organize his thoughts while stalling for time, “I suppose I could make another dentist appointment but…”

“Excellent!” she cut in. “Then tomorrow at 3:15 in your room. Thank you,” and the phone clicked off.

* * * *

The Millers arrived twenty-five minutes late. Bill's last class ended at 3:05 and his official day was over at 3:15. Although he frequently stayed until nearly four, preparing lessons and getting materials ready, he was still annoyed at the bullying manner in which Mrs. Miller had insisted on this immediate appointment. He decided he would wait a half-hour and then leave, but at 3:40 Dr. and Mrs. Miller appeared at his classroom door.

"Sorry to be late," she said curtly, and Bill considered it a perfunctory, throwaway line, like the way everyone said "God bless you" automatically when someone sneezed.

Mrs. Miller introduced her husband, who offered Bill a wan, tired smile and a limp handshake before taking a seat next to his wife on the other side of Bill's desk. Dr. Miller was a big man probably, Bill guessed, in his late forties, somewhat older than his wife. His massive frame was taking on fat and his heavy eyebrows and drooping eyelids made his eyes almost invisible. His mouth curved downward at both ends, adding a perpetually stern look to his jowly face. Bill couldn't imagine him having a pleasant bedside manner.

Mrs. Miller launched immediately into her mission.

"Our daughter Rachel seems to be having some problems in your class, and we thought that if you were made aware of her issues, it could be helpful to you in making her feel less nervous."

Once again, Mrs. Miller had startled Bill with her crisply aggressive manner, but this time he was also confused by her matter-of-fact assertion of Rachel's "problems" in his class.

"We're only in the third week of school, Mrs. Miller and I can assure you that I don't see Rachel having any problems in my class."

She stared at him like a parent who has lost patience with a child. Opening her pocketbook, she produced two folded pieces of paper and, unfolding both, handed one to Bill.

"Perhaps this will help explain what I'm talking about," she said, a peevish tone creeping into her voice. "This was the first assignment Rachel completed in your class."

Bill glanced at the unfolded paper and instantly recognized it.

"Yes," he said, shaking his head. "I asked students to write on their personal feelings about poetry. It was an open-ended topic, just intended as an icebreaker, really. I wanted to get them to start thinking about poetry and I had already discussed with the class that all kinds of poetry could be found everywhere in everyday life: in the lyrics of songs, on greeting cards, in hip-hop and rap and even…"

Mrs. Miller impatiently waved her hand and cut him off.

"And how did you rate Rachel's essay?" she asked curtly.

"Well, I didn't rate it at all, Mrs. Miller. I was trying to get the students to open up and honestly talk about how they experienced poetry in their lives."

"But you made a number of comments on her paper," she said, her voice rising in accusation.

"Yes, I did," Bill replied, "but as you can see, they were positive responses to what Rachel had written, all intended to encourage her to continue to explore her feelings and observations about poetry."

"So your comment about your liking Bob Dylan's lyrics too was intended to encourage her to do what? Listen to more Bob Dylan?"

Bill felt like he was on the witness stand being grilled by a prosecuting attorney.

"No, not to listen to more Dylan, but, yes, possibly to examine more of his lyrics for their imagery and symbolism and rhythm and imagination and interesting juxtaposition of words and…"

He felt himself on a defensive rant and paused, then continued on a new theme.

'I'm trying to find the 'hook,' that is, any kind of poetic form that a kid already likes without realizing it's poetry, and then use that interest as a motivation to explore other kinds of poetry."

He stopped abruptly when he saw Mrs. Muller waving a second sheet of paper in front of him.

"Please read this," she said impatiently.

Bill took the paper and scanned it. It was typed and had a title, My Enjoyment of Poetry. It was a full-page essay, double-spaced, with four paragraphs. In clear, simple sentences, with no spelling errors, it dealt in the most general way with the joys of discovering poetry in one's life, including vague references to Shakespeare and Wordsworth. While it was trying to be ingenuous and sincere, it had a sophisticated overlay that Bill immediately detected. Before Bill could finish reading the last paragraph, Mrs. Miller spoke.

"What do you think of this writing?"

"Well," Bill said, choosing his words carefully, "it's clear and clean, but I'm not sure that the writer is showing any genuine interest, any passion, for what's being said."

His comments were greeted with another dismissive wave of Mrs. Miller's hand.

"Nonsense!" she said. She was leaning forward, her eyes boring into Bill. "You mean to tell me that the second piece of writing isn't much better than the first?"

Bill felt the heat of her stare and again chose his words carefully.

"From the standpoint of organization and grammar and spelling, yes, but what does this have to do with Rachel's classwork?" he asked, thoroughly confused.

Mrs. Miller sat back in her chair and let out an audible sigh.

"Mr. McGregor," she said – it was the first time she had used his name – "Rachel is an extremely shy, high-strung child who wilts under any kind of pressure. She simply falls apart. She crumbles."

She paused, as if waiting for a response from Bill, and when he said nothing, she continued.

"When you outlined your course requirements the other night, you mentioned several reaction papers that students would complete in class, which would form a good part of their final grade.

"Yes, I did," Bill said, nodding affirmatively.

Pointing to the two pieces of paper Bill held in his hand, Mrs. Miller spoke in a low, dramatic voice.

"Both of those essays were written by Rachel. The first one was written in class under the worst possible conditions for her, and the second one was written the same day, at home, that evening, in her room where she wasn't experiencing any stress. Both her father and I assured her that you only wanted her best effort, and you would be understanding of how any work in class, with a possible time factor and her distress at seeing all the other students writing furiously, would not – could not – show you what she was capable of."

"And?" Bill said, not sure where this was leading, but mesmerized by Mrs. Miller's throaty, impassioned delivery.

"And," Mrs. Miller repeated the word with explosive force, rocketing forward in her chair, her right arm resting on Bill's desk and her hand extended toward the papers he was holding, "we are asking you to see Rachel not just as another student but as a bright, sensitive girl with special needs, and to make accommodations for those needs by allowing her to do all her assignments at home.

Mrs. Miller sat back and folded her arms, her eyes never leaving Bill's face, challenging him to refute the argument and the conclusion she had put before him.

Bill was both dazzled and outraged by this parent's temerity, and while he could admire the fierceness with which she fought for her child, his innate sense of fairness told him that what she was demanding was impossible. Then a word she had just used suggested a plausible plan of action.

"Mrs. Miller," Bill said, summoning the most soothing tones he could muster under her aggressove stare, "you mentioned that Rachel was a girl with special needs. I'm sure that what you say is true and I just haven't had time yet to focus on those needs, while you, as her mother, know them intimately…"

Mrs. Miller's eyes grew larger and seemed to change shade from dark to light, as she responded to Bill's positive words. Bill drew a deep breath and continued.

"Perhaps you're not aware of a formal process here in our district for acknowledging students with special needs and meeting those needs through an individualized educational plan. I'm referring to the Committee on Special Education."

Mrs. Miller exploded out of her chair, her eyes flashing and her voice strident, as she leaned toward Bill.

"That's not the answer!" she shouted. "You think I'm going to jeopardize my daughter's fragile self-esteem by having her officially declared a child with problems?"

Then, right there in front of him, Bill saw a remarkable transformation in Mrs. Miller's face. One minute it was taut with angry indignation; the next minute it crumpled into spiraling lines of fear and defeat. Tears overflowed her eyes and streamed down her cheeks. Abruptly she turned away and walked to the windows, holding her back stiffly, wiping her face with a tissue she must have been clutching throughout their meeting. The room was silent and Bill was fumbling to say something when Dr. Miller broke the silence. His baritone voice vibrated with authority.

"What my wife has been trying to explain to you, Mr. McGuire..." – Bill was jarred by his new name but was so grateful for any pacifying speech at this point that he said nothing and Dr. Miller continued – "is that Rachel indeed has a special condition – a condition with a technical term that I won't bore you with, but one which a number of my colleagues who have examined Rachel have identified, and I can supply you with the names of these colleagues, or I can give you their written evaluations."

Dr. Miller paused and smiled – never had Bill seen such a condescending smile – and then said, "We were hoping that we could avoid any formal classification since we don't want to hurt her chances of getting into a really good school."

Mrs. Miller turned toward Bill and spoke from across the room.

"We were hoping that you would be understanding and see you way to helping Rachel without giving her name a black mark. We've tried everything: tutors, psychologists, private lessons for anything she expressed an interest in, but the school has never made her feel special."

Her voice quivered with these last few spoken words, and she was clearly struggling to regain her composure. She walked back to her seat, folding into it like some wounded animal, the tissue still clutched in her fisted hand and lines of weariness crisscrossing her face.

Bill felt bludgeoned, cornered. Still, he knew that they were both waiting for his response. Now he played his final card.

"I see how deeply concerned you are about Rachel, and I can understand how you want her to have every chance to do well. But I hope you can also see that if I were to allow Rachel to complete all assignments at home, under ideal circumstances, as you, yourselves, describe them, it would be putting all the other students at a disadvantage unless I allowed all students to do all work at home."

Bill's voice trailed off as he realized that he was giving the Millers an opening for suggesting this very approach. Curiously, they did not follow up on this idea, choosing instead to remain focused exclusively on Rachel.

Dr. Miller responded: "No doubt the other students are perfectly capable of performing well in a classroom setting, but Rachel isn't."

Bill decided on another approach and said: "Since my poetry course is an elective, perhaps it would be best for Rachel to drop it and take something else that is less stressful to her."

Mrs. Miller spoke with controlled anger: "But she likes you and doesn't want to leave. We just want her to be given some consideration."

Then, as an afterthought she blurted out, "Don't you have any empathy for your students? How can you call yourself a caring teacher? What difference would it really make if you let her complete her assignments at home? No one else would have to know. She could do all the writing activities in class and then the next day quietly hand you the same activity done over at home. How does that hurt anyone?"

She raised her hand holding the tissue to her face as tears again welled up and she continued.

"She's struggled all through school and now, at this crucial point in her life, she's developing a negative self-image. I just want her to have a chance to shine, to really feel good about herself, to boost her confidence, to know that she's special. Is that so much for a parent to ask? Really, I just don't understand your obstinate position."

Everyone stopped talking, and the three figures sat stiffly in a triangle, etched by the slanting afternoon sun. An angry monologue was silently racing across Bill's brain.

Sure, lady, let the kid do everything at home, and since you're so anxious that she shine, why not give her a little help, like writing the assignment for her. As far as you're concerned, this isn't a public institution with standards and ethics and a level playing field for all students; this is only a forum to make your daughter shine, no matter how contrived and underhanded and artificial that "shining" is!

Bill recognized that everything he knew to be fair and honest and just was being violated by this bullying pair of parents, and he struggled with his growing indignation. He was angry and tired, but resolute. This must end!

"I'm very sorry, Dr. and Mrs. Miller, but you're asking me to enter into a private arrangement with you and your daughter that, in my judgment, would be unethical on my part, unfair to my other students and ultimately bad for your daughter. I assure you that I'll do everything I can to help her succeed in my class but I can't accede to your request."

Dr. and Mrs. Miller rose from their seats.

"I knew this was a waste of time," she said to her husband, ignoring Bill.

"This matter isn't ended, young man," said Dr. Miller in a patronizing tone. "You've got a lot to learn about being a teacher at PS."

"I'm sorry," was all Bill could think of to say. He extended his hand to Dr. Miller but both parents abruptly turned away and headed for the door.

* * * *

The following week Bill learned that the Millers had gone to see Mrs. Baker.

"I told them 'no way,'" she said breezily during a chance meeting in the faculty lounge, "but you're definitely on their shit list at this point. They couldn't say enough bad things about you. Of course, what they're asking for is outrageous. They're well known to the staff as always arguing over grades and looking for an edge. The kid's out a lot and they claim she's got issues that we're not addressing. But be careful! They're a powerful force in this community."

Bill said nothing, but he was relieved to hear his department head's dismissive opinion of the Millers' request.

Rachel had been absent for several days after his meeting with her parents, and he thought that perhaps they had changed their minds and taken her out of his class. He checked with the guidance office and learned that no formal request to drop his class had been made. When Rachel finally appeared in his class, she handed Bill a note from her mother, tersely stating that Rachel had been home ill, due to stress. Throughout the forty-minute class period, Rachel displayed her usual behavior: sitting quietly, rubbing her hands repeatedly, staring down at her desk and only occasionally casting sidelong glances at other students who were actively participating in the group discussion.

When the bell rang ending the period, Bill walked to her desk and asked if she could stay for a minute. She blushed, fumbled with her books and nodded yes. He waited until the other students had left and then took a seat across the aisle from her. He spoke in a low, calm voice.

"Rachel, I guess you know that I met with your parents last week."

Her head jerked up and a frightened look came into her eyes. He spoke quickly to reassure her.

"Nothing serious! We all just want to be sure that you're enjoying the class and feel comfortable here."

Rachel stared straight ahead and began rubbing her hands together.

"Are you enjoying the class?" he asked cheerfully.

"Yes, I am," she answered in a barely audible voice, still staring at the front of the room.

"And is there anything I can do to make you feel more relaxed in class?"

She changed her gaze from the blackboard to her lap and folded her arms. She was silent for several seconds and seemed to be concentrating on forming an answer to Bill's question. Then she unfolded her arms and, turning her head, looked at him for the first time. Now her words came quickly, as if expelled on one long, courageous breath.

"Mr. McGregor, this is my favorite class. I love poetry and this is the only place where I get to hear anyone talk about poetry. I mean, I've even written some poems, but my mother found them in my desk and told me I was wasting my time and my spelling was terrible and I should be practicing essay writing for my college applications. She didn't want me to take this course. It's the first time I've disobeyed her and I'm not sorry. You're a good teacher and you respect what the kids have to say."

She looked down at the floor and continued in a softer voice. "But I do get very nervous when you call on me. I just get tongue-tied and I can't get the words out to say what I want to say. But I'm listening to everything that everybody else says."

Bill could see tears at the corners of her eyes. He wanted desperately to sooth her, to pat her on the shoulder, but he was mindful of the strict prohibition against touching students.

"Let's form a pact, Rachel. I promise not to call on you in class unless you raise your hand, but here's what I ask in return. You take any topic we've been discussing in class and, when you're at home, write me your personal opinion on it – not long and nothing formal – just a few sentences, and don't worry about spelling or punctuation. This will be a private exchange of ideas and opinions on poetry between the two of us…"

Rachel interrupted him with alarm in her voice.

"But my mother wants to see all my homework and corrects everything."

I'll bet she does, Bill thought, but made another suggestion.

"Then why don't you write your thoughts down during your study period and drop them in my mailbox in the Main Office?"

Rachel smiled and shook her head vigorously.

"Yes, I could do that, and it would be just between the two of us. I'd like that."

"Then it's a deal!" Bill said, rising from his seat. "By the way, I hope you're feeling better."

"Oh, I'm fine," she said. "I have big tests in two of my other classes at the end of this week and my mother made me stay home and study for them. She says I need lots of time to concentrate so I can do really well."

Rachel rose, gathered her books and scuttled across the room. At the door she turned and smiled. "Thanks, Mr. McGregor. Thanks a lot."

Then she was gone. Bill stood in the empty classroom and joyfully reminded himself that this was why he loved being a teacher.

* * * *

In the days that followed, Rachel kept her part of the agreement, and Bill was stunned by the volume of writing she placed in his mailbox each day. She revealed more aspects of her personality than he could ever have hoped. She commented on the topics discussed in class and seemed to have total recall of what every student said, elaborating on why she agreed or disagreed with particular comments. She offered her own interpretations of poems and revealed a keen mind and a sly, ready wit. She loved verbal puns and usually included one or two in each of her communications. She made references to her poor spelling but always in a humorous way, and because Bill only responded each day to the content of her writing, she wrote freely, her thoughts unimpeded by spelling inhibitions. In his responses Bill often used the very words she had misspelled; in this way, he felt, he was modeling rather than correcting.

Every night, Bill would prepare his lesson plans for the next day and read student writing assignments from his freshman composition classes and correct any review quizzes he had given that day. He always kept Rachel's notes for last, and considered them a treat. No matter how tired he was late in the evening, he tried to respond as fully as possible and found himself repeatedly remarking on the astuteness of her observations and how it was a shame that the other students could not enjoy and benefit from them.

One day in Mid October, the class was discussing a sonnet by Robert Browning and debating two interpretations. Bill was seated on the front of the teacher's desk, enjoying the lively debate among his students and offering comments to help them clarify their points, when out of the corner of his eye he saw Rachel tentatively raise her hand. At first Bill thought he had been mistaken, but the hand was definitely up – not the arm raised high above the head like all the other students who competed for attention, but only the hand elevated in front of her face. The expression on her face seemed riddled with anxiety but the hand stayed up. When Bill called her name, all talking in the room ceased, so startled were the students after more than a month of classroom banter, to have a contribution volunteered by Rachel.

She spoke slowly in a low voice, her eyes never leaving the teacher. Bill kept supportively shaking his head up and down, urging her on, and smiling. The longer she spoke, her words seemed to flow more easily and her face became more relaxed. Instead of making comments in support of either of the two interpretations under discussion, she offered a third interpretation, giving ample evidence from the sonnet to support her assertions. By the time she finished speaking, several students were nodding in agreement, but others wanted to debate her view. Furiously they waved their hands, some even half rising out of their seats. Their arguments were posed as questions directly to Rachel, and to Bill's amazement, she didn't flinch from defending her position and responded in a steady, calm voice.

The discussion, with Rachel as the central participant, lasted until the bell rang, and three students surrounded her desk, eager to continue the dialogue. As Rachel crossed the room, still engaged in conversation with another girl, she gave Bill a big smile. He, in turn, was grinning from ear to ear.

* * * *

Bill was still reading student papers when the principal arrived. Stuffing everything into his already bulging briefcase and grabbing his Styrofoam cup of coffee, Bill followed Dr. Mathews into the principal's office. It was a spacious room enhanced by a high ceiling, beige carpeting and dark wood blinds at the windows. At one side of the room was a large mahogany desk facing two brown leather club chairs for visitors. At the front of the desk was an embossed wooden nameplate, with the name Dr. Francis Mathews. Behind the desk was a long console, also mahogany, with several framed pictures of Dr. Mathews's wife and two daughters, posed informally on a ski trip, a camping excursion and at Christmas time. On the other side of the room was a large, round, mahogany conference table surrounded with more leather club chairs, all on wheels. Bill noticed that there were no pictures on the walls.

Dr. Mathews motioned for Bill to take a seat at the table and both men removed the lids from their coffee containers and took sips before the principal began speaking in his usual cheery, if somewhat distracted, manner, for as he spoke, he was examining his daily calendar that his secretary had left him.

"Bill, thanks for coming in early to meet with me. We've got a bit of a problem that I'm sure we can quickly nip in the bud."

The principal paused, and Bill, startled by this announcement, registered a surprised look but said nothing. Dr. Mathews continued, still smiling.

"The Millers have been in to see me and they're really steamed over your refusal to give their daughter a few accommodations regarding homework."

Before he could reflect on what he was doing, Bill interrupted the principal.

"It's not homework; it's classwork. Did the Millers tell you exactly what they wanted me to do?"

Bill recognized the indignation infiltrating his voice. Dr. Mathews took another sip of coffee and spoke in a casual way.

"Something about substituting more homework for some classwork because the girl found your class very stressful"

He leaned toward Bill and waved a finger. "Who knew you were such a slave driver?" he joked, but Bill saw no humor in any of this, and, straining to keep his voice calm, he replied:

"The Millers wanted me to exempt Rachel from all written assignments and tests given in the classroom and allow her to complete all work at home. They showed me a sample of a personal essay that she had first written in class and then did over that night, and, frankly, the second version was completely different from the first and strongly indicated a helping hand. No, a controlling hand!"

Bill felt his words growing in vehemence and stopped. Dr. Mathews still sported a thin smile but his eyes were blank. Airily waving his right arm as if he were pushing away the details that Bill was presenting, he said:

"They brought me copies of reports from other doctors saying that Rachel was suffering from a high anxiety disorder."

Again, Bill, entirely on reflex, interrupted the principal.

"But they refuse to have her brought before the Committee on Special Education and have her classified"

He felt the anger rising in him and struggled unsuccessfully to remain calm and professional. He could hear his voice becoming shriller but he continued.

"In my opinion, the only thing this girl is suffering from is the intimidation of over-zealously ambitious, controlling and manipulative parents. She is shy, and she is anxious but they're making her that way with their constant watching and criticizing and badgering her to do better."

"That describes more than half the parents in this school," Dr. Mathews said wearily.

"Maybe," Bill responded, "but she's a great kid, sensitive and reflective, and she and I have a good rapport going and I know she likes my class."

"It's not the girl's view that's important here. It's the parents," Dr. Mathews said in a quiet voice, as if speaking to himself, while he gazed distractedly toward the window.

Bill was stunned by this observation and sat silently, reflecting on the jolting implications of this last statement.

Dr. Mathews, as though recovering from some momentary reverie, jerked his head back in Bill's direction and took another sip of his coffee, followed by a long, audible, deep breath. He was still smiling but his tone was heavy when he spoke.

"Bill, I told the Millers that I'd discuss the situation with you and get back to them in a few days. My meeting with them was last Friday and here it is only Tuesday morning and they've been on the phone to several members of the Board of Education, including the board president who's their next-door neighbor, and he's called me, along with two other board members, and they're pleading the Millers' case. They've also called the superintendent and he called me at home last night and he wants this issue resolved."

A vision of community politics that Bill had never entertained before suddenly appeared to him, but he rallied to the challenge.

"How can we, in good conscience, give in to these unfair demands, no matter who is mistakenly pressuring us to do so?" he asked, gazing steadily at Dr. Mathews.

The thin smile left the principal's face. He avoided Bill's steely stare and, mindlessly turning his coffee container around and around, looked down at the table when he spoke.

"I'm afraid that conscience has to give way to pragmatics in this case. He continued, after a momentary pause, in a low, flat voice. "Bill, the simple fact is that you don't have tenure. Now, as you know, it's the Board of Education that awards tenure to both of us. My concern is that the Millers are bad mouthing you so much to various members of the Board that, come this time next year when you'll be up for tenure, those Board members could have formed a very negative impression of you and vote not to award you tenure."

"But surely," Bill blurted out, "you and Mrs. Baker would support my candidacy."

Never lifting his eyes from the table, Dr. Mathews responded.

"Yes, of course we would. But our Board members are not educators and they can be heavily influenced by what they hear from friends and neighbors, and social pressure can be a powerful influence in their thinking."

The scenario that Dr. Mathews was sketching was so unexpected and so relentlessly unfair in its implications that Bill could not have had his innocence and naivety ripped away in any quicker, more forceful manner. He stared mutely at the table, his mind racing as one thought collided with another and his spirits, weighted down by the vagaries of a world so suddenly glimpsed, plummeted.

"Frankly, Bill," Dr. Mathews continued, "once they form an opinion of you as being unresponsive to the needs of kids, no matter where that accusation comes from, there might be little that either I or Mrs. Baker could do to dissuade them."

Now he stopped spinning the coffee container and looked directly at Bill.

"So I'm urging you to see the reality of this situation for both our sakes."

"You want me to comply with the Millers' demands?" Bill asked, his voice full of disbelief.

The principal's reply was quick and emphatic:

"I want you to recognize the unique circumstances of this issue and find the one solution that will get the Millers off your back and the superintendent and the Board off mine." As an afterthought, he added, "You know, Bill, I'm up for tenure later this year, and I don't need this ill will."

"I see," responded Bill quietly, as he rose from his chair and without ceremony headed for the door.

Dr. Mathews also rose and came around the conference table, placing his arm around Bill's shoulder. Speaking in a cheerfully conspiratorial tone he said: "Don't be upset by this, Bill. This is just a little bump in the road that we have to get around. You always have to keep the big picture in mind. We'll both look back on this, years from now, and have a good laugh together. No one has to know. It's a private matter. And the child would benefit from less pressure, don't you agree? I know you'll do the right thing."

The principal opened the door and stopped there, and Bill passed through the doorway, quietly closing the door behind him, seeing now with perfect clarity what he had to do.

Turning Corners

Dr. Philip Madison sat in his office alone, entering a few notes in the file of the patient who had just left. From across the hall he heard Judy, the receptionist, saying,

"The doctor will be with you in just a moment." Then she closed the door to his examination room and opened the door to his office.

"Your next patient is here, doctor," Judy announced casually as she placed a thin folder on his desk. "She's new. Comes from out of state – New Jersey, I think she said."

Dr. Madison acknowledged this information with a silent nod, not wanting to interrupt his writing the final sentence in the last patient's folder. When he finished writing and glanced up, Judy had already exited his office, closing the door behind her. He reached across his desk and picked up the folder, opened it and saw that it contained only basic information about the next patient.

Name: Mrs. Helen Burke

Age: 76

Address: Penny Drive, Asheville, North Carolina

He'd have to work up a medical profile, he thought, seeing the remaining forms blank. Get her medical history sent down from her previous doctors in New Jersey. Routine work, really, and vaguely unsettling.

Philip Madison was a young doctor, only thirty-two, tall, good looking, with an athletic build conditioned by early morning workouts at the gym and five-mile runs on the weekends. He had recently joined the long established private practice of two older doctors when their caseload became too much for them to handle, primarily because of so many northerners retiring to the Blue Ridge Mountains area. Both doctors knew Philip, whose father was their golf partner. They had made an offer that he had eagerly accepted.

As new patients came to the office, they were automatically assigned to Dr. Madison. Although by nature a man of easy empathy and broad compassion, his exuberant youthfulness and robust personality often caused him to feel a yawning gap between himself and the many fragile, sometimes querulous and often anxious senior citizens who now comprised a significant portion of his patients. He could diagnose their symptoms and treat their ailments, but he sensed about them an unspoken fearfulness underlying any surface gaiety that made him feel awkward and inadequate in their presence. While conscious of these feelings, he was determined to do his best, but he did not relish still another septuagenarian patient.

He crossed the hall with Helen Burke's folder under his arm and opened the door to his examination room. Extending his hand, he said in a hearty voice, "Hello, Mrs. Burke, I'm Dr. Madison."

The woman facing him, seated on the end of the examination table, extended her hand and offered him a broad, pleasant smile.

"Hello, Doctor. It's nice to meet you."

Her voice had the thinness of age, with tinges of reediness, but it also conveyed an energetic vivacity that seemed forced.

Dr. Madison made a quick visual appraisal. Helen Burke looked considerably younger than her listed age. Really more like sixty-six than seventy-six, he thought. Her symmetrically shaped face and even features had neither that pinched look nor the web of wrinkles that he often noted in women of her age. A few lines around the mouth and some more at the corners of her eyes, but otherwise the skin was smooth and unblemished, and the chin firm. Dark gray hair, short and curly, framed her face, whose dominant feature were definitely the eyes, large and vividly green, with an inner sparkle and an alert, direct gaze. She was thin but looked robust rather than frail.

"I understand you've recently moved here from up north," Dr. Madison said, demonstrating a friendly interest in this new patient.

"Yes. From New Jersey," she said in a cheerful tone.

"And what brought you to our beautiful area?" he asked while opening her folder and placing it on the counter that ran along one wall.

"Well, I've been coming to the Asheville area on vacation for years. I used to come with my husband and daughter, but now that they're both gone, I decided this would be a great place to start a new life."

"I'm sorry for your losses," Dr. Madison quickly said, feeling he was plunging into deep waters.

"Thank you," she said in a quiet, even tone, with only a slight tremor in her voice, then added: "I lost my husband ten years ago this June – a massive heart attack – and my daughter died of leukemia three years ago." Her voice was trailing off. "She was only forty-seven."

"Do you have other children?" Dr. Madison asked, hoping to divert her attention from these sad memories.

"No," she said quietly, the corners of her mouth drawing down. "No other children, no family."

Her gaze shifted quickly. She looked off in the distance as if watching familiar ghosts. Then she perked up, threw him a sharp glance and smiled.

"That's why I'm free to go where I like and I chose to come here and make a fresh start. Just me, myself and I," she said and laughed, but the laugh trailed off quickly and a forlorn look flickered across her face for an instant and disappeared.

Dr. Madison had taken the ballpoint pen from the pocket of his white coat and scribbled a note on the empty page of Helen Burke's medical history. "No family – new to area – living alone – cheerful personality."

"Who was your doctor in New Jersey, Mrs. Burke?"

He was careful not to call her Helen. One of the first patients he had been assigned upon joining this practice was an elderly man, a retired college professor, Arthur Bascomb; he remembered him as if it were yesterday. He had entered this very room and greeted the patient with a hearty "Hi Arthur, I'm Dr. Madison."

The man gave him a withering look and said: "You look like you're not even thirty, and I'm more than twice your age, and if you expect me to address you as Dr. Madison, then I request that you address me as Dr. Bascomb. You have an M.D. and I have a Ph.D., so let's keep the playing field even and show some mutual respect."

Older people, he was quickly learning, could be prickly and unpredictable.

There was a pause as Mrs. Burke seemed to ponder this routine question..

"We'll have your medical records sent to this office with your permission," he said matter-of-factly.

She flashed him another smile.

"Well, Doctor, except for my dental records, which I don't think you're interested in, there are no medical records."

Dr. Madison looked at her curiously. "I'm not sure I understand. Who was your primary physician in Jew Jersey?"

Still smiling, she said with a throaty chuckle, "No one. I didn't have a physician, primary or otherwise, back in New Jersey. I haven't been to a doctor in more than twenty years."

Puzzlement registered on Dr. Madison's face and a nervous edge crept into his voice.

"You mean you haven't been ill in the last twenty years?"

"Nothing that would warrant my seeing a doctor," she replied, still chuckling.

Dr. Madison leaned back against the counter and folded his arms across his chest.

"Then what kind of illnesses have you had, even if you didn't see a doctor?" he asked.

"Just the usual – colds, the flu once, cuts and bruises from accidents around the house. Oh, yes, and a bad case of poison ivy three or four years ago."

She ended her inventory, then added as an afterthought: "Fortunately, my next-door neighbor was a retired nurse and she always looked out for me."

"And you've never seen a doctor or gone to a hospital emergency room in all that time?" he asked, with obvious incredulity.

"Oh, I forgot," she replied quickly. "I stepped on a rusty fish hook about six years ago when I was visiting a friend at her lake house. I was just coming out of the water when I felt a sharp pain in the heel of my foot and I picked my foot out of the water and saw this horribly rusty fish hook dangling from my heel. My friend got it out and then she insisted on taking me to the local hospital where they gave me a tetanus shot. I think I still have the card stating when I received the shot."

"And that's all?" he asked with a rising pitch to his voice.

"That's all. Absolutely," she said quietly

"You've never had a checkup, a complete physical exam in twenty years?"

"Probably more like twenty-five," she said.

Then, in an effort to explain what she sensed was, to this doctor, so unusual, so odd, so unbelievable a history, she told him that she didn't believe in checkups, didn't believe in constantly looking for things that might be wrong with you – the body would let you know in its own way – didn't believe in any preventative regimen of pills, shots and countless visits, not to mention rivers of money, to specialists.

"I went to a dentist when I had a toothache or to get my teeth cleaned, and I went to an eye doctor when I needed to get new reading glasses," she said, a defensive note creeping into her voice, "but otherwise I've been very well. I watch my weight, eat sensibly, exercise regularly and don't go looking for trouble. My mother used to say, 'Trouble will come soon enough and find you, so you don't have to look for it.'"

She finished her monologue and sheepishly grinned at the doctor, who stood motionless with astonishment at both her history and her point of view. Among his elderly patients he found far more to be hypochondriacs than stoics. And while he marveled at her independence, he was concerned that she hadn't accepted the modern medical evidence of all the silent killers that could attack the body and, if not detected at an early stage, prove fatal. Then he remembered that she was seventy-six and seemed to be in pretty good shape for someone who had ignored the medical profession for almost a quarter of a century. Still, he thought, many serious things could be lurking under that healthy appearance.

"I assume that you don't take any prescription medications," he said.

"Not in the last thirty years or more," she responded.

"What medications did you take before that?" he asked.

"Something a doctor gave me when I was going through menopause. I forget the name of the drug, or the name of the doctor, for that matter," she said dismissively.

He was still mentally grappling with everything she had told him when a new thought came to him and he asked: "What brings you here today?"

Her legs were dangling off the side of the examination table and she crossed them at the ankles. Her arms were resting casually on her lap, and she brought one hand up to her throat and absently stroked it with her fingers. Her eyes took on a clouded look again, leaving his face and gazing at some distant, unfathomed point. She spoke softly, her words coming in halting clusters.

"Well, for more than a month now I've been experiencing lightheadedness nearly every day. Sometimes I can ignore it but other times I feel so dizzy that I have to lie down for a bit until it passes. Then two days ago I was down on my hands and knees scrubbing my kitchen floor and I must have passed out because the next thing I remember I woke up and I was lying on the floor next to the bucket."

Dr. Madison reached for the sphygmomanometer.

"Let's check your blood pressure," he said, motioning toward her left arm.

He noted the clouded look that once again appeared in her eyes, and her whole body seemed to become tense as she offered him her arm.

Moving closer to her, he tucked the lower portion of her extended arm between his arm and side. He felt her fingers grip his arm as he pushed the loose sleeve of her blouse up and wrapped the medical cuff around the upper portion of her arm. As he inflated the cuff, his head was only a few inches away from hers, and he could smell a mild perfume coming off her body. She smelled fresh and clean, and he thought that the scent was so delicate that it must come from a scented soap rather than even the lightest perfume. He finished pumping air in the cuff and had just pressed the release button valve and was holding his stethoscope to her lower arm when in this intimate doctor-patient moment it happened.

He felt her firm grip on his arm growing tighter. Her head tilted forward, covering the short distance between their bodies and rested gently on his chest over his heart. Motionless it stayed there for only a second, light and feathery, but then her head bore into him and she trembled, as quick gasps of air and thin, barely audible sobs escaped from her throat. Then she was weeping, deeply, continuously, and her whole body was shaking and he felt the wetness from her tears seeping through his starched white doctor's jacket and his dress shirt, and her fingers gripped his arm in a death vise, as if she were clinging to a life preserver in a turbulent, dooming sea.

Without moving he heard the pulse returning and automatically took note of the numbers: 148 over 96. Not good, he thought. He slowly removed his stethoscope from her arm with his free hand while she continued to clutch his left arm. Her spasmodic sobs and tears came unabated.

Dr. Madison was gripped with surprise and confusion. Nothing in his training or his limited doctor-patient experience had prepared him for this. He tried to formulate a response that would be professionally appropriate, but his insides were churning and he was seized with uncertainty and self-doubt and could think of nothing to say.

He looked down on the head of curly gray hair against his chest, bobbing up and down with her sobs, and, acting solely on instinct, he placed his free hand there, patting her head gently but saying nothing. Her sobbing, softer now, continued, and they remained frozen in this position, locked in an indissoluble human bond. His single instinctive act of commiseration instantly brought him clarity of vision, a sudden sharp pain of understanding. This understanding flowed into him with overwhelming force, nullifying any doubt or confusion. She was weeping for all the possibilities of life, he thought, past and future, realized and forsaken, for all her losses and her dreams deferred, for the uncertainties lurking on the darkening horizon, and for the eternally fleeting comfort of a human touch. He recognized and accepted his role in this tableau and suddenly felt expansive, peaceful and assured.

Point System

TUESDAY

Goddamit, how many frogs do you have to kiss before you find a princess, Pruitt asked himself while nursing a rum and coke in the lounge of his local Italian restaurant. Over six months now since I've been meeting women on the internet dating services and still no winner, he thought. He hated wasting time and money and, besides, at fifty-four, he had no time to waste. He knew exactly what he was looking for, so his posted profile of the lady he hoped to meet was short and straightforward: Honest, mature, attractive, in-shape lady under fifty, financially independent, athletic, adventuresome, looking for long-term relationship.

Pruitt had purposely avoided including all the romantic clichés about long walks on the beach and candlelit dinners and nights by a fireplace or gazing at the stars. He had also excluded "likes to cuddle," since he thought this was just a code phrase for sex, and if any female wasn't interested in sex, why the hell was she looking for men on the internet..

His first, and very pleasant, surprise had been the large number of women who had responded to his profile and picture; his second surprise was how many of them either ignored the requirements he had listed or lied about their own attributes. His biggest surprise was the number of "players" he had encountered: women, ignoring his long-term relationship quest, who thought his picture was "cute," and who were just looking for sex and no commitments. Both flattered and aroused by them, he had enjoyed the thrills and the sex, but he soon recognized that these brief, exciting interludes weren't furthering his goal of a permanent relationship.

Now he was averaging two new dates a week and he felt he had the first meeting down to a science. After emailing a few times back and forth and progressing rapidly to getting a lady's phone number, he always kept his phone conversations short, preferring to arrange a meeting quickly. It was only in person that he felt secure in gaining a realistic appraisal of the woman. His mental checklist of qualities and attributes that he was seeking never varied. He could adroitly steer the conversation to cover all the important topics, and he didn't waste time. Within twenty minutes of meeting a lady, he could tell if she was a viable candidate for further exploration.

Pruitt looked at his watch and saw it was four-fifty. This date had been set for five. He liked to get there early and position himself in his favorite booth facing the door so he could make a quick appraisal of the lady's overall appearance before she spotted him. He always chose this restaurant for a first meeting because it was close to his home and he could plead a hectic business schedule as an accountant to avoid traveling far. Also, he preferred to meet for drinks, and then, only if the lady met his criteria, suggest extending the date to dinner in the adjoining dining room. The lounge was not crowded at this time of day, and his favorite booth not only had a clear view of the entrance but the recessed ceiling light shone directly down on this booth, giving him a good light to examine the lady's appearance.

He saw her come in the front door and pause to get her bearings. She looked taller that the 5'6" she had listed on her profile, but at 6'1' he wasn't intimidated. He stood up and waved, and she quickly moved toward him, her arm extended and a warm smile on her face.

"Hi, Valerie," he said. "I'm Pruitt."

"Hello. It's nice to meet you," she said in a high-pitched voice.

She made eye contact only briefly before looking away. She removed her coat and slid into the booth. He moved into his side of the booth and watched her as she made little nervous gestures, placing her coat and bag on the seat, and adjusting the bracelets on her wrists.

"Any trouble finding the place?" he asked, all the while evaluating her appearance.

For starters, she didn't look forty-seven, the age she had listed on her profile; more like early fifties, he guessed. MINUS ONE. She was definitely on the plump side, certainly not thin as he liked them, but not so fat as to be undesirable. The white silk blouse she wore captured the curve of her plump breasts, but the jewelry – bangle bracelets on each arm, two rings on each hand, a broad gold necklace and gold hoop earrings – he found excessive. MINUS TWO. Her face was pleasant, with even features and dark, expressive eyes, but her skin was bad, with large pores that she tried to conceal with too much makeup, and her short hair, caught in the arc of the recessed ceiling light, was dyed a monotone auburn and looked frozen in place with gels or sprays. MINUS THREE.

"How long have you been living in this area?" she asked, interrupting his mental appraisal.

"For about two years, now," he said. "since my divorce. You know how it is: The wife gets the house and the husband gets the boot."

He flashed a broad smile to hide the tinge of bitterness in his voice. She returned his smile and asked, "How do you find this area?"

"By following a map," he said with a cocked eyebrow, pleased to show her his lighter side.

Her smile momentarily faded, as she pondered his answer, but then returned, and she responded.

"Of course, but how do you like living here?"

She seemed to have quickly caught on to his sense of humor. PLUS ONE.

"I like it," he said with little enthusiasm. "It's close to my office, and the condo I'm renting is near the beach. It's fine for now."

His voice trailed off. He didn't care to reveal his loneliness in finding himself, after thirty years of marriage and three grown kids, cast off and alone. He wanted to focus the conversation on her.

The waitress approached the booth. Valerie ordered a glass of white wine, and he, another rum and coke.

"You're new to this area, aren't you?" he asked.

“”Not really,” she said, her eyes shifting to some abstract point in the leather booth as she seemed to be weighing her response. “I’ve been away for many years but I came back recently to take care of my mother.”

He avoided frowning and quickly asked, “Is she ill?”

“Not anything major…just old age. My father passed away last year, and she seems unable to cope without him.”

“Does she have other children?” he asked gently, hoping there might be several siblings who could share this burden.

“No. My brother was killed in Viet Nam,” she said quietly. “So it’s just Mom and me.” A faraway look came into her eyes.

“That’s a heavy responsibility,” he said, mustering a sympathetic tone. MINUS FOUR. “What about your children?” I remember your mentioning that you had two grown kids. Do they help you with your mother?”

She rested her arms on the table and looked down at her bracelets while she spoke.

“Well, my daughter, Jessica, is married to an Italian – a real Italian, from Italy – and they live in Florence permanently, with only occasional visits to the States. And my other daughter, Terry, is a junior in high school and living with me, but you know how kids are: not too reliable. And, besides, she’s young and has her own life and I don’t want to burden her.”

“I thought they were both grown?” he said, smiling to hide his disappointment.

“Yes, well, nearly,” she said and looked up as the waitress returned with their drinks.

“You seem to fit the profile of the generation that’s caught in the middle,” he said after the waitress had left, “taking care of a parent and a child.”

“Yes,” she said, and weariness seemed to flash across her features as she gazed down at her drink, then raised it to her lips, her bangle bracelets jangling with this motion.

Lots of responsibilities, he thought. MINUS FIVE.

She put her drink down and looked directly at him.

“How old are your children?” she asked.

“My oldest child, Jennifer is twenty-five. Bud is twenty-three and Jimmy is twenty-one.”

“Do any of them live with you?”

"Definitely not!" he said, too sternly, he felt. "Jimmy just graduated from college, and all my kids knew that I would support them through college or until they turned twenty-one, but after that, they were on their own. Bud recently moved back with his mother while he gets his master's degree, but that's between her and him, and I have nothing to do with it. I don't believe in all this malarkey about kids' returning home and being treated like kids again, no matter how old they are!"

."What must you think of me," she said with a small giggle, "moving back to my parents' home at my ripe old age."

He realized that he might have spoken too sternly on a topic that he felt strongly about," so he flashed her a broad smile and changed the subject.

"How long have you been divorced?" he asked, mentally running through the few facts she had included in her internet profile.

She took another sip of her wine before answering.

"Actually, I'm in the process of getting divorced," she said, gazing down at her wine glass and absently turning it with her fingers.

"Then you're legally separated?" he said.

"No, we never went through that step," she said in a lower voice tinged with sadness. "We'd been married for over thirty years and were just drifting apart. Then when my father died and my mother refused to leave her home and I came here, Ted – that's my husband – announced that he wanted a divorce. He'd fallen in love with some woman at work."

Still legally entangled, he thought. MINUS SIX.

She raised her eyes to his and gave him a forced half-smile.

"I guess you can't get to be middle-age and not have accumulated some baggage," she said, taking another sip of her wine.

"Yeh," he acknowledged. But you've got more than most, he thought.

Trying to keep the mood upbeat, he changed the subject.

"So, what do you do to keep in shape?" he asked. "You look like you're in great shape," he lied.

She actually blushed. He watched her skin turn pink below her beige makeup.

"Well, Ted and I used to play a lot of golf, but now I'm afraid I don't have a regular workout routine. And every time I get on a scale, it shows!"

She paused, looking at him expectantly, and he supposed that she was waiting for him to say something flattering but he didn't.

"I've been meaning to join a gym," she continued, "but just haven't gotten around to it, what with my mother and Terry and work and all."

No regular workout regimen. MINUS SEVEN

She had given him the perfect lead into another important topic on his list.

"What kind of work do you do?"

She rearranged her bangle bracelets, then drained the last drop of her wine before answering.

"I'm a dental hygienist."

Not much of an income from that, he thought. He wanted a woman who could bring as much to the table financially as he could. He thought of how hard he had worked to become a partner in his small accounting firm, and since his ex-wife was a teacher and it was she who had wanted the divorce, she asked for no alimony. He wanted to enhance his life style with a new lady, going fifty-fifty on everything. That wouldn't be possible with this lady. MINUS EIGHT

As far as he was concerned, it was over.

They spent the next ten minutes talking about the area, about traffic, about restaurants, about her job, about anything that was of no consequence to him, for he was just going through the motions.

Valerie glanced at the approaching waitress, and he quickly checked his watch: Five-twenty-five. The waitress asked if they'd like another round. Valerie looked at him, smiling. He couldn't terminate the meeting so abruptly, so soon.

"Sure," he said.

They fell into their first awkward silence before the waitress quickly returned with their drinks. He played with his drink and adjusted the cocktail napkin under it. Then she looked directly at him.

"I must make a confession," she said, half smiling but her eyes had an earnest, pleading look. "You're the first person I've agreed to meet since I put my profile on the dating service a month ago."

He feigned a look of supportive interest, and she continued.

"This is all so new to me…meeting men through the internet. I haven't been on a date in over thirty years, and I guess you can see that I'm nervous. Your picture looked so kind…and so respectable with your suit and tie."

"It's the picture they use at my firm," he interjected.

She looked down at the table and her tone became forlorn. She spoke as if in a private reverie.

"If anyone had ever told me that I'd be here at this point in my life – meeting a total stranger – well, I would never have believed it."

Her voice sank to a lower register.

"But everything has changed so quickly and I get so lonely, especially at night, after Terry and my mother have gone to bed. And I keep thinking how nice it would be to have someone to share things with."

Her eyes were moist, and a tear escaped and wandered down her cheek. She quickly brushed it away, her bangle bracelets accentuating this brief movement with noisy clashes.

"Look at me, going on like this!" she said in a brighter tone, as through recovering from a trance. She took a sip of wine and smiled. A sad little smile, he thought. She reached across the table to where his hands were resting by his drink and quickly squeezed them and then, just as quickly, withdrew hers and turned away, looking embarrassed.

Another frog, he thought. Needy and pitiful and hoping to be rescued. Well, lady, I'm not the valiant prince type who rides up to rescue you from all your troubles. What's more, you're no princess!

He was annoyed. Not just that another first meeting had proved disappointing, but here it had taken an unexpected turn into heavy melodrama which he hadn't expected, never saw coming. He felt put upon, tricked into feigning sympathy that he didn't feel. His patience was short. What right had this woman, a total stranger, dammit, to dump all this emotional baggage on him. That wasn't playing by the rules. Now he would have to be all mushy and sympathetic, when all he wanted to do was terminate the date and get the hell out of there.

He reached across the table and touched her arm.

"I understand. I understand," was all he could come up with, but her broad smile told him that was enough.

Another awkward silence as they busied themselves with sipping their drinks. She spoke first.

"I've been going on about myself and haven't given you a chance to say much."

"Not at all!" he protested. "I like to learn as much as I can about any lady I meet for the first time."

He saw a shadow pass across her face.

"Have you been meeting many ladies?" she asked quietly.

He paused, knowing that this was an area he didn't want to get into, but then his vanity mastered him.

"Let's just say it's been a steady stream," he said, smiling.

"How long have you been…been doing this?" she asked

"For about six months now, off and on," he said.

"You must have many funny stories."

"A few, but they're mostly sad," he said, thinking of all the frogs.

"And no one special in all that time?" she asked and shifted her eyes to the table.

"Not really," he said, and he through he saw her wince. "You know how it is. There has to be that special chemistry – that meshing of personalities and mutual interests, when two people are at similar points in their lives and can go forward as equals. It's not as easy to find as you think."

He had said too much, and there was another awkward silence as she continued to stare at the table, turning her wine glass.

Determined to regain the initiative, he said, "Do you like to watch sports: baseball, basketball, football, soccer?"

She hesitated as if weighing her answer. Then, in a barely audible voice and with a slight shrug of her shoulders, she said, "I'm afraid not."

The air seemed thick, and it was becoming harder to speak.

Goddammit, he thought, this is too much! I've got to put an end to it.

Sweeping his arm up to his eye level and staring at his watch he said, "Oh, Oh, I'm in trouble!"

She looked up from the table.

"We have an emergency meeting at the office…the partners…we were hit with a potential law suit today…got to get back."

Her face seemed to collapse, but all she said was, "I see."

"Sorry to cut this short," he said, signaling for the waitress, "but you stay and finish your drink."

Her eyes were moist again, he noticed, and he talked faster, eager to escape.

"Very nice to meet you, Valerie," he said, rising from the booth. He patted her shoulder. Then, for his exit line, he found himself uttering the universal lie, "I'll call you."

She smiled wanly, never lifting her eyes to his, and said nothing. He paid the bill and was quickly out the door.

Another frog dispatched in under an hour, he thought, breathing in the cool evening air. Such a sad little frog! Then he was already looking ahead to getting home and hitting the internet for his next date.

THURSDAY

His watch said five-fifteen. She was fifteen minutes late. He'd wait another fifteen minutes, then leave. Damn! She looked so beautiful in her picture, he thought. Really a knockout! Her profile was brand new, and he had emailed her immediately, breaking his rule and giving her his phone number. She called and sounded wonderful on the phone: a warm, husky voice rippling with laughter. He quickly set up this date, and now he wondered if he had been the first guy who had responded to her profile and then other guys had closed in, and she had decided not to meet him. He glanced at his watch again but knew that he'd wait longer than fifteen minutes.

The waitress brought him his second drink. She was young and friendly.

"No luck yet?" she asked brightly, flashing him a big smile. After seeing him on so many dates at this same Italian restaurant, she knew his story.

"Not yet, Lee," he smiled back, "but you know what they say: You have to kiss a lot of frogs before you find a princess."

She laughed and placed his rum and coke along with a small dish of peanuts on the table of his favorite booth.

"Don't give up hope," she said cheerfully before walking away.

"Never do," he said to her back, admiring the shape of her legs.

He tossed a few peanuts into his mouth and was raising his drink to his lips when he saw her come in. His arm stopped in mid-motion and he stared. My god, she's really lovely, he thought. Before he could stand, she spotted him and was striding quickly toward the booth.

"Pruitt?" she asked in a voice that instantly reminded him of Kathleen Turner's: husky and deep, with soft edges.

He stood up and realized that she was nearly as tall as he, at least five-eleven in heels, or probably more like a full six feet.

"Hi, Chris," he said, conscious of the few peanuts still lodged in his mouth.

She took his extended hand in hers and he was surprised by the firmness of her grip.

"Sorry I'm late" she said in that voice that already was beguiling him, "but traffic was a bitch."

She removed a bright wool shawl and casually flung it into the booth along with her bag.

"Where's the powder room?" she asked, and he pointed to a corner of the lounge.

He watched her walk away, the discernible curve of her butt visible beneath her sleek beige dress, and the long, well-shaped, plump legs quickly gliding across the wood floor, her high heels making clicking sounds. She was gone for what seemed to him a long time before he saw her coming toward him.

She really looks like a model, he thought, but with larger breasts. His pulse started to quicken. She had a superb figure. Even Lee, the waitress, was staring at her as she gracefully slid into the booth across from him. Now all her features were caught in the glare of the recessed ceiling light, and he was aware that he was staring too intently, but he couldn't help it. He was ensnared by her striking beauty, the planes and hollows of her face, the perfect symmetry of her features, the large, heavily lashed brown eyes that looked directly – almost defiantly – at him, and the thick honey-blond hair that fell in soft, casual layers to her shoulders. The eyes were heavily made up, and he could see under the direct light that she wore a good deal of makeup, but, he had to admit, the overall effect was fascinating. He couldn't stop staring at her.

"You look a bit older than your picture," she said straightforwardly, breaking the silence and his long stare. She laughed, as if dismissing the observation. She looked no more than mid-thirties, although she had listed her age as forty-one. He was suddenly conscious of his age.

"Yes, well it was taken a few years ago," he admitted, "for my firm."

"You're an accountant, right?"

"Yes, a partner in an accounting firm," he said, suddenly eager to impress her.

He blushed under her direct stare as she studied his face closely.

"You've aged very well," she said finally. "Except for a little gray at the temples, you've hardly changed since that picture was taken."

He felt himself blushing harder, like some pimply teenager.

"So, are you going to buy me a drink?" she asked in a teasing tone, glancing toward the bar.

He signaled for Lee, the waitress, who was observing them from the bar and quickly came to their booth. Chris ordered a Tanqueray martini on the rocks, "Double olive, please." As she turned her head toward Lee, Pruitt admired her striking profile and strong jaw line.

"Now, Pruitt," she said, turning back to him and flashing another dazzling smile – perfect teeth, he noticed, and wondered if they were capped – "tell me about yourself."

He knew that this was not following the usual pattern of his first dates where he always asked the questions, but her striking looks and strong personality had so captivated him that he didn't care. He didn't care if she was taking the lead; he didn't care if he was acting like a nervous schoolboy; he didn't care even if she was a player, for now that thought came to mind. He was bewitched by her and wanted to be in her presence, to listen to her speak, to take in her beauty, to meet her approval, to touch her, to make love to her.

"Well," he began, clearing his throat as though he were about to give a public speech, "I'm fifty-four, as you know; divorced nearly two years, with three grown children – no responsibilities there. I'm six-feet-one and a hundred eighty-five pounds." He was aware of the hint of pride in his voice. "I work hard and play hard. Work out at the gym three times a week and run five miles on the weekend. I like to swim, ski and roller blade."

Her face registered surprise at this last activity.

"And I enjoy watching sports on TV, especially basketball. I played a little in high school."

"I'm a Celtics' fan," she interjected. "Played a little, myself, in school."

He beamed.

I live alone," he continued, "don't smoke; drink moderately. I thought about getting a dog when I moved into my condo but decided that it would tie me down too much. I like to travel. Didn't do much of it all the time I was married – just local vacations with the kids – but now I take a big trip once a year. Went to England, Scotland and Ireland two years ago – I'm Scotch-Irish – and France last year. Have plans to visit Spain and Portugal this year."

He paused, realizing that he'd been running on, encouraged by her approving smile.

"I don't like to waste time and I'm not very patient, but I think I have a good sense of humor, and I'm looking for a lady to share my life."

He took a sip of his drink and gazed directly at her.

"Now let's see what I know about you?" he said. "Your profile said you were forty-one – you look younger; attractive - you certainly are; in shape – that's obvious; divorced, no children, a lawyer, and looking for a soulmate, someone adventurous and very open minded."

She nodded affirmatively.

"You forgot that I love all kinds of food, jazz and traveling," she said in a teasing tone. "And I also ski, but didn't mention that. I've done a bit of roller blading, but didn't mention that either."

"It seems as though we have a lot in common," he said, recognizing for the first time that he hadn't registered one MINUS since she entered the lounge.

He had forgotten to check out her jewelry but now he saw one cocktail ring as she took a sip of her martini and noted her small gold earrings. A bright, multicolored scarf around her neck was the only touch of color, kept in place with a small gold pin. Everything was a PLUS.

Her hands were large but graceful, and after all, she's a big woman, he thought, like those big super models that have perfectly proportioned bodies but big frames, like Heidi Klum and Tyra Banks. Her nails were long and painted a soft shade of pink.

"How long have you been divorced?" he asked.

"Over five years now," she said, and he was again conscious of that marvelously husky voice. "I was only married for three years before I decided that I wanted a totally different life."

She smiled and ran her hand through her hair, so shiny in the glow of the ceiling light, he noted.

"I can't believe that in five years someone hasn't snatched you up," he said.

"I'm very choosey!" she said with mock self-importance, but then her expression changed and she looked directly into his eyes. "I'm looking for a man who isn't your run-of-the-mill guy; someone who thinks out of the box and is very secure within himself."

"And how do you decide if a man meets those criteria?"

"I have my ways," she said mysteriously, cocking an eyebrow and forming a half-smile, but she offered nothing more and changed the subject.

"How would you describe yourself politically?" she asked.

"That's a little difficult to answer," he said. "I'm a registered Republican, but lately there have been so many factions within my party that it's hard for me to place myself. I'm not a neo-con and I'm certainly not one of the evangelical right wingers.

I definitely believe in fiscal restraint and a strong military, but not as aggressive as we've been lately."

"What about social issues?" she asked. "Abortion, stem-cell research, gay marriage, affirmative action?"

His answer was spontaneous.

"I'm basically a libertarian, I guess, so I don't want many restrictions placed on my freedoms by the government. I have pretty mixed feeling about abortion, though, especially when I read the statistics about how many fetuses are aborted in the U. S. each year, and around the world, too. But then I tell myself that if all those babies were born, and they had babies, our population explosion would be unsupportable in terms of space and natural resources, so that's the trade-off, so to speak."

He stopped to take a sip of his drink, and she sat quietly, waiting for him to continue.

"I'm not too sure about affirmative action," he said. "I think there should be an even playing field to compete in." Then he found himself making it personal. "No one gave me preferential treatment. My parents were typical working-class people and I was the first one to go to college in my generation, and I worked my way though school."

He dropped the subject, dissatisfied with his answer, and she didn't register any response.

"And stem-cell research and gay marriage?" she asked softly.

"Well, since I don't have any strong religious beliefs and don't practice any religion, I'm not opposed to stem-cell research. And as for gay marriage, why the gays want to imitate us, when our divorce rate is over fifty per cent, is beyond me, but if that's what they want, go ahead."

"You don't think that would be undermining the institution of marriage and our notion of family?" she asked.

He couldn't decide from her tone what her own position might be, but he felt she was testing him and he wanted to please her.

"Marriage, when separated from religious beliefs and practices, is a binding contract between two people who willingly enter into it. What difference does it make if it's between a man and a woman, or two women or two men? Live and let live –

that's my motto. And a family should be anything you want it to be, as long as there's love and mutual support."

He was pleased with these opinions and searched her face for a reaction, but although she continued smiling, she gave no hint of her own opinion. Before he could ask her how she felt about these issues, she leaned forward and captured him with those beautiful eyes.

"Pruitt, do you believe in God?"

This grilling is getting into some serious territory, he thought, but his answer was forthright.

"The jury's still out on that," he confessed, smiling. "A personal god that's involved in each of our lives and keeps a checklist of all our actions, offering us eternal rewards or punishments in a life after death: No. A superior being who created everything, the First Cause, so to speak: Yes."

She leaned back against the booth and shook her head while laughing softly.

"You're an interesting guy. Quite the philosopher! Not your average accountant, I'll bet."

He was uneasy about having been drawn into such revealing topics on a first date, but he felt happy that she seemed to approve of his answers.

"So did I pass some kind of test?" he asked brightly.

"The jury's still out," she said, imitating his own words in a teasing tone, but he was encouraged.

The waitress approached their booth and asked if they wanted another round. Pruitt looked at his watch and was surprised to see how much time had elapsed since Chris's arrival. He wanted to continue this date, definitely.

"Why don't we move into the dining room and have dinner," he suggested, and she readily agreed.

As they left the lounge and walked into the dining room, the few people at other tables were clearly staring at her, and he felt a surge of pride in being her escort. We make a fine looking couple, he thought. She's a knockout!

The conversation flowed easily throughout dinner. They discovered they were both an only child and both harbored a secret love for dirty jokes, and they started to share their repertoire, like two pals over a beer at the local pub.

She has a marvelous laugh, he thought: deep and throaty and full. He loved the way she erupted with laughter, throwing her head back, her hair swirling in shimmering waves and the multi-colored scarf around her neck floating below her exquisite face and strong jaw. Her face had a sculpted quality to it, he thought, as if some artist had created her from clay. He wondered if she had had some plastic surgery but could see no signs. Still, it was so perfect, so mesmerizing!

He asked her about her work and discovered that she had a private practice.

"Wills and divorces and real estate—the usual stuff, nothing special," she said, but he knew from what his own divorce had cost that there was good money in these mundane matters. He asked her about her childhood and learned that she had been born and raised in the Mid-West and had only relocated here after her divorce. When he gently inquired about her recent dating history, she was vague.

For every question he posed to her, she had two for him, and while his were mostly factual, hers were more abstract and psychological. And provocative! What was his greatest fear? What really made him happy? What was his concept of an ideal relationship? What was the wackiest thing he had ever done? What had he always dreamed of doing? What did he think of the feminist movement?

These questions, while challenging and throwing him off guard, were put to him with such casualness and encouraging, teasing smiles, that he surrendered to her charm and found himself willingly revealing more intimate details about his history and character than he had ever thought possible on a first date.

She's bewitched me, he thought, bemused.

They had lingered over coffee, and then over refills, and then he suggested an after-dinner cordial, and he had never felt so positive, so hopeful, so giddy with expectations. He had an uncanny feeling that she knew and understood him, even more than his ex-wife ever had. She had drawn him out from his protective shield and caused him to relinquish his reserve and control.

This is magic, he thought. She's so damn comfortable to be with, but so alluring. She's direct and honest, yet there's a mysterious quality lurking at the edges that I can't decode. She's fascinating! Truly fascinating!

His impulse was to invite her back to his condo where he hoped to reenact the love-making he had been fantasizing about all evening, but he was uncertain as to how she might respond, and he didn't want to rush things and break the spell. He decided that he'd let her take the lead.

The waitress approached their table and asked if they wanted anything else. Chris shook her head, no. He had lost all track of time and checked his watch: it was ten-thirty. He looked around the dining room and saw that they were the only remaining customers.

"I guess we'll have the check, Lee," he said, disappointed that the evening might be coming to an end.

Chris excused herself and, taking her purse, headed for the Ladies Room. He sat quietly, reflecting on the wondrous evening they had had.

She does take a long time in the Ladies Room, he thought, chuckling to himself, for this was the only small MINUS he had registered all night. Besides, he thought, the wait is worth the results. She's like a dream girl. I feel so comfortable with her and she's the hottest woman I've ever dated.

She finally returned and stood by the booth.

"Too much coffee," she said smiling, and he smiled, too, at this intimate reference. She reached for her shawl

He stood up.

"I hate to end this date," he confessed.

"All good things…," she said, without ending the saying, draping the shawl around her shoulders. She was giving no sign of anything further tonight.

"I'd really like to see you again, Chris," he blurted out, with no rehearsal.

"Well, sailor, we can probably arrange that the next time you're in port," she said in that teasing tone that he found so enticing.

"When?" he asked eagerly, as they walked toward the door.

She smiled but didn't answer, which momentarily threw him into a spasm of uncertainty and doubt. They walked a short distance until she stopped beside a green Jaguar.

"Here's my buggy," she said, turning to face him, her beautiful eyes locked into his. "I've really enjoyed this evening, Pruitt."

"So have I," he said quickly. "More than any I can remember."

Her voice took on a deeper pitch.

"I'd like to see you again, but I don't want to start off on a false note," she said softly.

He had no idea what she meant. He felt an overwhelming urge to wrap her in his arms and kiss her, but something in her look held him back.

She opened her purse and took out a folded piece of paper and pressed it into his hand.

"Please don't read this until you get home. Then, if you still want another date, call me. Goodnight"

She smiled, squeezed his arm, and was in her car and pulling out of the parking lot before he recovered his wits, so unexpected was her last action of the evening. Clutching the folded paper, his mind racing furiously as to what the paper could possibly say, he hurried to his car and, once inside, switched on the overhead light and read her note.

It was two pieces of paper, and her handwriting was bold and sloppy.

Dear Pruitt,

I'm writing this note in the Ladies Room so forgive my scribble. This was my first date since my divorce – yes, that's right – five years ago – and I didn't know what to expect.. Your picture and background made you seem like a very conservative man and I wanted to test things with someone like you. I never dreamed the date would go so well. You're a nice, attractive guy, and while I like you, I'm not sure that we're compatible – not because of any personality differences but because of my history. You'll remember how I told you that I left my spouse because I wanted a new life. I truly wanted a new life – as a WOMAN. The last five years have been spent turning Christopher into Chris, and you were my test run. I am now fully a woman in every way, anatomically and otherwise, but I don't want to fly under false colors. From the way this evening went, I believe this will come as a surprise to you and you'll need time to think "out of the box," and assimilate this information. I'll certainly understand if you find the adjustment in thinking too hard to make. Thanks for a memorable evening.

Chris

He read the note again just to be sure his mind was registering what was written. Then he sat in his car for a long time, absorbing the startling revelation, too shocked, really, to believe it. She was so beautiful, so statuesque! How could that be a man? But it wasn't a man. If he understood her note, it had taken five years to transform herself. Correction: himself. That's why every feature was so perfect! And that body! At least, what he had seen of it. He vaguely remembered a word for people who changed their sex. What was it? Transvestite? No, that's guys who dress up as women, he told himself. Then he found it: transgender. He suddenly recalled the tabloid headlines about a model who had appeared in a James Bond movie as one of Bond's girls and later it was revealed that she was a transgender. And she was gorgeous, like Chris!

He shook his head in disbelief and told himself that this was like science fiction: a man transforming himself so completely that he became a totally convincing and beautiful woman. He reviewed the evening, looking for signs. Her height and large frame: No, many women are tall and big-boned. The large hands: that went with her general size. The voice? But Kathleen Turner isn't a transgender, is she?

His mind took a different tack, and he had a "eureka" moment.

"That's probably why I felt so comfortable with her!" he shouted. "She knows how a man thinks and feels."

He flashed back to the joke telling session – just like two guys having a beer and swapping dirty stories. He thought about her note again and how she had specifically said that she was anatomically a complete woman, and his lustful curiosity was aroused.

"What the hell," he said aloud to himself, "maybe she's the best of both worlds!"

Then, in frustration, he shouted, “Welcome to the twenty-first century, where science fiction becomes reality and kicks you in the ass,” and he hit his fist against the steering wheel.

He had finally found a princess but she had once been a frog – a big bullfrog – he told himself, half in humor, half in dismay. Still, this jolting experience was so strange, so alien to anything he had known in his fifty-four years that he felt he was venturing into uncharted territory where he was unsure and vulnerable.. His natural inclination was to retreat, to be safe. He saw the lurking dangers, the confusion and the doubts that lay in wait for him, and, as a naturally cautious man, he shrank back.

He suddenly felt very tired. He started his car and pulled out of the parking lot, heading for his condo, where all the lights would be out and the silence would, again, be deafening. He was speeding ahead, mindlessly, all the while seeing her beautiful face. He knew now that she had spoiled him for any other woman, and he felt achingly lonely.

Would You Believe?

When the Indian family moved in next door, I told my husband Charlie that this was the last straw and I wanted to move. With the two Asian families down the block and a black family around the corner, our neat little gated community was becoming an outpost of the United Nations. Charlie just chuckled and gave me a tolerant smirk that I always find infuriating.

"I happen to know for a fact," Charlie said, "that the heads of all these families are professionals – lawyers and doctors and such – so they may not like living next to us, since I'm only a building contractor."

I laughed and told Charlie to remember that in America money talks and we were as good as anybody, especially now that he was building the big strip mall across town.

"Besides," I said, "we own the biggest house, with the biggest plot of land, and we have the only house with an electrified fountain in the front yard, for when company's expected, so they probably envy us."

Anyway, I sat out on my screened-in side porch when the Indian family moved in, and I could see everything. And let me tell you, it was a strange sight to behold, right here in Ohio, the heartland of America. The husband was tall and thin and as dark as a black man, and he wore a white turban and had a thick black beard. His wife was not quite so dark but she had black hair that she wore in a braid hanging down nearly to her waist, and she wore sandals and a sari, like something out of the Arabian Nights. They had all this heavy dark furniture and lots and lots of cushions that the truckers kept hauling into the house, while a boy, who I'd say looked about ten and was as dark as his father, was scurrying around and seemed to always be under foot. I noticed a Mercedes parked in front of the moving van but it was a smaller sedan than ours.

I watched this scene for a good hour and then decided that since it was a warm day, I'd do the neighborly thing and offer them some iced tea. Of course, I have no idea what Indians drink, but it's the thought that counts. So, I got out my best pitcher and filled it with Crystal Light Iced Tea and put it on a tray with three tall plastic glasses, decorated with palm fronds, and marched over to their driveway and introduced myself.

They were pleasant enough, I have to admit, and the boy had nice manners, and they all thanked me for the tea, which they seemed to enjoy. Well, we were standing on the side of the driveway so we wouldn't interfere with the movers, and they told me their name – Gupta or Gudna or something strange and foreign sounding like that – and their first names were even stranger, and I tried to pronounce them and they laughed

"I know it's difficult to pronounce," the wife said softly, "so everybody calls us Nolly and Jed."

They looked to be in their forties, which put them on the younger side of the people in our gated community, since most of us are in our fifties, like Charlie and me, or even their sixties.

They invited me to sit on their front porch where the movers had already delivered a set of rattan couches, but I didn't want them to think that this was a social visit, and, besides, in trying to twist my brain around their foreign names, and with the movers whizzing by me with so much heavy furniture, and the sun beating down, I was eager to make a hasty retreat.

Then I saw it. Basking in the sun at the far end of the front porch was a large yellow cat with distinctive black facial markings, very exotic looking, I thought, like the whole family.

"Is that your cat?" I asked, and the wife smiled – she had a very sweet smile – and said it was really their son's cat.

I had asked them a few polite questions, just to get some idea of who these strange people were, and they were telling me that they were both professors at the university.

"Now, living here, we'll have a much shorter commute to work." Jed happily explained

I was relieved to hear that they weren't part of some Hare Krishna sect that begged or sold incense on the streets, like the ones I had seen on my one and only visit to New York City, when Charlie dragged me to a contractors' convention many years ago.

Now I was really anxious to get out of the sun and back into my house, so even though there was more iced tea in the pitcher, I didn't offer them a refill when they finally drained their glasses. I was just about to say goodbye when I felt something brushing against my leg and looked down to see my dog, Sparky, and realized that I must have left the side gate open when I was carrying the tray. Nolly looked very nervous when Sparky started sniffing her sari, but I assured her that although Sparky was a big dog, he was very gentle and friendly. She relaxed a little, and Jed drew Sparky's attention by patting him on the head.

I had just turned toward my house when Sparky spotted the cat at the far end of the porch, and in a flash, he was on the porch and racing toward the cat. The cat seemed to leap straight up into the air and landed on the porch balustrade, but only stayed there until Sparky, in a mad dash, was almost upon it, and then the cat made a huge leap over Sparky's rushing body and streaked through the opened front door. Sparky had smashed into the porch railing, which slowed him down for only a second before reversing direction and following the cat through the front door.

We all stood motionless as both the cat and the dog disappeared inside the house, and then we heard a loud noise and one of the movers cursing a blue streak, and we all rushed into the house. A large, heavy chair was lying on its side, as two movers were bending to lift it. The cat was perched on the top of a china breakfront, breathing heavily, its black eyes gleaming, and Sparky was staring up at it, barking furiously.

I could see that Nolly was clearly upset.

"Sparky is always kept in our yard but I forgot to close the gate," I explained. "I promise you that this will never happen again."

Grabbing Sparky with one hand, and balancing the tray and pitcher and glasses with the other, I said goodbye, again promising that there would be no repeat of this incident, and dragged the reluctant dog home.

The next time I saw the Indian couple was about a week later when they came to my door with a covered dish and thanked me for welcoming them to the neighborhood. It's a good thing

Charlie wasn't home because he would have invited them in. I thanked them for the food, which turned out to be some curry concoction that Charlie said was very tasty, but I don't like spicy foods. They stood there, smiling, and it was a little awkward.

"I'm sorry I can't ask you in," I said, "but I'm just on my way out to meet my husband."

This wasn't true since Charlie was at a lodge meeting. They left, and then I had to leave too, in case they were watching the house, so I got in the Mercedes and drove to the mall and did some shopping and then returned home an hour later. After that, we'd wave and call "Hi" to each other if we were coming or going, but I kept my distance.

Weeks passed, and one night Charlie and I came home about eight-thirty from a church social, and before we drove the Mercedes into the garage, I noticed that the side gate was open and was annoyed that the lawn crew must have left it open, and Sparky was probably out again. He never strayed too far, and after we had parked the Mercedes in the garage, Charlie whistled and I called Sparky's name. In just a few seconds we saw him coming through the side gate, with something hanging from his jaws. As he came closer and the lights along our driveway made him clearly visible, I saw what it was and sucked in my breath and grabbed Charlie's arm. The Indian family's yellow cat, its fur covered with dirt, was hanging lifelessly from our dog's mouth. Sparky pranced up to us, his tag wagging, and dropped the dirty dead cat at our feet

We both stood frozen to the spot, staring down at the carcass. I couldn't believe that Sparky had killed the cat, but he, too, was covered in dirt.

"They must have been struggling in the dirt and then Sparky probably broke the cat's neck and it was quickly over," Charlie said.

My mind was racing a mile a minute, thinking of how hurt the Indian family, especially the boy, would be at the loss of their pet. Then I had some terrible other thoughts.

"The Indian family could sue us for not keeping Sparky on our property and maybe even insist that Sparky be put to sleep as a menace to the community," I said with alarm.

Charley must have been thinking along the same lines because he clearly looked worried. Then I started hatching a plan to avoid all these embarrassing, and possibly costly, entanglements. I quickly outlined it to Charlie, and he agreed.

First, we shut the side gate. Then Charlie picked up the cat and brought it into the house while I took Sparky behind the house and used a garden hose to wash the dirt and grime off. After drying him, I locked him in the basement and joined Charlie at the slop sink in our laundry room where he was rinsing off the cat. I ran upstairs and returned with my hair dryer, and we gave the cat a blow-dry.

We waited until after midnight when all the lights were out next door. Then Charlie went quietly through the side gate and tiptoed up to the neighbor's front porch and left the dead cat by their front door so that it would look like the cat had died there. I watched from our upstairs window to make sure no one saw Charlie. He scurried home and we went to bed, but I didn't sleep a wink, worrying that we had forgotten something that would cause the Indian family to suspect Sparky.

For the next week we avoided our neighbors. Charlie left for work very early and I stayed mostly at home, with our curtains drawn. As the days passed and no one was banging on our door with an accusation or a legal notice, I began to relax, feeling that the worst was over.

One morning I was out at my mailbox and I saw Nolly coming toward me with a big smile, so I wasn't too nervous.

"We received a notice about the annual homeowners meeting. Can you tell me, please, what this is all about?" she asked.

"Our main focus will be deciding as a community if we want to switch from electricity to natural gas for our home heating," I explained.

We chatted briefly about the weather, then parted, and no mention was made about the cat.

The day of the homeowners meeting came and Charlie and I were just taking our seats when in walked Nolly and Jed. They saw us and made a beeline for the empty seats next to Charlie. Jed was still wearing his turban but now they were both wearing jeans. After saying hello, I pretended to be studying the printed agenda we had picked up at the door, but Charlie was chatting away with Jed, so I felt obliged to make small talk with Nolly.

"How does Joey like his new school?" I asked.

"Oh, he likes it very much, but he misses his cat," Nolly replied.

Now, I'm not an actress but when the situation calls for it, I can be as phony as the next person, so I lifted my eyebrows in confusion and said, "What happened to the cat?"

At this point Charlie abruptly stopped talking to Jed and was waiting for Nolly's reply, but it was Jed who picked up the story.

"It's really a great mystery," Jed said, "because our cat had died of old age and, at Joey's insistence, we buried it in the back yard, only to find it several days later, all clean and lying on our front porch."

Well, at this point, as you can imagine, I nearly fell out of my chair, and Charlie placed his hand over his face, but any fool could see that he was chuckling. I poked him in the ribs, but he couldn't stop. Nolly and Jed were staring blankly, so I quickly said that Charlie occasionally suffered from shortness of breath and I grabbed Charlie's arm and led him outside. Then Charlie started laughing so hard that I was afraid he might have a stroke or something. I didn't see what was so funny.

I finally got Charlie calmed down, and we went back inside for the meeting. When we got to our seats, I was surprised to see Harriet Trusdale standing with Nolly and Jed. Now Harriet is one of the snootiest women I've ever met. She thinks she's better than everyone else just because she can trace her family back practically to the American Revolution and because her husband has the biggest car dealership in the state – at least that's what the newspapers say. She acts like she's sweet and humble, dresses real plain, and their house isn't exactly a showplace, like ours, but from what I've read, she's on the board of a lot of charities and serves on all sorts of committees. If you ask me, that's just showing off. You wouldn't find me running around all day to committee meetings when I could be home in my beautiful house, enjoying my TV soaps.

I tried to be friendly with Harriet when her family first moved in. I went to her house, two blocks away, and brought her a batch of my homemade molasses cookies. She invited me in and I noticed lots of antiques, nothing like the smart modern furniture I have. She was very nice and made us some tea and we chatted a bit. I mentioned that Charlie was starting to build a big strip mall across town and had been one of the builders involved in our gated community, just to let her know who she was dealing with.

"Since our husbands are both successful business men, we probably have a lot in common," I said, "and I should warn you about those people in the community you should probably avoid – the foreigners and such!"

I was about to say more when the strangest look came over her face, and she interrupted me and said she just remembered an appointment, and ushered me out the door so fast that I still had a cookie in my hand. After that, I had invited her and her husband twice to dinner at our house, just to show that we were as good as them, but both times she made some excuse.

So now I said "Hi Harriet," in a polite and breezy way, as if I barely remembered her, and she gave me a brief smile and a "Hi" right back.

Nolly was chatting away with her and then I heard Harriet say, "Don't forget dinner with us on the twenty-second," before she hurried away to her seat as the meeting was about to start. Well, I couldn't believe my ears, and all through the meeting I was so agitated, I couldn't pay any attention to what was going on. I just couldn't figure out why Harriet would be friendly with Nolly and Jed and not with Charlie and me, when we had so much more in common. But then I thought, it's a free country, and if Harriet wanted to take up with the likes of them, be my guest. As for me, I'll keep my standards, thank you very much, when it comes to those people.

Course Change

A half hour before landing in New York, Bob had a splitting headache. He knew it was coming; he just didn't know at what point in the course of a long flight it would strike. If he spent more than four hours on a plane, he always got a headache. And they had been delayed over an hour on the runway in Los Angeles before taking off, which didn't help. Was it the endlessly recycling air? Maybe just his cranky state of mind after being cooped up for so many hours, his long legs stretching into the aisle and then constantly being drawn in, as people passed his seat on their way to the toilets. Or maybe, in this case, it was his anxiety and uncertainty about what they would find in New York.

He looked across the aisle and saw that his wife, Kay, was still sleeping, something he could never do on any flight unless he was heavily drugged. Jealous of her peaceful state, he gently nudged her shoulder and her eyes opened.

"I need some Tylenol," he said.

Wordlessly, she pulled the small carry-on bag from beneath her feet and rummaged through an outer compartment until she found the right bottle and handed it across to him. He fumbled with the child-proof cap and finally got it open. Quickly shaking out two tablets, he swallowed them, one at a time, without benefit of water, a feat his wife always marveled at. He handed the bottle back to Kay.

"We're landing in a half-hour," he said, and she nodded while placing the bag back under her feet.

He knew how painful this trip was for her. For him, too. It wasn't just the awkwardness of the present situation and the uncertainty of the future; it was the horrors of the past. Everything was converging at this point in time, and gentle diplomacy, a light touch, was vitally needed when too many raw emotions would be huddling just below the surface, but must be kept in check. Kay was much better at this than he was. He watched her as she unbuckled her seat belt and stood up. She smiled down at him and patted his shoulder briefly before disappearing down the aisle. That one small, reassuring gesture and he was instantly flooded with emotion.

Kay was his rock. In all their thirty-four years of marriage, she was the keel of their marital ship – he liked to use sailing metaphors – the ballast in the choppy seas of their family's voyage, keeping him on a steady course, really a remarkable woman, calm, loving and supportive. He needed her now more than ever to help him stay focused on the one goal of this journey, the only reason they had come: to keep from losing their granddaughter.

Bob laid his head back against the seat and closed his eyes, hoping the Tylenol would take effect quickly. How different their last two trips to New York had been, he thought, recalling the happy memories of just a few years past. First it was the trip to celebrate Peggy's unexpected wedding. After finishing her law degree at Columbia, she had gotten an offer from a prestigious law firm and had decided to stay on in New York City. She was working very hard, very long hours, she told them when she'd call every few weeks. Then, out of the blue, she called to say, in short breathless snatches, interspersed with nervous giggles, that she was getting married to a young lawyer from her firm, Tony Palmer, and it was going to be a very small, informal ceremony the following Saturday, but could they please come? Of course they could.

Such a spontaneous and unexpected decision by their cautious, methodical, map-your-life-out-long-in-advance daughter took them by complete surprise. Bob had always dreamed of, and saved for, a big church wedding and walking Peggy down a flower festooned aisle, but he had to settle for a brief ceremony in a judge's chambers, followed by a celebratory dinner at a fancy restaurant. Tony's parents were on a tour of China, so the wedding party was only six: the bride and groom, two friends from the office who had served as witnesses, Kay and he.

In the two short days that he was with Tony, Bob had trouble forming an opinion. Tony was a good looking young man and pleasant enough, but there was a lawyerly exactitude, a crisp control and a cool reserve that presented a barrier to forming any impression other than a superficially appealing one. Kay sensed it too, but they reassured themselves that they had years to get to know and appreciate Tony.

The bride and groom left the next day for a week's honeymoon in Tahiti, and he and Kay returned to California. A few months later, the call came announcing that she was pregnant, and when the due date was stated, they both recognized that it was only seven months after the wedding date but said nothing to each other.

On the second trip to New York Bob could barely wait for the plane to land, and he was the first one out of his seat when the seat belt sign went off, flinging open the overhead compartment and hauling the roller suitcase down with one jerk, then waiting impatiently for the plane's door to open and everyone in front of him and Kay to file out. Tony was waiting for them, waiving his arms when they came through the doors of the baggage area into the crowded concourse filled with people greeting the arriving passengers.

"Hi, Kay. Hi, Bob," he called when they were still about twenty feet away, and Bob had rushed forward and, for only the second time, wrapped Tony in a bear hug, ignoring the outstretched hand. Neither he nor his son-in-law was demonstrative by nature, and the only other time he had hugged Tony was on the day of his and Peggy's wedding, but this was an equally special day.

"How's the proud father?" he nearly shouted, and Tony laughed good-naturedly and gave Kay a kiss on her cheek.

"Just great!" Tony said. "Are you eager to see your new granddaughter?"

"We can't wait!" Kay said, and all three were beaming.

They hurried to the parking area where Tony had left his car, and in the forty-minute drive from the airport to the hospital in Manhattan, they talked of nothing but Peggy's delivery – it had been a C section because of minor complications – and the baby's statistics. Finally they were at the hospital, embracing Peggy and holding little, perfect Sarah Ann. The happiness that radiated from both parents and grandparents was a mental snapshot that Bob would always carry with him, trying to offset the horrible images that followed.

Just ten months after Sarah Ann's birth, their beloved, Peggy, their only child, was dead. Brain cancer: totally unexpected but then insidious and quick and lethal. Another hospital room; Peggy in the last moments of her short life, only twenty-eight years old, surrounded by her shocked husband and her grieving parents. When Tony brought Sarah Ann to say goodbye to her mother, the child was clearly frightened by the strange surroundings and seeing her mother lying so still in the bed with tubes sticking out of her and monitoring devices making unfamiliar sounds. She recoiled in fear, and, burying her face in her father's chest, cried hysterically. She was not brought to the wake, and she did not witness her father's stunned look throughout the burial service at the cemetery, or her grandparents' numb, mask-like expressions.

Bob returned to Los Angeles, but Kay stayed on for a month after the funeral, joining Tony's mother in taking care of Sarah Ann and looking after Tony, who was trying to adjust to his new situation. Kay called Bob every few nights to report on things, including the anger and resentment phase that Tony was now exhibiting. After the first month, Tony made it clear that he was determined to get on with his life and didn't expect, or want, Kay's help any longer. Kay then returned to California. In the ensuing months Bob and Kay talked about relocating to New York to be near Sarah Ann, and Bob started making arrangements to sell his electronics business and their home, but when they mentioned their plans to Tony about six months after Peggy's death, his response was startlingly cold.

They called Tony frequently and sent clothes and dolls and toys and cards to Sarah Ann, and always asked Tony for pictures, but few came. They decided they would make another visit to New York, and Kay called to tell Tony they would be coming.

There was a long pause and finally Tony said, "Just now, that's not a very good idea, Kay." Another long pause; then Tony said, "I was going to call you. I'm getting married."

"Oh, I see," was all Kay could say in a faraway voice.

"I need a wife, and Sarah Ann needs a mother," said Tony defensively, and, again, Kay could only say "I see," in a soft, fading voice. "Well, congratulations," was all she could finally muster.

"Thanks. I'll call you, Kay," Tony said before hanging up.

Kay told Bob the news in a slow, monotone voice, and they both sat quietly together, digesting and expanding the meaning of this announcement.

"How could he do this, so soon after Peggy's death?" Bob finally said angrily. "It's not even a year!"

"Sarah Ann will have a new mother," Kay said reflectively.

"No! She'll have a new stepmother!" he said defensively.

"She's too young to even remember us," Kay said, and he saw her eyes getting misty. "Oh, Tom," she cried, "We're losing our only grandchild!"

He put his arm around her and she spontaneously huddled against him, quietly weeping.

"I promise you, Kay, we're not going to lose her," he said with far more conviction than he felt. "Tony will respect our rights as grandparents. You'll see."

* * * *

They sent a wedding present to Tony and his new wife, Joanne, and they got a brief, formal thank-you note. The return address indicated that they had moved out of Manhattan to Long Island. Kay wrote to Joanne, saying that if there was anything special Sarah Ann might need, or want, she and Bob would be guided by Joanne's recommendations for Christmas or birthdays. Several weeks went by before Joanne wrote back with a note that was short and chilly, saying there was nothing special that she could think of. Then she mentioned that she was pregnant. Kay seized on this news to write Joanne again, congratulating her and asking if Joanne would mind if she and Bob called once in a while to speak to Sarah Ann, who, at nearly two, they assumed must be talking by now. They got no response, and Bob could see, in the ensuing weeks, how troubled Kay was. Finally, he couldn't stand to see the weight of concern that Kay was carrying, and he picked up the phone and called Tony and Joanne. It was early evening back east. Tony answered the phone.

"Hi, Tony. It's Bob," he said with too much forced cheeriness.

"Oh, hello, Bob," came the response, clearly surprised and unenthusiastic.

Bob plowed ahead, speaking in a quick staccato.

"We're just calling to see how our wonderful granddaughter is doing."

"Fine…just fine," was the hesitant, lukewarm answer, but Bob was determined.

"How about putting Sarah Ann on the line so we can say hello to her and she can hear our voices?"

A long pause before Tony replied.

"I'm sorry, Bob, but this isn't a good time. We just put her to bed."

"At seven o'clock?" Bob said, tinges of disbelief and anger slipping into his tone.

"Well, yes," Tony answered evenly. "She had a very busy day and after dinner she was very tired."

"Okay, Tony, I understand," he said, trying to be conciliatory, but desperation was rising in him like a drowning man gasping for air. "But just tell me when would be a good time to call and speak to her. Please."

The air hung heavily around another long pause.

"That's really hard to say, Bob," said Tony, irritation now discernible in his voice.

Bob knew that he couldn't afford a rupture, so he retreated, switching to a placating tone.

"Then why don't we leave it to you. When you find any time that's convenient, maybe this weekend, just give us a call. We won't stay on long, I promise. We just want to hear her voice. Except for church on Sunday morning, we'll be home all weekend."

Bob could hear the desperation in his own voice

"Yes, Bob, I'll try," Tony said, but he didn't make it sound like a firm commitment.

"Please do, Tony. It would mean so much to Kay. And to me, of course. We'll look forward to it. Please."

A click on the other end. Bob turned to Kay who had been listening from across the room, and he saw the disappointment in her face.

"He promised he'd call us. Probably this weekend," he said with sham optimism.

Kay nodded, but she clearly wasn't fooled, he thought.

The weekend passed with no call from Tony, and every time the phone rang that weekend, they both rushed to answer it. His anger and frustration grew with each passing hour of that Saturday and Sunday, and by Sunday night he was in a quiet rage, unable to concentrate on anything, jumpy and irritable. He felt trapped, defeated. He couldn't call Tony again. What could he say? You promised to call – well, sort of – and you didn't. Why the hell couldn't you? He recognized that Tony was calling all the shots and all he and Kay could do was plead and wait. When it was after ten, New York time, he gave up all hope. They both took a sleeping pill and went to bed.

The next morning he got up at dawn and went for a long walk. When he returned to the house, Kay was in the kitchen and the coffee was already made.

"We're going to New York!" he announced in a fierce voice that would brook no opposition.

Kay sat at the kitchen table, her English muffin before her, untouched.

"When?" was all she said.

"Immediately! As soon as we can get the plane tickets. I'm calling Tony today."

Kay nodded, then took a bite of her muffin. Bob filled a mug with coffee and felt relieved. Somehow, in making this decision and forming this plan, he was moving forward and not just angrily grappling with the distance and the silence and the uncertainty. He was asserting himself, tackling the issue, staking his claim. This was not a time for further discussion, and, in some unspoken intuiting of his mood, Kay was silent. Her acquiescence confirmed the rightness of his call for action. He left the kitchen and, with his mug of coffee, strode into the den like a general in a victory parade. When he returned to the kitchen twenty minutes later, Kay was at the sink.

"It's done," he said with a hint of pride. "We leave next Tuesday, ten-fifteen in the morning."

Kay was rinsing her breakfast dishes, her back to him.

"Now call Tony," she said dryly.

"Yes," he said, still feeling purposeful. He glanced at the wall clock. "I'll wait until it's ten-thirty New York time and I'll catch him at work."

In some quirkily ebullient mood he returned to the den and read the paper, checking his watch regularly until the time arrived for the call to Tony.

Joanne answered the phone, and when Bob announced who he was, she said, "Oh, yes. Just a minute," and he could hear her speaking a good distance away from the phone but couldn't make out what she was saying. Not very friendly, he thought. When Tony came on the line, Bob steamrolled ahead, ignoring Tony's less-than-enthusiastic tone, and announced their arrival date and time.

"Bob, I wish you had called me first, before making these plans. Joanne isn't feeling well; she's having a difficult pregnancy. And we just finished converting our guest room into a nursery, so we don't have any place to put you."

Bob would not be deterred.

"No problem, Tony," he said with forced cheerfulness. "Just give me the name of a nearly hotel or motel, and I'll take it from there."

"Okay. And how long were you planning on staying?" Tony asked, weariness creeping into his voice.

"Just five nights. I have to be back for a company meeting next Monday," Bob said.

Tony gave him the number of a Holiday Inn that he said was about a half-hour from their house, and Bob scribbled the number down.

"Great!" Bob said. "So we'll call you on Wednesday morning to get directions to your home."

"Bob, the mornings can be rough. Joanne usually has morning sickness. Better make it the afternoon."

Instantly, Bob's anger flared, but he held it in check. "Okay," was all he said, adding, "See you soon," before hanging up. Then he quickly called the Holiday Inn and made a reservation with no problem. It was done. Everything was in place. Come hell or high water, they were going to see their granddaughter!

* * * *

They had rented a car at the airport. The drive from the Holiday Inn to Tony's house took close to an hour, and all that time Bob was on the lookout for another inn or motel that was closer, but he saw nothing. When he had called the house, Tony answered and said he was taking the day off from work. Now, as they pulled into the driveway of a small white colonial house with dark green shutters and a detached garage in the rear, Bob saw Tony trimming a hedge at the side of the property.

Tony put down the trimming shears and walked over to the car. Kay jumped out and kissed Tony on the cheek, then Bob and Tony shook hands, but there was no enthusiasm in any of Tony's actions. They were all like players in some long-running drama, just going through the motions, Bob thought. Tony led them inside the house, past a small living room and formal dining room, and they followed him to where a modest kitchen flowed into a family room. Joanne and Sarah Ann were at the breakfast table. Joanne got up from the table and both Kay and Bob moved forward quickly.

"We're so happy to meet you," Kay said with a big smile, hugging Joanne. Following his wife's example, Bob embraced Joanne, but from the stiffness of her body and the waxen smile on her lips, he could see that Joanne was neither happy nor at ease with their visit. But now their attention was focused entirely on Sarah Ann.

Kay moved next to the highchair where the little girl was sitting, with a dish of applesauce in front of her. Kay bent down so that her face was very close to Sarah Ann's and said, "Hi, Sarah Ann. I'm your grandma."

Bob stood a few feet away, watching everything closely. The child, still clutching the spoon with which she had been eating the applesauce, looked at Kay briefly with large, solemn eyes, said nothing and then returned to spooning her applesauce.

"You might be confusing her, Kay," Tony said quietly. "She calls Joanne's mother 'grandma.'"

Bob saw the quick shadow of disappointment pass across Kay's face.

"Oh, yes," she said in a neutral voice. "Then I could be Nana or Granny, which were the two names I had for my grandmothers."

Tony and Joanne said nothing, and Bob now moved to the other side of the high chair. As he studied his granddaughter's face he could see only mild traces of Peggy, for Sarah Ann seemed to be a true composite of both her mother and father. Around the eyes and the mouth Bob could trace Peggy, but the dark hair and ruddy coloring and long nose were strictly her father's.

"What name isn't already taken that she can call me?" Bob asked with too sharp a tone, he felt.

"She calls my father 'grandy' and Joanne's father, 'grandpa,'" Tony said.

"But he's not...." Bob said and stopped in mid-sentence, trying to control his resentment that the new wife's father had precedence over him, the real grandfather, in deciding what name Sarah Ann would call him.

"I guess that leaves me 'grandpop,'" Bob said quickly and bent closer to Sarah Ann with a big smile.

"Can you say 'grandpop'?" he asked Sarah Ann directly.

The child returned his gaze for only a moment before glancing away and looking at her father, without saying a word.

"Oh, please, may I hold her?" Kay asked.

"Sure," Joanne said, glancing at Tony.

Kay lifted Sarah Ann from her highchair and held her at half-arm's length, smiling directly into the child's face.

"What a big, beautiful girl you are!" she trilled, gently swaying the child to and fro.

Sarah Ann seemed to be studying Kay's face intently but then she began to squirm and to push away from Kay who was attempting to hug her. Little grunts of anxiety or displeasure – Bob couldn't tell which – were now coming from Sarah Ann.

"Down!" she yelled forcefully, repeating the word again.

Bob moved in and took the child from Kay and held her high over his head, thinking to distract her, but this motion only scared her and she swiveled her head in Tony's direction and started to cry. Tony stepped in and took the child from Bob.

"She's cranky now. It's time for her nap."

Tony handed Sarah Ann to Joanne who moved into the hall toward the stairs, the child solemnly gazing back at the strangers before disappearing up the stairs. Tony motioned to two sofas facing each other, separated by a coffee table, in the family room. Bob and Kay sat on one and Tony sat opposite them.

"Joanne and I discussed your visit," Tony said, "and we thought it would be best if you were introduced to Sarah Ann through her normal routines."

Bob thought irritably that Tony sounded like a lawyer reading the codicil of a will: professional and distant, with unimpeachable certitude, lacking all warmth. He felt a flush of anger rising to his face but Kay came to his rescue.

"That's a good idea. She has to get to know us…to feel comfortable with us," Kay said, nodding her head vigorously as if convincing herself of the reasonableness of Tony's mandate, and her instant capitulation made Bob more annoyed.

"But we were hoping that we might take her someplace on a special outing – a park or a zoo," he said assertively.

"Well, let's see how the first few visits here go," Tony said with the same dispassionate tone that left no room for appeal.

"We're not going to steal her, Tony," Bob blurted out, and then fell silent, regretting his outburst.

Tony stared at him and made no reply. Kay filled in the stony silence.

"It's just that we have so little time and we'd like to get to know her and have her know us."

Joanne returned and joined them, sitting next to Tony on the opposite sofa.

"Would anyone like something to drink?" she asked with a half-smile.

She was definitely pretty, Bob thought, in that tall, slim, good skin and healthy hair way. Her lips were thin and her eyes too deep-set to be striking. No signs of her pregnancy yet, but any tummy protuberance would form a sharp contrast to her pencil-thin profile. She looked no more than early twenties and Bob suddenly realized that he knew nothing about this young woman who would be raising his granddaughter.

‘I’d like a soft drink if you have it,” Bob said, smiling directly at Joanne, but Tony jumped up.

“What about you, Kay?” Tony asked, heading toward the open kitchen.

“A glass of water, please,” Kay responded.

Tony quickly returned with the drinks and Bob saw that no lunch or snacks were being offered.

“Your home is lovely,” Kay said. “I love that hutch in your dining room.”

“Thank you,” Joanne said. “It was my grandmother’s.”

“So, how did you two meet?” Bob asked.

Tony and Joanne exchanged glances.

“At a dinner party,” Tony said. “Joanne’s father is a senior partner at my firm.”

Bob chuckled. “Marrying the boss’s daughter, eh?”

Tony made no response.

“I hear you’re having a lot of morning sickness,” Kay said.

Joanne sighed and ran her fingers through her long, lustrous brown hair.

“Well, it’s gotten a little better these last few weeks, but I’m just tired all the time and it’s hard with Sarah Ann.”

Joanne’s voice trailed off and she looked embarrassed to have mentioned Sarah Ann as a drain on her energies to Sarah Ann’s grandparents, whom she didn’t know but were now sitting across from her.

Another awkward silence filled the room.

“Joanne’s mother is coming to help Joanne with Sarah Ann,” Tony said. “She arrives next week.”

“Where will she sleep?” Bob asked bluntly, recalling Tony’s announcement that they had no room in the house for him and Kay.

“We have a day bed in the nursery” Tony said, staring coldly at Bob.

Another person I don’t know looking after my granddaughter, Bob thought, but said nothing.

“Well, for the short time we’re here, Joanne, I’m happy to help you all I can,” Kay said.

“Thank you,” Joanne responded, with little animation.

Thy sat there, two couples facing each other, really strangers, and the only thing they could talk about, since they couldn't talk about Peggy, was Sarah Ann. So Kay asked a lot of questions, and Bob listened to the answers, mostly coming from Tony, as Joanne wore an absent, tired look, and he learned about Sarah Ann's current vocabulary and when she had taken her first step, and her eating and sleeping habits, and her current delight with specific television cartoons. And somehow, with lots of pauses and awkward silences, an hour passed, until Sarah Ann's voice calling "Mama" announced that her nap was over. Bob was startled to hear Sarah Ann call for her mother until he realized that Joanne was now the child's mother, and Peggy wasn't even a memory.

Joanne brought Sarah Ann downstairs and she smiled at her father and looked briefly at Kay and Bob before heading over to a large box of toys in the corner of the family room.

Kay and Bob sat on the floor next to the child, and Kay immediately moved into Sarah Ann's world and, with vocal patterning, broad facial expressions and physical gyrations, kept the child amused for a good hour. Bob participated some, but mostly watched attentively, transported back to similar scenes with Kay and Peggy as a child, and a tight lump formed in his throat. By the end of this play time, Sarah Ann seemed comfortable with both Kay and Bob and was demonstrating her vocabulary in describing her toys and dolls and how she wanted the adults to participate in her make-believe games.

Tony then announced that he was taking Sarah Ann for a walk and invited Kay and Bob to join him, while Joanne excused herself and went upstairs for a rest. When they returned from a walk around the neighborhood, and Joanne was still not up, Kay softly suggested that she'd be happy to prepare some food for Sarah Ann. Tony agreed to this, and he and Kay prepared a separate meal for Sarah Ann since Tony was ordering takeout for the four adults.

Joanne reappeared, looking more tired than before her nap. They sat in the breakfast nook and ate an assortment of Chinese dishes that Bob couldn't pronounce or decipher the ingredients of, the table strewn with white cartons with the little metal handles, and clear plastic packets of sauces and a generous supply of paper napkins. They ate mostly in silence.

Bob suggested that he treat everyone to dinner out the next night, but Tony explained that Joanne was both lactose and gluten intolerant and on a restricted diet, and they seldom ate out. Kay then suggested that she and Bob could buy groceries and make dinner for Tony and Joanne. Tony seemed lukewarm to this idea and Joanne said nothing.

With rising frustration, Bob said, "Great idea!" That's what we'll do. Joanne, you can tell us what you can't eat, and I'll still bet that Kay can fix us a delicious dinner."

Joanne smiled and said, "It's time for Sarah Ann's bath."

Joanne took Sarah Ann up for her bath and Kay went with her. Tony had made coffee and the two men sat alone at the breakfast table, sipping the coffee and playing with their spoons, not making eye contact. Finally, Bob spoke.

"Tony, we've all been through a lot these last few years, and I see how you're getting on with your life and I can't say I blame you, but Sarah Ann is all we have now…" Bob's voice faltered and he took a sip of coffee to recover. When he felt sure that he had his emotions in check, he continued. "We'd like to have a role in our granddaughter's life, and I'm sure you can appreciate this."

Idly stirring his coffee during Bob's speech, Tony stopped and looked directly at Bob.

"How do you see that role, Bob?"

Bob wasn't prepared for that question, but he struggled on.

"Well, we'd like to keep in frequent touch with Sarah Ann, of course, and, as I mentioned to you, we're seriously thinking of relocating to this area so we can be near her and spend time with her. And then, when she gets a little older, maybe we could take her on vacations or trips with us."

His coffee spoon still gripped in his hand, Tony was staring intently at Bob but said nothing.

"And don't forget," Bob continued, "Kay is the perfect baby sitter."

Tony dropped the spoon on the saucer, and it made a sharp clang. The pupils of his eyes grew larger and darker.

"Let me share some things that you might not be aware of," he said, and Bob heard the sarcasm in his voice. "I loved your daughter but I wasn't ready to get married, wasn't even thinking about getting married, when Peggy told me she was pregnant. Knowing your daughter, I knew it was my child, but this put everything in a whole new light. Peggy told me she was perfectly willing to have the baby and raise it as a single Mom and never identify me as the father or make any claims on me. And when I asked her how we had slipped up – she had insisted on being in charge of our contraceptive measures – she confessed that she had wanted to become pregnant by me but not for the purpose of forcing me into marrying her. She just felt a great desire to have a child at that time in her life, she said. Well, I admired her independence and her grit and I did love her, although we had not been together that long, so I decided, what the hell, I'll marry her and be a father."

Tony paused and stared into his coffee cup for several seconds before jerking his head up and continuing to speak. His words came faster, tinged with anger, and he struggled to keep his voice low.

"But there was one thing your daughter didn't tell me, Bob. One vital fact she left out. She knew she had a brain tumor and she knew it was inoperable and it was only a matter of time. How much time, or how little, was the only thing she didn't know. That's why she wanted a baby, and that's why she was willing to marry me: because she wanted to play house and be a wife and a mother in the little time she had left. She wasn't honest with me and I didn't learn the truth until a few months before she died. So she took me on this roller coaster ride, and by the time I got off, I was a husband, a father and a widower with a baby daughter."

Tony glanced down at the table. His voice was steely. "And now you show up and want to have a role, as you call it, in Sarah Ann's life."

Bob started to speak, but Tony raised an open hand to silence him.

"But I want to forget the last few years, to put them behind me! Sarah Ann is too young to even remember her mother. Joanne is her mother now. And always will be. But you want to spend time with Sarah Ann and take her on trips and tell her all about her real mother just to gratify your own needs, but what will that do to Sarah Ann? To Joanne and me? You want to hover over our lives like some dark shadow, confusing Sarah Ann and reminding me of Peggy's dishonesty, her duplicity, her…"

"We have a right…" Bob stammered, meeting Tony's stare. Tony's jaw was clenched, his lips constricted.

"Than I think you'd better consult a lawyer, because you're not welcome in this house or in this family."

Dumbfounded, Bob stared across the table at this young man whom he knew so little about, who was really a stranger and yet was deciding a major course in his and Kay's life. The gauntlet had been thrown, the challenge shrilly stated, and in an instant, he and Tony had become enemies, forever divided over their only link: a child whom they both loved. Bob's thoughts were racing and, unexpectedly, he found himself blurting out one last appeal for compassion.

"Sarah Ann is the only grandchild we'll ever have!"

He saw Tony's face soften for a fleeting moment before resuming its clenched set.

"I'm sorry," was all he said, and Bob knew that no appeals would change Tony's resolve.

The impact of this brief conversation in terms of both its revelation – Bob and Kay had also been kept in the dark about Peggy's tumor until her last months – and Tony's intended exclusion of him and Kay from Sarah Ann's life, was so staggering that Bob struggled to rise from his chair. Anger, frustration, desperation made him disoriented in time and space. He felt tears welling up and, like a drunk, he tried to focus on any object in the room to regain his physical equilibrium. Impassively, Tony remained seated.

Bob was aware of Kay's voice floating down the stairs and then she and Joanne came into view. Kay looked at Bob, and concern instantly registered on her face.

"We're leaving!" was all he said, his voice cracking.

"Why?" Kay asked, clearly startled.

"We're leaving!" Bob thundered, and he was already heading toward the door.

"Tony, what's wrong? What happened?" Kay pleaded.

Tony, glancing at Joanne, said nothing.

"Oh, my god!" Kay yelled, as she turned to Joanne who now locked eyes with Tony, and silence filled the room. "Please," Kay wailed in a quivering voice. She watched Bob disappearing out the front door. "Please," she cried again, facing Tony, her arms outstretched, a desperate and confused supplicant. Then, seeing the impenetrable resolve in Tony's fixed stare, her arms fell helplessly to her sides, and, abandoning all hope of reconciliation, she hurried after her husband's retreating shadow.

Uncle Billy

Dear Professor Hogan,

I know this assignment was to write about an unforgettable character from fiction and to tell what made the character unforgettable, but the more I thought about this topic, the more I wanted to write about Uncle Billy, a real-life person, because right now he stands out in my memory as much more unforgettable than any character I've read about in books. Since you've told us several times in our Freshman English class that we should be independent thinkers and be more creative in responding to our readings and our lives, I decided that you wouldn't mind if I wrote about a person instead of a fictional character.

Uncle Billy wasn't my real uncle. He wasn't even related to me but I've known him all my life. He lived around the corner from us. He worked with my father at the local gas company and they drove to work together. All the kids in my neighborhood called him Uncle Billy. Next to my parents, he was my favorite adult.

You told us to include a physical description of the character so here's mine. Uncle Billy was tall and skinny and had a long nose and nice teeth and a beautiful smile. He was always smiling. He had a booming voice and a loud laugh and he had nice black hair that he always kept in a crew-cut. As a little girl I remember being fascinated by his big hands because I had never seen such big hands. Not even my father had hands like that. Uncle Billy had what my father called a lazy eye. One eye looked in a different direction from the other eye, which was a little weird and sometimes the kids made fun of his eyes but he took no notice of them.

You also told us to include the personal traits of the character and Uncle Billy had many memorable traits. First of all, he was very jolly and he had a lot of enthusiasm. Whenever he came to our house, my two brothers and I would laugh at all the funny stories and jokes he would tell us. My parents always enjoyed his company too. He and my father went fishing together. Uncle Billy loved kids although he didn't have any of his own. His wife died when I was about five and he lived alone in the house he inherited from his parents after they died.

Uncle Bill could fix anything. When the head came off of my favorite doll, I brought her to Uncle Billy and he returned it to me a few days later as good as new. When the wheel fell off of my doll carriage, Uncle Billy fixed that too. When the kids complained to their parents about any toy that was broken, they were usually told to take it to Uncle Billy. When any of the fathers in the neighborhood were planning some big project in their houses, they would usually consult Uncle Billy and he was always happy to offer advice but then he'd show up while a father was working on the project and offer his help. I bet Uncle Billy has worked on more houses in my area than any professional carpenter, plumber or electrician.

Uncle Billy loved baseball. He got all the kids from the neighborhood and organized a boys' team and a girls' softball team and we became part of a community league and Uncle Billy was our coach. I played third base and sometimes the left outfield. He was always very patient and supportive. He told us that our goal should not be to win but to play our best and give a hundred per cent effort.

Sometimes Uncle Billy would invite us all over to watch a big league baseball game. He had a finished basement with couches and chairs and a big television set. He gave us popcorn and pretzels and soda while we were watching the game. Uncle Billy would shout at the players on the screen if they made mistakes or he'd holler at the empires if they made a bad call but he was always laughing and never really angry. He'd also point out good moves the players were making that he said we should imitate. After the game, we'd all troop upstairs to the kitchen where we'd have ice cream and Uncle Billy would put out lots of stuff for us to make ice cream sodas or sundaes. Some Saturdays a few of the kids' fathers would join us to watch the game and they seemed to have a good time too. They'd get into the spirit of it and shout and laugh with Uncle Billy.

I always thought Uncle Billy was a really good listener. A lot of kids confided in him about troubles at home with their siblings or their parents, or at school with teachers or other kids, or just about anything that was bothering them.

Uncle Billy loved to restore old cars and always had one in his driveway that he was working on. A kid would stroll over to Uncle Billy's house and find him in his driveway working on an engine and they'd start to talk and the kid would open up and tell Uncle Billy his problems. Uncle Billy would stop tinkering with his car and invite the kid to sit on his front porch where he had some wicker chairs and a glider. Many times I'd go by Uncle Billy's house and see him with some boy or girl sitting on the porch, talking quietly. He always seemed to have some advice for solving a problem. I, myself, had several talks with Uncle Billy when my two older brothers were giving me a hard time, and he suggested how I might deal with them and I followed his advice and it worked pretty good.

I also remember when I was in seventh grade going to Uncle Billy about a boy in my class who had been very friendly to me and I liked him a lot, but then one day he refused to talk to me and gave me the silent treatment every time we met outside of class. Uncle Billy told me a story about when he was in the eighth grade and had a crush on a girl named Patricia and they would talk and joke around at recess, but then another girl whispered to him that Patricia was telling everybody that he was a jerk and was making fun of him behind his back. He was very upset so he avoided Patricia and refused to speak to her. Then one day Patricia came up to him in the playground with tears in her eyes and asked him what was wrong. He told her what the other girl had said and Patricia said that none of that was true. It was all lies, she said, and she cried. Uncle Billy believed her and they got back together and went to the eighth grade dance together. Then Uncle Bill told me that I should speak to the boy directly and ask him what was the matter.

The next day at school I got up my courage and went up to the boy, who was standing with his friends, and said I wanted to speak to him. He stared at me as if he never saw me before and said, "Get lost!" and all his buddies laughed. I turned red with embarrassment and ran back into the school. When I told Uncle Billy what had happened, he said that boys had a very awkward age when they wanted to be friends with girls but their buddies made fun of them and held them back. I thought this was a lame excuse and I was pretty mad at Uncle Billy for a while, but when I returned to school after the summer vacation, the same boy had grown about a foot and we were in the same eighth grade class and he chose a seat next to mine and was very friendly again, and we wound up going to our end-of-year dance together. All the kids knew that he was my boyfriend and now he didn't care. In fact, he liked it.

As I've said, Uncle Billy was a very good listener and it wasn't just the kids who went to him for advice. Lots of men in the neighborhood talked about their problems with Uncle Billy, and my father used to say that Uncle Billy was an escape valve for people to let off steam. We had this one family down the block, the Andersons, and Mrs. Anderson drank a lot and when she got drunk, she was a mean drunk, as my father used to say, and she'd attack Mr. Anderson and hit him with anything she could get her hands on. She'd yell and scream and call him names and you could hear her all over the neighborhood. Many times Mr. Anderson would escape and run to Uncle Billy's house and stay there until the next morning when Mrs. Anderson had calmed down. One night Mrs. Anderson ran after him and stood outside of Uncle Billy's house and screamed for her husband to come out. Then she yelled that she would break all the windows if he didn't come out right away. Uncle Billy came out and spoke very quietly to her and convinced her to go home and walked her back to her house. We heard all about this later from the Cramer family who lived next door to Uncle Billy.

I think Uncle Billy loved Halloween more than the kids. He'd always dress up in some great costume – a clown, a wizard, a hobo – nothing scary, and he always had lots of candy or bubble gum to pass out to all the kids who went trick or treating door to door. The traffic on one of our streets was getting bad and one Halloween when I was about nine, a little boy was hit by a car while crossing the street and seriously injured. Then all the parents started to worry about letting their kids go out alone to trick or treat. Uncle Billy spoke to my father about an idea he had, and the two of them went to see the principal of my elementary school and the next year there was a big Halloween party at the school. Everyone came in costumes, even the parents and the teachers and the principal. There was a haunted house and a castle bounce and a magic room of funny mirrors and games with prizes and a big parade of all the kids around the gym. Then the kids went to each of the classrooms down one corridor to go trick or treating and parents dressed as witches or goblins or pumpkins would give out candy at each door. Uncle Billy and my father directed all the heavy traffic in the corridor and kept everyone moving. We all had a great time and didn't mind not doing any real trick or treating around the neighborhood. This party at the school became our community Halloween tradition and is still going on.

At Christmas, most people in our neighborhood had big Christmas trees, even some of the Jewish families, and you could usually see them all lit up through the living room windows. It always put me in a real holiday spirit when I walked around the streets I had known all my life. Uncle Billy's house was always the showplace that we all wanted to see. He started decorating right after Thanksgiving and I'd pass by and wave to him when he was up on his roof setting up a sleigh with Santa Claus in it and four reindeer spread across the roof. All the shrubs in front of his house would be lit with blinking colored lights and on his front porch he had a beautiful life-size crèche and he even had some bales of hay to suggest a manger. If you went by his house on Christmas Eve, Uncle Billy would be dressed as Santa Claus, standing at his front door and waving to everyone and yelling Merry Christmas to all who passed by.

Professor Hogan, you told us to pick out one scene in the book where the character stood out the most but I'm writing about a real person so I'll tell you about one scene with Uncle Billy that I remember more than anything else.

Thanksgiving at my house was always a crazy time and when I became a teenager I didn't look forward to it because all my aunts and uncles and cousins and my grandparents would come to our house and people were always pinching my cheeks and hugging me so tight I could hardly breathe, and asking me silly questions about school and boys. One Thanksgiving, when I was fourteen, I escaped from the house as soon as our Thanksgiving dinner was finished and all the adults were playing cards and all my cousins were having a ping pong contest with my brothers down in our basement. It was just starting to get dark as I turned the corner and came to Uncle Billy's house. There were no lights on in his house and no cars in his driveway except for the latest car he was restoring. Suddenly I started thinking about how Uncle Billy spent Thanksgiving. I knew he didn't have brothers or sisters but maybe he had other relatives who invited him for dinner, or friends. Then I saw the flickering light of a television coming through his living room window. I was curious so I walked up onto the porch and peeked in.

Uncle Billy was sitting in a big leather chair with a snack table across his legs and a thawed frozen dinner, still in its black plastic container, on the table. I glanced at the TV screen and saw it was showing reruns of the New York Thanksgiving Day parade with all the floats and balloon characters and marching bands and crowds of happy, cheering people. The flickering light from the television hit Uncle Billy's face and I saw the strangest thing. Uncle Billy had a smile on his face but there were tears running down his cheeks. He was smiling and crying at the same time and I couldn't decide if he was happy or sad. Seeing him like that, in that darkened room with the TV and the frozen dinner, made me feel sad. I tiptoed away.

I never mentioned what I had seen at Uncle Billy's house to anyone. A year went by and I asked my parents if we could invite Uncle Billy for Thanksgiving dinner. They said he probably was spending Thanksgiving with relatives or friends. I never let on what I knew but I said that just in case he wasn't, it would be a nice gesture to offer an invitation. I could see that my mother was too preoccupied with getting everything ready for the holiday to give my suggestion much thought, so I pestered my father to ask Uncle Billy when they rode together to work.

A few days later, my father told me that he started talking to Uncle Billy about Thanksgiving and when Uncle Billy said he didn't have any special plans, my father invited him to join us and he accepted. On Thanksgiving Day he came with a beautiful bouquet of flowers and a box of chocolates. He was very jolly and told funny stories and all my aunts and uncles liked him. As people were leaving, they said this was the best Thanksgiving ever. My father told Uncle Billy that he'd just have to spend every Thanksgiving with us. This made me very happy.

Two years ago, right around my sixteenth birthday, Uncle Billy died suddenly of a massive stroke. It was only when he didn't show up for work that my father walked over to his house and looked through the living room window and saw Uncle Billy. When my father described the scene to me, I burst out crying. Uncle Billy was slumped in his big leather chair with a snack table and frozen dinner in front of him and the television on. I immediately thought back to that Thanksgiving Day when I saw the same scene and I was so sorry that I hadn't rung his bell just to wish him a happy Thanksgiving.

It turned out that Uncle Billy had no relatives and my father made the arrangements for his funeral. My family and only a few of his co-workers and neighbors attended it. Afterwards, a lot of people said they had intended to go but it just slipped their minds or they were too busy.

I still think of Uncle Billy whenever I walk around my neighborhood and pass his house. He gave so much to our community and I don't know how much we gave back to him. So I hope, Professor Hogan, you can see why I had to write about Uncle Billy and tell you about him because he was the most unforgettable person I've know. Someday I'd like to write a book about him and then maybe in some future Freshman English class you're teaching, a student might choose Uncle Billy as the most unforgettable character he or she has read about. Wouldn't that be great? And you heard about him first. Thank you.

Marilyn Packard

Past As Prelude

Adam Fletcher stood shivering in the cold November rain, protected only by a thin sweater, refusing to go back into his house. A chorus of voices, booming and shrill, called to him from the front porch, entreating him to come in out of the rain. He ignored them, standing like some mute statue at the end of the short driveway with his back to the voices, his arms folded, his legs rooted. He refused to let anyone see that he was crying. The sodden sweater pressed in upon his thin frame; his sparse hair lay limply across his forehead.

The chorus of voices from the porch grew sterner, less supplicating, more demanding. Among the voices Adam could distinguish those of his two sons, Matthew and Russell, and his daughter, Margaret, with the rest forming a cacophonous background.

"Dad, please come back in," boomed Matthew.

"You'll make yourself sick," added Russell.

"Stop acting like a child!" shouted Margaret, clearly annoyed.

Yet no one stepped off the porch and approached him, so volcanically had he erupted from the dining room table and stormed out of his house. He was both a loving and intimidating father, he knew, and at this moment his children, even if they were all grown up, were cowed by his angry outburst coming at the end of a tense and heated discussion following his announcement.

He felt the muscles of his arms start to tremble from the cold. This was one hell of a lousy way to spend Thanksgiving, he thought. How differently everything had turned out from what he had expected!

He had started the day with much excitement and high spirits. Up at 6:30, his usual time, he walked Bently, his black lab, on their routine two-mile course through his suburban neighborhood while visualizing the events of the day. At seventy-six, Adam had a keen sense of time's passage and was grateful, particularly on holidays, for comforting celebrations with his family. This Thanksgiving was special as the first one since his wife's death six months ago. Married for fifty-one years, Annie and he had presided over the Thanksgiving table in this very house for the past four decades. Their four children, now all with families of their own except for the youngest girl, Emily, who could never seem to settle on just one man, saw this house as their locus of continuity, their vault of history. No matter how widely dispersed across the map, they returned here every Thanksgiving, like homing pigeons on automatic pilot, he thought, with spouses and a growing number of children in tow, to reconfirm their membership in the clan, to reestablish bonds of familiarity and place.

Entering the kitchen through the back door, he fed Bently and then made his breakfast, brewing extra coffee for Emily who had arrived last night and was still sleeping in her old room that she had shared with her sister Margaret. He stood at the bottom of the stairs and called up to her.

"Emily, rise and shine, honey. We've got to get the show on the road. Lots to do."

He was singing snatches of arias from his favorite operas while washing his breakfast dishes when Emily shuffled into the kitchen and came up behind him at the sink, wrapping her arms around his tall, thin frame while resting her head on his back.

"Morning, Dad" she said in a voice still choked with sleep.

Adam chuckled contentedly. "Coffee's ready," he said.

Emily shuffled into the breakfast nook while Adam poured a cup for her and then one for himself. They sat opposite each other across the round oak table where so much of his family's history had been played out and where Annie's ghost would most often appear.

This child of his was lovely, he thought, as he sat silently for a few minutes taking in her beauty while she tentatively sipped her coffee. The morning sun spilled across the room, haloing her copper hair and strong profile. Of his four children, she was the one who most resembled her mother in both looks and temperament. Margaret and the two boys were more like him: cocky, careless, sharp-eyed and thin-skinned. But Emily, his youngest, was Annie's child and Annie's gift to him and Annie's strongest legacy. Emily was calm, flowing, reflexively generous and tender.

"So how's my shiny penny this morning?" he asked with a wide grin, using a nickname he had given her as a little girl. Now this thirty-three-year-old tall, angular woman with her large brown eyes and soft, expressive mouth, her wide forehead and strong dimpled chin, and that thick, curly copper hair – Annie's hair as a girl – that ran riotously across her temples as she bowed to sip her coffee, was a vision he wanted to drink in and feel happy about.

"I'm fine, Dad," she said with her wide, crooked smile. "Just give me a minute to focus."

He was eager to tell her his news. Given her expressive nature, her response, he was sure, would be the most enthusiastic, while his other children would no doubt be more restrained, more deliberative. Yet he had a flair for the dramatic and an eye for the big scene and, in fairness to the others, he decided to hold off on saying anything until the right moment, which he had already set in his mind and rehearsed many times, like an actor gearing up for his opening night.

Each sip of coffee revivified Emily a little more, and soon they were chatting about the family and preparations for Thanksgiving dinner. Mrs. Higgins, the lady who came in every afternoon to cook dinner and do a bit of cleaning, now that he was living alone, had offered to make the full Thanksgiving dinner in advance but he wouldn't hear of it and Emily understood and agreed. More than anything he wanted the time-honored, peculiar family rituals of this holiday: the kitchen crammed with people laughing and joking and arguing over who should do what, while savoring the smells from the turkey and the pies and the other dishes baking in the two ovens; the counters filled with platters and mixing bowls and casserole dishes and plates and half-empty wine glasses, as roars of approval or disappointment erupted from the adjacent family room over gains or losses of favorite football teams, and everyone rushed in to catch a glimpse of the unfolding contest; incorporating the special dishes that relatives brought and welcoming new guests to the feast; getting out the special table cloth that had been his mother's and the good china that he and Annie had been given for a wedding present all those years ago and which had been treated so reverently, even by the kids when they were young, that in more than half a century only a few cups and plates had been broken and carefully mended by Annie.

His oldest son, Matthew had suggested that the family might go out for Thanksgiving dinner this year but he immediately vetoed the suggestion, longing to see his family gathered once more around his dining table. Besides, this was how he pictured the scene when he made his announcement, and a restaurant just wasn't the right setting for such an important event.

After two cups of coffee, Emily was ready to start the day. The wall clock by the refrigerator read 8:45 and their family custom was to have dinner around two. The one concession to Annie's absence was the decision that his two daughters-in-law would bring several of the meal's customary dishes, prepared in advance, so, as Emily reviewed what had to be done, the list was relatively short.

"Okay, I'm back among the living," Emily said as she rose from the table and headed for the sink. "Time to get the turkey stuffed."

As she reached behind the kitchen door for one of Annie's aprons, Adam reflected that in one minor respect Emily differed from her mother. Like her mother, she loved to cook, but, unlike her mother, she was methodical, disciplined and precise, while Annie had been intuitive and creative. He had marveled at his wife's great flair in the kitchen, her natural, exuberant talent for all things culinary, and he had been proud of the compliments she received when friends dined with them. When anyone had asked Annie for a recipe, she was exasperatingly vague: a pinch of this, a dollop of that, a smidgen of something else. He knew this vagueness was not from any vain desire to hoard special recipes but was, rather, a true reflection of her creative, spontaneous approach.

Adam carried the turkey from the second refrigerator on the back porch into the kitchen and Emily gently shooed him away as she organized herself for work. He left willingly for it was clear that the division of labor traditionally observed by him and Annie on this holiday was now to be honored by Emily. He knew that he had never been much of a hand around the house, but Thanksgiving was special, when he savored his role as head of the family, and he had insisted on participating fully in preparing for the family gathering. Annie had indulgently assigned him the task of setting the table, first bringing up from the basement the extra leaves to extend its length and then gathering the extra chairs from across the house to accommodate the estimated number of guests. They always recognized that any member of the family might show up with someone added to the entourage at the last minute, but this was a practice that he and Annie had always welcomed, for no one, they felt, should be excluded from a family gathering on this day.

The extra table leaves felt surprisingly heavy as he hauled them up the cellar stairs and he begrudged this sign of his advancing years, but still his spirits were buoyant as he maneuvered them into place, anticipating the happy, noisy scene to come around this very table. He returned to humming snippets of opera arias as he scoured the house for the requisite number of chairs.

He found three in his office, or retreat room, as Annie called it. His thoughts wandered back to the first time he had beheld his office. It had originally been two rooms and a shared bath for two live-in servants when this Victorian house had sheltered a family much larger than his, and live-in servants were the norm. By the time he and Annie occupied the house, they had never thought of having live-in servants, mostly because they could never have afforded them when the kids were young and his private law practice was just getting started, and also because Annie's mother, Marion, had moved in with them after Annie's father died. Marion had been a great help to Annie until she suffered a stroke and retreated to her room for the last year of her life. The two servants' rooms, off the kitchen, down a short corridor, had become storage rooms for the kids' toys and sports equipment and Christmas decorations; otherwise they were forgotten. Then, on one of his birthdays – he couldn't remember which, but all the children were still young and Marion was still healthy – after his favorite leg of lamb and roast potatoes and creamed spinach dinner and Annie's home-made birthday cake with the vanilla butter-cream frosting that he loved, and the chorus of Happy Birthday and the successful blowing out of all the candles on the cake and the gleeful presentation of the little hand-made presents from the kids and a handsome tie from Marion, Annie had led him by the hand down the short hallway, followed by the giggling, excited children, to the former servants' wing.

The two rooms were now one commodious space, furnished with a large, walnut desk, two leather wing chairs, a wall of bookcases and a sofa large enough for napping, as Annie pointed out. Hanging on an ornate hook next to the door was one of those hotel signs saying Do Not Disturb, that Annie's sister, Gert, had "borrowed" from a hotel the last time she had visited Atlantic City. With the children clustered around her, jostling and giggling and closely gauging their father's surprise reaction to this special birthday present, Annie made a short, informal speech, stating her opinion that every family man deserved his own private space, a sanctuary to which he could retreat from the noise and cares of family life, to work, to read, to reflect, to relax. The children understood and agreed to a new house rule that they were never to disturb their father when the Do Not Disturb sign was posted on the door handle. Annie, too, observed this rule except for some emergency.

Now he stood surveying the room with the same furniture and the same tan, patterned wallpaper above the dark wood wainscoting, the bookcases crowded with his old law books and tomes on hobbies he had taken up and abandoned through the decades, and he saw Annie as she stood before him that night so many years ago, and he could hear her voice and see her eager smile and recognize how thrilled she had been to surprise him with this major undertaking that she, in conspiracy with the children, had brought off. He reached out as if he could touch her, as if he could thank her again – if he ever thanked her at all – for this marvelous present, this telling gesture of love and thoughtfulness, like so many, many gestures she had rendered in their long shared history, and suddenly he was crying softly, aching and lonely.

She still inhabits this home, he thought: every room, every piece of furniture, every family picture adorning walls, bureaus and the piano. Every routine that he now did perfunctorily reinforced her absence but also made her a living presence, closer to him than ever. The house, he knew, was much too large, and his two boys, in recent phone conversations with him, reluctantly asked if he had given any thought to selling it. He said no, and he knew that he would give no serious thought to it as long as Annie's palpable presence in all these rooms was comforting him. He recognized that it was her home even more than his. She had reigned here as the tent pole of family life; as its central nervous system. Her heart resided here. He knew that he had merely been a player, donning the role of father and lord of the manor at his pleasure, then escaping to other realms he inhabited.

From the kitchen he heard a glass shattering against the stone floor and Emily emitting a complicated series of curses. Wiping his eyes, he hurried to see what had happened and discovered her on her hands and knees, picking up glass shards from a pool of cranberry sauce. He rushed to her side.

"Be careful, Dad. There's glass all over the floor. I'm sorry for this mess. As soon as I finish cleaning up, I'll just run out and see if I can get more cranberry sauce."

"Don't worry, honey," he said quickly. "Your mother always kept a good supply of cranberry sauce in the pantry because she knew I liked it not just for Thanksgiving."

Emily would not permit him to assist in the clean-up so he left the kitchen and resumed arranging seats around the dining room table.

By his calculations there were seventeen people expected today: Matthew and Charlotte and their two children; Russell and Maria and their three children; Margaret and Skip and Timmy, their only child; Aunt Bambi, the youngest and last of his father's generation who, at eighty-six, was only ten years older than he, and Uncle Fred, her husband – no children there; Henry Ferguson, his old army buddy, divorced and alienated from his only daughter; Emily and himself. He counted a total of seventeen chairs but then added another one, remembering a widowed neighbor of Margaret's whom Margaret had casually mentioned during her last phone conversation with him a few nights ago.

"She's a lovely person, a widow, and she doesn't have any relatives in this area, so I thought…"

"Of course," he interrupted her. "Bring her along."

As he arranged eighteen assorted chairs around the dining table, he was grateful that the room was so generously proportioned to accommodate big family gatherings. He recalled with a smile that when his grandchildren were little, their parents had suggested that they be seated at a separate adjacent round table bought in from the breakfast room, but Annie and he would not hear of it, insisting on the entire family being seated around the one family table. Now, of course, his grandchildren were either in their late teens or early adulthood and the question was moot.

From the massive breakfront that occupied one long wall of the dining room, he extracted the extra pads for the table leaves, then the huge linen and lace tablecloth that his mother had given them when they first moved to this home. Next he removed the white bisque china with the plain gold rim that was always used for holidays and birthdays. Finally, from the sideboard he took the Waterford crystal water goblets and wine glasses that he and Annie had collected over years, and the four Tiffany hurricane candle holders. Returning to a deep drawer in the breakfront, he removed a large, suede-covered box containing the good flatware, service for twenty-four, and set the appropriate utensils at each place. In the center of the table he set a large vase filled with leaves and flowers, all of autumn hues, that Emily had brought.

Stepping back to survey his work, he saw Annie coming through the kitchen door, strands of copper hair plastered against her forehead shiny with perspiration, wiping her hands on her apron – the full-size flowered kind that went over the head and covered the entire front – her eyes sparkling with pleasurable anticipation. She was always full of praise and congratulations, expressing awe at his table setting talents. Each holiday, every year, her enthusiastic remarks were about the same, including the final "I think you've really outdone yourself this time, dear." And each holiday, every year, he stood at the other side of the table, like a preening young child, forever basking in this ritual of inspection, culminating in the caressing waves of her warmth and approval.

His eye was drawn to the far end of the table next to the bay window and the potted jade and philodendra plants. There in regal splendor, isolated from the motley assortment of seventeen chairs surrounding the table's sides and other end, stood his chair, a massive sculpture of ornately carved walnut legs and arms, with a vivid red leather seat and back, topped by more Gothic wood curlicues. The chair was nearly six feet tall; a chair straight out of medieval royal mead halls, fit for the knights of the Round Table, but actually a nineteenth century Episcopal bishop's chair that Annie had impulsively purchased at auction and presented to him on the first wedding anniversary they had celebrated in their house. It was accompanied with a note in which, if he remembered correctly, she had said something about every man being king in his own castle and since he was the king of her heart, as well as this castle, it was only fair that he have a regal chair befitting his position. Then she closed, as she did on every one of their fifty-one anniversaries, with "Thank you for loving me and for being such a wonderful husband."

During the early years of marriage, these words, while always gratifying, also evoked an unusual degree of self-examination on his part, as he reflected on his relationship with Annie and acknowledged definite areas for improvement. His law practice, his community work and fraternal organizations, all of which, he felt, were necessary connections that contributed to the success of his practice, kept him away from home many evenings and left the major burden of raising four kids and managing a household squarely on his wife's shoulders. Even his avid pursuit of golf on weekends and some vacations, a sport he did not share with Annie, he justified as solidifying social and business connections. She never questioned, never reproached him, and she managed everything so seamlessly, whether a dinner party for twelve or having the roof repaired or adroitly managing the household budget or sending their kids off to college, that his life rolled on merrily, and he took scant notice of the strong underpinnings she provided. He would resolve in those rare moments of reflection to be of more help, or at least more verbally grateful, but these resolutions would quickly dissipate as inert contentment settled on him once again, and Annie cheerfully, effortlessly carried so much of the marital load.

Then she was gone, after a series of severe headaches, a routine checkup, a shocking diagnosis and a mercifully short but graphically horrific decline, mitigated only by anodyne drugs and her unconquerable spirit. During those four months he lived as if in a dreamscape where he didn't breathe, he didn't think, he didn't feel, so overwhelmed was he by this catastrophic eruption in his life. Routinely, he would sit for hours by her bed, ignoring the hospice personnel who cared for her, holding her hand, sensitive only to any tremors or pressure he felt through her fingers, interpreting these as her intimate, final communications with him. During those long hours of silent vigil he never cried and hardly ever spoke. He was both vaguely aware of, and oblivious to, his children and their spouses and his grandchildren surrounding Annie's bedside and gently steering him through the daily rituals of the living. Everything – time, people, events, decisions, consciousness, itself – was blurred, suspended in an agony of shock and disbelief.

After the rituals attending her passing were completed and he returned to the even greater shock of a house, a life, a world without her, he was surrounded by solicitous and loving people but existed in emotional isolation, relieved only by conjuring Annie's image, her voice, her smile, her gestures, in every nook and cranny of the home they had shared for nearly four decades. Ever generous, she came willingly.

While the aching void dominated his waking hours and intruded on his attempts to sleep, he eventually sought relief in the company of others, slowly resuming limited social interactions. He also found escape in concentrating on the mundane activities of everyday life. As his children saw his renewed independence, his immersion in scheduled rituals and his revived interest in family life, their focused concern for him gradually receded until it became a peripheral alertness, an underlying theme, to be shared and discussed and evaluated among siblings but mostly relegated to the corners of their busy, complicated lives. With the help of Mrs. Higgins, the new housekeeper they had first forced on him but whom, later, he obligingly accepted, Dad was doing fine, seeing old friends, calling them for news of the family, giving special attention to Bently, getting out and about, keeping fit and active and exhibiting both his old cheerful personality and a renewed interest in daily life. They accepted his surface decorum as indicative of his true frame of mind and, relieved of a heavy emotional weight, got on with their lives.

He stood motionless in the dining room, lost in memories of the past but brought back to the present with a surge of feelings:

happy and proud to be presiding again over an assemblage of family and friends, the patriarch of a large and spirited clan. Annie had died in May and now, six months later, the family was gathering for the first big holiday without her. And he had his news.

* * * *

He had helped Emily baste the turkey and wanted to be of more help but he sensed he was getting in her way. She had gently conveyed this feeling, just like her mother, he thought, so he took Bently for his midday walk and, upon returning a half-hour later, saw from the cars in the driveway that his three other children and their families had arrived. His excitement mounted. Now the merriment would begin, he thought and the day would go as he had pictured it and then he would tell them. He and Bently bounded up the five steps to the porch and burst through the front door to join the noisy throng. He was quickly surrounded by his children, their wives and his grandchildren, kissed by the females, hugged and patted by the males. As he engaged in these rituals of greeting, he was conscious and proud of the fine looking descendants he and Annie had produced – their contribution to the human flow. He observed, too, that both his boys and Margaret were eyeing him closely for signs of change in him so he feigned an extra measure of exuberance to defeat any suspicions.

Everyone moved past the living and dining rooms to the family room at the rear of the house where a football game in progress was displayed on the huge flat-screen TV that all the children had given him and Annie for Christmas just two years ago. Annie had marveled at its size and picture clarity, contrasting this behemoth with their first tiny Philco set. Annie, he recalled, was always expressing awe and delight with the technological advances she had witnessed in her lifetime. The grandchildren arranged themselves in casual clusters on the furniture and the floor to follow the game while the adults bustled about, preparing the meal, getting in each other's way and talking in high pitched, animated tones as if competing for attention.

After delivering their compliments on his table setting, they politely told him that his further service was not required, and he found himself seated next to Amy Chandler, Margaret's widowed neighbor. Adam judged her to be a woman in her late sixties, although nowadays, he admitted, women looked years younger than their actual age. Annie certainly did, up to her quick decline. He remembered how fond she was of repeating the advice of some celebrated beauty – he couldn't recall the name – who said that women should take ten years off their age until they turned seventy and then they should add ten years to their actual age so that people would still marvel at how good they looked. Annie would repeat this advice, then confess that since she had married and had children so young, the only way she could deduct ten years from her age was if her boys agreed to the same stratagem, which, since they had both started losing their hair prematurely, would have made them nearly freaks to be balding at, say, nineteen, instead of twenty-nine. "No," she said, "I'll always have to admit my age and be grateful if anyone thinks I look younger."

Adam had always thought Annie beautiful and desirable at any age, and now he saw her in the kitchen, surrounded by her daughters and daughters-in-law: tall, angular, smiling, gently directing the bustling activities, secure and happy in the bosom of her family.

His concentration was interrupted by Amy Chandler's voice commenting on what a lovely home he had, and he turned his focus to her. She was on the plump side, though not fat, he thought. She wore a dark brown pant suit and a white silk blouse with a ruffled collar. Her eyes were kind, he noted, but her face was generic, with no distinctive, interesting features, and he judged her continuous smile to be full of artfulness. He also noticed that her teeth were of uneven color, some white, some gray. Her short hair was dyed a monotonously even light brown and had that lacquered, helmeted look, with a slight indentation on one side where no doubt she had slept on it after having it set and sprayed into rigid form. He thought of Annie's hair, long and shimmering like burnished copper in her youth, then short and prematurely white – only momentarily gray – in middle age, sweeping back from her broad forehead in natural waves, soft and silky and inviting to his touch. Again, Amy Chandler's voice intruded on his meditation and in recognition of his role as host, he resolved to give her his full attention.

"It's very kind of you to include me in your family gathering," Amy said, gently laying a hand on his arm. "I've heard so much about you from Margaret that I feel I know you already and I was very eager to meet you." She now locked eyes with him and lowered her voice to an intimate range. "I'm so sorry for your loss, Adam. I know how you must feel, especially on holidays like this. I lost my Dan just over two years now, and it's very lonely, isn't it?" She paused as if waiting for his response, but when he said nothing, she continued. "Both my daughters are settled in California with families of their own and they always invite me for Thanksgiving, but I've got circulation problems and the long plane trip is so tiring that I just can't do it every year. So I was delighted when Margaret invited me to join you." She tilted her head closer to his and squeezed his arm. Her voice was almost a confessional whisper. "It's the companionship I miss the most and the sharing of everyday, little things. Don't you agree?" Still gripping his arm, she flashed him an intimate smile.

He was dumbfounded by this head-on assault, her practiced sincerity, her references to shared feelings, her conspiratorial invitations to intimacy. He was aware that he was staring at her with a fixed smile as he struggled for a casual response that discouraged her forwardness when the room erupted with triumphant shouts as someone on the big screen scored a touchdown. Bently, who had been lying quietly by Adam's feet, joined the revelry with loud barking, and in the dog's exuberance Adam found his escape. Quickly excusing himself, he left Amy and taking Bently by the collar, led him to his office. Once there, he spent several minutes consoling Bently for separating him from the festivities before closing the door and returning to his quests. By this time, Amy had joined the women in the kitchen and he vowed to avoid any more quiet chats with her for the rest of the day.

He observed from a distance how Emily had clearly taken her mother's place as director of activities in meal preparation, apparently to Margaret's annoyance, for as the eldest daughter she seemed to feel that this role rightfully belonged to her. In vying with Emily for leadership, however, the differences in their personalities could not have been more forcefully demonstrated to Adam. Margaret ordered; Emily requested. Both his daughters-in-law and even Aunt Bambi ignored Margaret's instructions, complying only with Emily's suggestions, and Margaret soon relinquished the field. He watched the women parading through the family room to the dining room, like priestesses of some culinary god, carrying platters, covered dishes, water pitchers and assorted serving utensils, with Matthew bringing up the rear, proudly holding the golden brown turkey. With Russell's help, Adam brought up several bottles of wine from the basement, opened them and placed them on the sideboard. Only twenty minutes after the time that he and Emily had aimed for, family and friends gathered round the heavily laden table for their traditional Thanksgiving feast.

Before seating themselves, they all held hands while Adam, happy in his role as patriarch, said grace. He gazed down at the far end of the table and saw Annie, her apron gone, head bowed, eyes half closed, with just a trace of a smile forming on her lips. She always expressed admiration for his "original and eloquent prayer" each Thanksgiving, he remembered, though he felt that the conventions of this holiday demanded a good amount of repetition. Still, he tried each year to express gratitude for the bountiful meal, the blessing of family, the gift of friends, the joy of being together and sharing this day, using new phrases, not omitting a few humorous references to the turkey's sacrifice or the holiday traffic. Again this year, he had sat in his office and prepared his remarks, jotting down themes or salient words as quick reminders. His overriding rule was to keep it short, but this year he knew he would exceed his usual brevity for there was the absolute necessity of adding one more theme.

As he reached the final sentences of his prayer, he felt a slight quiver and a loss of volume in his voice, and he took a deep breath before beginning his peroration. He was aware, too, that his hands were trembling slightly, entwined with Margaret's and Emily's on either side of him, but then he felt a comforting squeeze from Emily's hand, through which Annie's strength and reassurance seemed to be coursing.

"We thank you, Lord, for all these manifold blessings and we gather together with loving memories of our wife, mother, grandmother and friend who enjoys Your presence now but remains forever with us in spirit. Amen."

Everyone murmured Amen but the last references to Annie left the group in a momentarily hushed, somber mood, broken quickly by Emily.

"Wonderful blessing, Dad! Now, everyone, dig in and eat! And remember, ladies, if you eat with one eye closed, it's only half the calories."

This silly, but perfect, remark seemed to restore good spirits, and Penny, Russell's twenty-one-year-old daughter, added that it was no calories if you ate standing up; then Matthew's wife, Charlotte, joined in the silliness by saying that if you ate with the lights out, you actually lost weight. Adam noted that a convivial mood now swept the table, as wine was passed among the guests and chatter and laughter erupted in small groups or with the entire table participating. Many comments praising the food and giving credit to the preparer of a particular dish were heard, along with self-deprecatory responses. Aunt Bambi's casserole, a spinach, onion, water chestnut and cheddar cheese concoction, annually received raves, much to the old lady's delight. Soon the grandchildren were taking second helpings. More wine was poured and then Emily and Margaret, assisted by their two sisters-in-law, cleared the table.

The family custom at this juncture, as coffee, tea, and pies – apple, pumpkin and mince – were being prepared for serving, was for everyone remaining at the table, one at a time, around the room, to give a brief recitation of recent personal events or accomplishments. This tradition, Adam recalled, had been started by Annie many years ago when the grandchildren were little and, distracted by all the meal preparation in the kitchen, she had wanted to be sure that she could focus on each child and not miss any family news. She had also suggested that each person mention some particular thing that he or she was thankful for. The children relished the idea of being the family's center of attention at this specially designated time and the adults willingly entered into the spirit of the recitation to please Annie, delighting in hearing her hearty laughter at their witty and often self-mocking remarks.

"I'd like to report," said Charlotte, affecting a glum look, "that in the last two months I lost seven pounds, only to gain them all back today. But I'm still grateful that I'm back where I started and not seven pounds heavier than my original weight. Tomorrow

I will immediately start my diet again in preparation for Christmas. In this way while I may never be thinner, I hope never to be fatter."

Timmy, Margaret's seventeen-year-old son, always centered his gratitude on beating his father or mother or cousins or buddies at one competitive sport or another. Adam recalled that this had been Timmy's theme from the time he was five or six.

Adam was always the last to speak. This year, instead of remaining in his imposing Episcopal chair, he broke with tradition by standing at the head of the table. This unexpected action, coupled with his sudden shift in demeanor, sent a mildly disconcerting tremor down the table, as everyone fell silent and the four women in the kitchen, alert to the sudden hush, stopped their work and moved to the dining room doorway. Adam adjusted his cardigan, cleared his throat and began.

"I'm grateful to my family and friends for the love and support you've shown me during this most difficult period. I know you have all been concerned about me and I've been aware of the small and large and not-so-subtle ways you've been keeping an eye on me. And I know that you want me to be happy. So today I want not just to thank you but to tell you that I'm okay. No, more than okay."

Adam paused, took a sip of water and then looked at each of the faces turned in his direction, all looking rather slack-jawed, he thought, but that would change. The moment was here. He cleared his throat and continued.

"For fifty-one years I had the perfect wife and found love and happiness and comfort beyond my expectations; really beyond what I deserved. Now I've been blessed to find another lady who loves me and whom I love and we are to be married at Christmas. I'm sorry that she couldn't be here today to meet all of you but she's with her two children and grandchildren in Pennsylvania. I know that when you meet her, you'll realize why I love her, and, after all, it's not often a fellow my age gets a second chance at happiness, a second time around, so to speak."

His light joke and wide grin were met with stunned, blank faces and total silence, broken only by Margaret's dropping a large glass water pitcher she had been drying. The shards of the smashed pitcher skittered across the wood floor but no one paid any attention. Then Timmy, Margaret's son, jumped up and, pumping the air with his arm, cried "Way to go, grandpa!" This, too, was met with silence except for Margaret's rebuke, "Sit down, Timmy!"

Adam noted the shocked looks on all the upturned faces but felt sure that the response was only temporary. He spoke again.

"I can see that this has come as a great surprise to all of you and, indeed, it's even a great surprise to me, but I know that you want the best for me, and this lady – her name is Christine – is the best thing I could ever hope for at this point in my life."

He remained standing, staring at his family for any sign of joy at his happy news but the silence surrounding him was overwhelming. Finally Matthew, his oldest child, rose from his chair and stood facing his father.

"Dad, I don't know what to say. You've taken all of us completely by surprise. It's just such a shock…with Mom gone such a short time and now you say you're already in love again and plan to remarry this Christmas."

Matthew paused and looked at his wife and sisters standing in the doorway, then back at his father, and his next words came in a strangled muffle of emotions.

"It just doesn't seem fair! Or right! Or proper! It's not respectful to Mom! To us! We don't even know this woman…this Christine. And you plan to marry her at Christmas? That's only six months since Mom…since Mom…" His voice trailed off and, shaking his head, he sat down.

Now Russell stood up and continued the themes started by his older brother.

"Dad, of course we want you to be happy but isn't this much too hasty? Can't you let the family meet Christine and give us a little time to get to know her and then, when we've all gotten used to the idea, you could think about marrying her."

Adam's blue eyes turned a darker hue and any hint of a smile left his face when Russell finished speaking and sat down. Adam saw in his sons' remarks the suggestion that he needed his family's approval before considering remarrying. This notion was so alien to his own concept of father and family head that he considered it gross impertinence and took immediate offense. But he spoke in a calm, deliberate voice.

"I'm sorry that it's hard for you to understand or to accept that I love this woman and she loves me. And regarding the 'hastiness' of our wedding plans, when you're my age, you don't make long-range plans. You grab what happiness you can find in the present and hold on to it and are grateful for it."

Standing perfectly straight at the head of the table, his eyes radiating a challenging intensity, he spoke in a formal, frosted tone. "I'm not asking you to let Christine take Annie's place. No one could do that. At this point in your lives, she's not going to be your new mother. She'll be my wife and companion. I feel sure that if you gave her a chance, you would all find her to be warm and honest…a gracious and lovely woman. But, frankly, whether you like her or not, or resent her or not, or accept her or not, is your choice and it's immaterial to me. We're getting married at Christmas and that's that! You .may take all the time you need to get to know her after we're married."

Having tossed the gauntlet, he sat down, feeling tired. During his last remarks, Emily had disappeared and now returned with a broom and dustpan and was sweeping up the shards of glass. In a timid, barely audible voice, Aunt Bambi now spoke.

"Adam, where did you meet this Christine?"

Annoyed, Adam responded. "I met THIS Christine at the Methodist Church thrift shop about three months ago when I took some of Annie's clothes there. She was bringing in some of her husband's things – he died about a year ago. She was all teary – eyed about giving his things away, and I understood how she felt and we started to chat and I invited her to lunch. And we've been seeing each other ever since.

Margaret, who had been standing in the doorway, immobile, still clutching the towel that had been drying the now destroyed pitcher, suddenly stepped into the room like a sprung coil and walked to the end of the table opposite from Adam and stood facing him. Her brows were knit low above her eyes and her dark stare never left her father's face. She spoke in a quick, peremptory tone, like a lawyer interrogating a hostile witness.

"And you never mentioned this lady to anyone until now?"

Adam tried to remain calm at this effrontery but his answer was tinged with barely suppressed anger.

"Why should I have mentioned it? We met. We had a lot in common. We had lunch and played golf a few times and went to the movies and I visited her home and she came here."

Margaret pounced. "She came here!" Her voice rose to a shrill pitch of indignation on the last word.

Adam could picture the color rising in his face but he still struggled to keep his voice low, yet when he spoke there was a noticeable quiver.

"Yes, Margaret, she came here. Mrs. Higgins made a lovely dinner for us. I didn't mention her to you because you all have very busy and independent lives and it was only a few weeks ago that Christine and I had a heart-to-heart talk and realized we both felt the same about each other. It might sound corny or lightning fast but that's the way it was, and the next night I took her out to Michele's Restaurant for a nice dinner and I proposed and she accepted, and today was the first time we were all together so I could announce our plans."

Margaret was relentless, desperate.

"But who is she? What do you really know about her – her history…her background…her family…her values?"

Adam rose quickly and pointed a finger at Margaret

"Margaret, you're being impertinent!" he shouted.

This thunderous declaration echoed around the room as Margaret, reduced to naughty child, her defiance crumbling, sank into a chair and everyone else looked down at the table. Overt sarcasm now flooded across Adam's words, which tumbled out of him in rapid-fire succession.

"While I did not engage the FBI to conduct a thorough investigation of Christine, I know all that's necessary to appreciate what a fine person she is and to want to spend whatever time is remaining to me with her at my side. She is a widow. Her husband was Malcolm Ridge, a tax attorney. She's sixty-four, and, yes, that makes her twelve years younger than I, and SO WHAT! She owns her own home, is financially secure and drives a late model Audi. She was born in Maryland, but grew up in Ohio. Her father was a Methodist minister and she is a practicing Methodist, and since I've never given strong adherence to any religion, this is not an insuperable barrier, don't you agree? She has a sister living in Virginia and an older brother in Arizona and her two daughters

– I can't remember their ages – are both married, both with children, both live in Pennsylvania and we plan to visit them shortly after we're married. As for other vital facts that you're so keen to know, Christine is a graduate of Vassar, where she majored in classical studies. She and Malcolm went on several anthropological digs and we hope to go on one together very soon. She's a good cook, although not as creative as your mother, enjoys tennis and golf, so I'm planning to take up tennis again, and she loves opera. She's an avid gardener, which I'm not, but I can learn."

He had been delivering these lines in quick, staccato fashion, barely pausing for breath, and now sweat was forming rivulets across his forehead and around his ears. He took a sip of water and resumed speaking, but in a slower voice, so low as if he were talking to himself. He saw Annie at the other end of the table, smiling.

"But all these things are just facts about the lady. What is essential is the way I feel when I'm with her: not so lonely or old or irrelevant. We talk and we laugh and we share our stories and we comfort each other and when I hold her, I feel alive again. She's warm and inviting and positive and she listens attentively and has a kind heart. She even likes Bently. And I don't want to be alone and face what's ahead without her. Maybe it's not the same kind of love I had with you, Annie, not as consuming and giddy and mindlessly spontaneous, but it's reassuring and invigorating and comforting and I think, Annie, you would approve."

Annie was beaming at him and shaking her head vigorously.

As if emerging from a trance, he was once again aware of the familiar faces surrounding him. He sat down and wiped his forehead with his napkin as weariness overcame him, and he momentarily closed his eyes. Conversations about his announcement now broke out around the table, snatches of which drifted up to him, but only vaguely, as he lapsed into a state of total lassitude, slumped in his Episcopal throne chair, looking diminutive and fragile.

"Where will they live?" asked Aunt Bambi in a low voice tremulous with age.

"Well, I hope they're not planning on living here," offered Margaret, refortified for battle.

"I thought about inviting Dad to live with us," said Matthew, "but now I couldn't bring a stranger into my home and feel comfortable."

"And it wouldn't be fair to Charlotte to bring another woman into your house," observed Russell.

"Maybe they'll live in Christine's house," suggested Margaret sarcastically. "Isn't that something to look forward to: spending holidays in a stranger's home, if she'd even invite us."

"They might sell both their houses and move into a condo, like the complex that Bambi and I now enjoy," said Uncle Fred

Amy Chandler, disregarding her role as guest, commented that "it seems all too soon and he's rushing headlong into something he'll probably regret but then the damage will be done."

"I hope they sign a pre-nuptial agreement," said Russell

"And Dad's will should be changed to protect all the grandchildren," said Matthew

"What about Mother's jewelry and all our family heirlooms, like everything on this table?" said Margaret, aggrieved and petulant.

"This is one hell of a mess!" said Russell

"But maybe they really do love each other," offered Aunt Bambi

Matthew banged his fist on the table and yelled, "Yeh, and maybe she just sees a pigeon!" Many heads nodded in agreement while other heads nodded in the opposite direction, suggesting their confusion.

Adam sat motionless, but his eyes were now keenly observing all these interactions of the people surrounding him, who continued their discussions about him as if he weren't present. From deep within him welled a disturbing, then infuriating recognition that a dramatic role reversal had taken place within his family: he was no longer regarded as the father but as the child. They were speaking like stern parents clearly annoyed with a naughty boy for his irresponsibility and lack of judgment, as if they bore the full burden of caring for him and suffered for his rashness; as if they were in charge of determining his actions because he was incapable of rational processes. All around him the buzz of voices

– angry, sarcastic, dismissive – grew until it was screaming in his ears, rendering him invisible, inconsequential., bringing shock and fury until he could contain it no longer.

Erupting from his seat with such galvanic force that the Episcopal throne chair toppled over, making a thunderous crash against the wood floor, his blazing eyes and flushed face made him a riveting force. All conversations ceased and again all heads turned to him. His mind fumbled for the words to denounce such callous treatment but all he could manage were gestures and grimaces. Encircling the room with a sweep of his arm, he could only sputter "How dare you!" again and again, as his indignation overcame all attempts of rational speech. Looking at his family and their bewildered, closed expressions, he could only point and utter accusations in short breaths, aware that his rising temper and truncated words were only magnifying his diminished authority and unappeasable hurt. His frustration was paralyzing him and he felt tears forming at the corners of his eyes, which, in his mind, signaled total surrender. He would not be reduced to a crying child for all to scorn and pity. He rushed blindly from the dining room, out the front door, across the porch, down the steps and stopped only when he had reached the end of his driveway. The rain pelted him but he didn't care, so embarrassed was he for his family and himself and this unexpected rush of events. Ignoring the voices entreating him to return to the house, he stood rooted to the spot, unable to wrap his mind around any plan of action, as the rain and his anger and his confusion washed over him, and the tears came and joined the flow of drops on his cheeks, and he was grateful for the camouflage and the isolation.

Suddenly he was aware of the warm muzzle of Bently sniffing his side, and he automatically dropped his hand to Bently's head and the dog licked his wet fingers. Next he felt a coat being thrown over his shoulders and then Emily was standing mutely by his side, entwining her arm with his. She was the only one, he thought, brave enough to approach him, and wise enough to sense that he would reject all direction, so she offered none; only the consolation of her presence. His focus shifted to her, and his concern for her standing unprotected in the chilling rain broke his paralyzing spell and he told her gently to go back. She smiled and squeezed his arm but didn't move. He raised one side of the raincoat to shelter her. She snuggled under his raised arm, against his side, and his love for her pulsed like a warm current. Still numb from his family's assaults but determined to get Emily out of the rain, he led her away from the voices, around to the rear of the house, with Bently following close behind. They entered the house through the back door, and he crossed the kitchen, still holding a protective arm around her and led her to his office where he invited Bently to enter, then immediately closed the door.

They sat facing each other in the worn leather armchairs, the dog lying at the side of his chair. He was calmer now and words finally came to him.

"They act as if I have to ask their permission to do anything," he said, dismissively, waving an arm toward the general direction of the dining room. "Goddammit, it's my life! They have no right to question me and object to anything I decide to do!" Then in a plaintive voice he said, "Why isn't anyone happy for me?" and added, "I know your mother would be."

Emily smiled, leaned forward in her chair and patted his knee.

"Dad, it's just so sudden and such a surprise that no one knows really what to say."

"Well, they sure as hell had a lot to say in there!" he thundered with a grimace of disgust.

Bently's head rose from his paws and his eyes studied his master's face for the meaning of the raised voice and the sweeping gestures. Emily moved forward to the edge of her chair and placed both her hands on his knees. Her voice was calm and soothing.

"Dad, we all love you and we know how difficult it must be for you without Mom, but she's been gone for such a short time and we never expected anything like this...that someone might take her place...and so soon!"

They sat in silence for several minutes, as the rain pelted the windows and Bently returned to resting his head on his paws, but his big brown eyes never closed. Emily continued to clutch her father's knees, as he stared down at his dog. When at last he spoke his voice was hollow and small. He looked directly at Emily and grabbed her hands and she saw the tears welling up in his eyes. His words came in a torrent.

"I can't live like this...I miss your mother so much and I want what I had with her...the warmth, the comfort, the caring...I need to share my life with someone and Christine feels the same way...and we want to be together for whatever time we have left. Can't you understand that?" His voice rose in pitch, suggesting both pleading and anger. Emily instinctively rose from her chair and in one quick movement embraced her sitting father, drawing his head into her chest, allowing him to hide his tears.

"Yes, Dad, of course...I...we do understand...and we want you to be happy."

She stroked his thinning white hair as a mother might soothe a child. "Just be patient with us...it's such a big surprise...we need a little time to adjust to everything."

He pulled his head back from her body and reached for a tissue on the table by his chair and wiped his eyes. Sternness crept back into his voice. "They can have all the time they want to adjust, but I'm not changing my plans one jot!"

"I know," she said, smiling at his determined squaring of his shoulders as he offered this declaration. "We'll support you, don't worry, Dad."

The room had grown dark from the early onset of evening and Emily switched on the floor lamp behind her father's chair.

"Why don't we rejoin everyone for coffee and dessert," she suggested lightly

He sat back in his chair and blew his nose.

"No. You go on. I need to be alone for a while."

"Alright," she said, laying a hand on his shoulder. "I'll save you a piece of pumpkin pie."

"And a piece of mince, too," he said.

Smiling, she left the room, closing the door behind her. Bently rose and placed his massive head on Adam's lap. Adam stroked the dog's head absently, for Annie was sitting in the chair that Emily had vacated, just as she had sat opposite him for so many years, behind this closed door when she wanted to discuss something with him that she didn't want the children to hear. He remembered fondly how she never violated the original rule she had made about this being his private sanctuary and had always asked his permission to join him, which, of course, he always granted, for he relished their discussion on issues concerning the family and their lives together.

"You do understand, don't you, Annie," he said, searching her calm face for acknowledgment. "I can't be alone…I just can't be alone."

In the nimbus of the floor lamp's light he saw the smile welcoming him to their secret understanding, and he felt peaceful and resolved..

With All Due Respect

The engraved invitation on heavy vellum paper read: "The Davis family cordially invites you to a brief memorial service for their much cherished Clara, to be followed by a backyard barbecue celebrating the homecoming of their beloved Ralph and the arrival of beautiful Sonia. Sunday, September 17, 2 PM, Cornet Lane, Sands Point. RSVP."

It arrived on a Saturday when I had slept late, following an exuberant party with friends and a lot of drinking, and on my way to the corner deli to get some breakfast I had stopped to get my mail. The lobby of my apartment building was, mercifully, empty so I didn't have to struggle to focus on making small talk with the many elderly ladies who seemed to always be in the corridor, the elevator or the lobby, usually accompanied by a small, yappy dog.

Patti Davis was the wife of Henry Davis, the founding partner at the large and prestigious law firm I had recently been invited to join, through the intercession of my father who had been Henry's college roommate at Yale. At thirty-one I was starting my second life, having lived on the West Coast for six years where I had worked as a high school English teacher, married and, three years later, divorced my college girlfriend and decided to return to my roots in New York City. I had also decided to change careers and had been accepted at Columbia University's School of Law. This was my first job after graduating from law school and, to my surprise, passing the New York bar exam on the first try.

Henry had invited me for dinner shortly after my joining the firm and, eager to please, I quickly accepted. I arrived at their large, rambling apartment on Park Avenue promptly at the suggested time, having already been greeted by a doorman, a concierge, and an elevator operator, to now be greeted by, first, a maid, then two barking lhasa apsos, followed by a little girl who told me her name was China, and, finally, Mr. And Mrs. Davis. My jaw was already tired from smiling so much.

"Welcome! Welcome!" boomed Henry, one hand around his wife's slender waist, the other hand holding a martini.

Henry was a dead ringer for Leslie Neilson, silver hair, baritone voice and all, with only a little more girth around the middle. Standing shoulder to shoulder with him was Patti, almost six feet tall in heels. She was Henry's third wife and, silhouetted against the baroque marble foyer, looked like his daughter, probably no more than mid-twenties, I thought. She was not beautiful in any classic way but she was definitely lush: big green eyes, aquiline nose with flared nostrils, full lips and luxurious honey brown hair that cascaded across her bare, perfectly tanned shoulders, drawing attention to ample breasts and a long flowing body full of seductive curves.

I saw Patti as every construction worker's dream girl, the type that garnered prolonged wolf whistles and vaguely lewd remarks at every construction site in Manhattan, no matter how demurely she might be dressed. But, judging from the clinging black strapless dress she was wearing tonight, I doubted that she ever dressed demurely. Hollywood, I thought, would see her as perfect casting for the third wife: what every mature, very successful man wants to come home to at night after a long day of wielding power and making lots of money, which in the eyes of the world, I reminded myself, equalized their assets.

Henry introduced me as the "young man I was telling you about," and Patti, moving swiftly past my extended hand, gave me a warm hug, intoxicating me with the smell of her perfume and those large soft breasts pressed against my chest. As strong an attraction as I instantly felt for her, as the boss's wife, she was strictly off limits.

"Welcome to the family," she said, revealing both a dazzling smile and a high pitched, little-girl voice, so discordant with her physical impression. I assumed she was referring to the firm's "family" which, with over fifty employees, was a pretty big family.

I was ushered into a cavernous living room that, with all its different seating arrangements, high, coffered ceiling, massive furniture and walk-in fireplace, looked like the lobby of some grand hotel. A second maid was offering canapés on a silver tray and a bartender was serving drinks from a temporary set-up in the corner. I didn't know most of the dozen or so people in the room, except for a few older members of the firm who, apparently still on their first marriages, introduced me to their tired looking wives and exchanged a few pleasantries before moving on. I headed over to the makeshift bar and ordered a double scotch on the rocks, feeling I needed to fortify myself for the evening's festivities.

Patti moved among the little clusters of dinner guests and I could hear her high pitched, almost shrill, laugh intermittently echoing around the high ceiling while I hovered by the bar, pointedly making small talk with the bartender to avoid looking like the odd man out. Then Patti announced that dinner was served and made a beeline for me. Grabbing my arm she leaned into me and in that little-girl voice said, "You're my guest of honor tonight and I want you to sit on my right." She giggled and, still holding my arm, we marched into the mammoth, vaulted and frescoed dining room, resplendent with glowing candles, sparkling crystal and shining white and gold tableware. Add a few more people and a couple of tiaras, I thought, and you'd think you were in Buckingham Palace dining with the queen.

I remembered very little about the rest of the evening except that the food was delicious, my wine glass was never empty and with Patti's constant chatter, my supporting role was to keep an appreciative smile on my face and nod occasionally as she steamrolled along. Like her voice and laugh, Patti's topics were those of a spoiled teenager, centering on shopping, parties she had recently given or attended, her two dogs whom she adored and referred to as her babies, the hard rock and rap music she loved, the beautiful Ferrari that Henry had just given her for her birthday and the celebrity gossip she had picked up from People magazine, evidently her major source of worldly information. Only at one point, when dessert and coffee were being served, did I manage to interject a question about how she had met Henry. With a lot of giggling she told me – in an intimate tone as though it were confidential information – that she and her live-in boyfriend at that time had been operating a dog-walking business.

"Henry and Louise, Henry's second wife, had a Kerry blue terrier and were one of our customers. Henry made it plain that he was attracted to me and sometimes when I was walking his dog, he'd run into me on the street. He told me later that he had planned all this. Anyway, he and Louise were about to call it quits and she took the dog and moved out and when I arrived at the apartment the next day, Henry told me that the dog and the wife were gone and would I like to have dinner with him sometime soon."

Patti paused to take a sip of wine, then continued.

"And, honey, I didn't even have to think twice," Patti said, her voice filling with excited laughter, her hand grabbing my arm for emphasis. "I always had a thing for older men and Henry was so attractive and he looked so sad, like a lost puppy, so I said yes right away and then at dinner he told me how unhappy he had been in his marriage – they'd only been married for less than two years – and how lonely he was. Well, my relationship with Todd, who was my boyfriend at the time, had gone flat and it was really only our dog-walking business that was keeping us together. Anyway, Henry and I started dating and then I dumped Todd and let him have the business and moved in with Henry and about six months after that we were married."

Patti sat back in her chair and flashed me a dazzling, triumphant smile as I uttered grunts of affirmation. Covering my hand with her own, equally large hand, she continued to smile and guilelessly said, "I like you."

In the following months, I was invited to several more social gatherings at the Davis apartment, none of which had much appeal for me but all of which I dutifully attended. The invitations were made to me either directly by Patti's calling me at the office, or casually by Henry as he encountered me in the corridors of our law firm.

"Come by next Wednesday for cocktails, six o'clock," he'd say and, smiling benignly, he'd add, "Patti's really taken a shine to you and I want her to have friends her own age." No mention was ever made of my bringing a guest. I felt obliged to accept these invitations, given my novice status with the firm and my general inclination to toadyism, so I trotted up to their Park Avenue palace and was a favorite courtier for Patti's gushing monologues.

Now this formal invitation had arrived by mail and was different. Patti had occasionally talked about their place in Sands Point, which I knew to have been at one time a bastion of the mega-rich like the Guggenheims, Goulds and Vanderbilts, whose ornate Italian palazzos, drafty castles and Mediterranean villas had long since been converted into museums, schools or country clubs, or had been razed. It was still an enclave of the really well heeled, mostly new Wall Street money, about thirty miles out on the north shore of Long Island, where Henry and Patti relaxed on the weekends. But September 17 was a Sunday and I'd have to take the train out to Port Washington and then take a cab to the house in Sands Point, self-consciously set at the tip of a peninsula. I begrudged having to surrender a Sunday, the only day I allotted myself for relaxation and seeing my friends. I had no clue as to who Sonia, Ralph and Clara were, and the commingling of a memorial service cum barbecue and homecoming celebration seemed bizarre. Still, caution and cowardice whispered in my ear, telling me I had to pay court, so I reluctantly told Henry that I'd be delighted to attend.

* * * *

In Sands Point the really impressive houses are mostly hidden from view but some of the homes on the smaller properties can be glimpsed from the narrow, winding lanes that crisscross this exclusive area. The taxi I got at the Port Washington station must have been doing a thriving business that day, for the minute I said Cornet Lane, the driver said, "Yeh, the Davis house." When I said yes, he added, "They must be having a pretty big party up there," and then we fell into silence for the short ten-minute ride into the bowels of Sands Point. We passed lots of gates and high hedges and caught only glimpses of massive houses representing every architectural style from colonial to ultra modern, mostly far from the road, sheltered and obscured among massive old trees.

At Cornet Lane – no number as part of your address, I gathered, reflected moneyed significance – we entered a long, winding gravel road that made me feel I was magically traveling through some Bavarian virgin forest until a gigantic neoclassical stone house came into view. We pulled into a large brick-paved courtyard where several dozen cars were parked, many of which competed for my attention with exotic nameplates and logos I had only seen in auto magazines.

I was greeted at the door by the same maid who always welcomed me at the Park Avenue apartment – Didn't this woman ever get a day off? – and directed to the rear of the house when the festivities were taking place. I walked quickly along a center hall the size of Cleveland, catching glimpses on either side of massive formal rooms, and stepped through a pair of Palladian style French doors onto an enormous flagstone terrace. Beyond the terrace was a sweeping lawn on which the entire Normandy Invasion could have been reenacted. The lawn, perfectly manicured, sloped gently down to the Long Island Sound and a dock, maybe fifty feet long, where several boats, some large and grand, some small and sleek, all bearing the stamp of costliness, were gently rolling in the rhythmically lapping water. Off in the distance, to my astonishment, I spotted the Manhattan skyline and the Triborough Bridge.

A throng that I estimated at more than sixty people was gathered on the lawn, some in small clusters, others in awkward isolation. Under a peaked trellis with striped side curtains I spotted the bar and, like the homing pigeon, flew straight to it. Here, too, I found the same bartender who serviced me so well at the Davis soirees in the city. I greeted him by name and having spent so much time in idle, nervous chitchat with him, I considered him a dear friend.

"Don't you ever get a day of rest?" I asked.

"Sure," he said, "but Mr. and Mrs. Davis like to work with people they know and this job pays double time including travel time, so I couldn't refuse." He smiled. "Your usual?"

I was thinking about being adventurous and trying a new drink when a pair of large hands covered my eyes and a not-so-subtle perfume assaulted my nose while a memorable pair of breasts dented my back. I played along with the childish "Guess Who?" game, saying Mariah Cary, Julia Roberts, the Ghost of Christmas Past, amidst squeals and giggles from behind me. Only when I said Barbara Bush did the game end on a less exciting note.

"I'm so glad you could come," she said in that voice that conveyed both authenticity and childish delight.

The afternoon sun haloed her hair, turning it golden, and her bold-featured, open face, with its flawless olive complexion and wondrous eyes, transfixed me with its inspired symmetry. She wore a beige dress of some material that seemed to slide like water over her body, discreetly suggesting every curve. Whenever she appeared before me, I was struck afresh by her exotic beauty and her earthy appeal, as though electromagnetic waves of desire vibrated from her pores and ricocheted out to every man not officially senile or gay.

"We're going to start the memorial service in just a moment, so grab your drink and head over by the pool." She blew me a kiss and rushed off.

I followed the crowd that was heading across the lawn and through an opening in a ten-foot-high, manicured hedge, where I saw the pool, suitably sized to host the next summer Olympics, and beyond that another smaller hedge that led to a rose garden with gravel paths. At the far end of the garden I spotted Henry and Patti and China, the ten-year-old, youngest child of Henry's first marriage, and a scowling, scruffily dressed young man who, by his severe acne and wispy, unkempt beard, seemed to be a late adolescent. Next to him was a tall man in a black suit, and they were all posed next to something covered in white canvas. Patti and China were holding small bouquets of flowers; Henry held a drink. The clear space where they had stationed themselves in the garden corner was small, only accommodating a few more people, so the rest of us streamed out among the garden paths, surrounded by the vivid scent of roses and the dull droning of bees. The tinkle of ice cubes against glasses set a gentle musical note as people shifted their weight from one foot to the other.

Patti took a step forward and clutching her bouquet with one hand, waved to us with the other, as though she were on the deck of a departing ship. She tried projecting her high-pitched voice until it sounded like a gale-force wind.

"Greetings to all, dear friends, and thank you for joining us today," she said, as though speaking at a high school graduation and assuming an air of appropriate solemnity. "As many of you know, we lost our beloved Clara a short time ago, and we felt it was only fitting to honor this precious member of our family with a final tribute in this garden that she loved so much and in which she spent so many happy hours romping with her constant companion, Sherry.

With each word she said, her voice became softer and more tremulous until it was nearly a whisper as she tried not to cry. She struggled on.

"The Reverend Parker has kindly agreed to say a few words."

Dabbing her eyes with a tissue, she took a step back as the man in the black suit stepped forward. He stood with his hands folded in front of him and a large, insincere smile across his face, waiting for the audience to be totally focused on him before he spoke. His strong, mellifluous voice easily reached the people in the rear of the crowd.

"Patti asked me if I would say a few words and I am happy to do so."

He gazed paternally at the audience as if he were congratulating them on the honor of his presence. He spoke slowly, with hand gestures adding dramatic flourishes.

"Now we know that the Lord God made man and woman and all the creatures of the earth. And in creating the animals He made those who would live wild and ferocious in the forests and mountains and jungles and deserts; and those who would be of use to man, like the horse and the donkey and the camel and the cow and the sheep; but then He made one special animal that would be man's constant companion, would guard his possessions and offer abiding love and loyalty and devotion. And this wondrous creature was the dog. From the earliest history of man, even back to a time before written history, when records of man's life were glimpsed only through drawings on cave walls, we see the dog always at his side, helping him in the hunt and serving as his loyal companion"

My mind's eye rambled though my college History of Art course and I couldn't recall any dogs depicted on the caves at Lascaux, but the preacher was on a roll as his voice slowly rose in pitch and increased its measured cadence.

"And no matter how much man advanced through technology and culture, no matter how sophisticated society grew and no matter how rich or knowledgeable or refined man became, there was the dog by his side in a bond that could not be broken."

The preacher paused, looking above the crowd, as though reading from a heavenly teleprompter before continuing in a rhythmic, hypnotic pattern.

"Whether you were a king in a shimmering palace or a peasant in a hut, THERE WAS THE DOG! Whether you were a rich merchant in a beautiful mansion or a shepherd sleeping in the fields, THERE WAS THE DOG! Whether you lived on the frozen tundra or in a tropical oasis, THERE WAS THE DOG! In the tenements of the city, in the ranch houses in the suburbs, in the farmhouses in the country, THERE WAS THE DOG! When man marched off to war, or ploughed his field, or herded his flocks, or hunted for his food, or sat by his fire, THERE WAS THE DOG!

I was tempted to shout "Amen" to each of the preacher's magniloquent phrases, since with each utterance of the word "dog," he seemed to half expect some audience participation. Now his voice ascended to its fullest volume and his breath came rapidly, with barely a pause between each sentence, delivered in staccato fashion.

"Who is with the young in their playful times, the middle-aged in their working times, the old in their quiet times? THE DOG! Who is a boy's best friend, a man's trusted companion and an old man's consoling presence? THE DOG! Who asks so little of us and gives so much? THE DOG! Who shows us the meaning of true friendship and loyalty? THE DOG! Who forgives our faults and encourages our gentleness? THE DOG!

His eyes flashing, his voice approaching a screech, his arms extended toward the sky, the preacher held us all transfixed as he bellowed, "As the angels surround the very God Almighty, who surrounds and worships us? The DOG!

The Reverend Parker, as if coming out of an ecstatic trance, drew a handkerchief from his pocket and wiped his perspiring brow, then paused for a moment to assess the effect he was having on his audience, silent except for the now audible sobs of Patti. I glanced around and saw several women dabbing at their eyes while the men stared stonily ahead. The Reverend continued on a softer note.

"Now I know that a lot of Christians believe that only man has an immortal soul, and only man enjoys eternal happiness with Our Lord. But I tell you the honest truth: That just doesn't make sense to me, for the Lord created this marvelous creature to be with man, and since the dog has fulfilled that mission so nobly, so willingly, so heroically, we can feel certain that the Lord would not deprive man of this happy company. No, my friends, I believe that in the next life the dog will still have his honored place at man's side, for surely the dog has pleased the Lord with his endless devotion and is deserving of a place in Heaven alongside his beloved master."

I marveled at how easily the Reverend Parker had just turned thousands of years of Christian doctrine on its ear.

Turning toward Patti and Henry with a broad smile, the Reverend assumed a more intimate tone.

"So we come together today to remember one special dog: Clara. A beloved member of the Davis family and a unique personality: full of life and a wide mischievous streak. When she bit people's ankles, she was forgiven. When she refused to be housebroken, she was forgiven. When she chewed the furniture, forgiven. When she dug up plants and flowers, forgiven. When she jumped on everyone, forgiven. When she stole food from the table or the kitchen counter, forgiven. And when she annoyed just about everyone with her constant barking, forgiven.

Patti was registering dismay at this extensive list of Clara's deficiencies, but I felt sure that the Reverend would redeem himself.

"And why was she forgiven, my friends? Because at the end of the day she would jump into China's arms and lick her face or lay sleeping in Patti's lap or curled up next to her friend, Sherry, and the sweet, loving dog under all that rambunctious behavior would be seen again and cherished."

Reverend Parker moved closer to where the canvas covered something.

"Henry and Patti and China and Ralph wanted her buried in this garden where she loved to romp and play and wrestle with Sherry. When the family comes here and walks among the beautiful roses, they will always feel Clara's presence and be comforted."

With a sweeping, dramatic gesture, the Revered pulled off the canvas covering, revealing a full-size, five-foot-by-five-foot granite tombstone with a running lhasa apso carved into the polished surface along with the words, "Clara, Beloved Friend and Companion, 1995 – 2006. Till We Meet Again."

Whether from standing in one position for so long, with the warm afternoon sun beating down on me while I drained my double scotch, or because I was a cold, heartless bastard, I witnessed all this dramaturgy with a gimlet eye and a mounting struggle to suppress a fit of giggles. When the headstone had been revealed, I swear I heard a few snickers ripple through the crowd. The cheeks of both Patti and China glistened with tears while Henry looked bored and Ralph looked angry and morose. Patti and the Reverend changed places. Gazing forlornly at the grave marker, Patti spoke.

"I have such wonderful memories of my baby and how she'd always greet me with such excitement when I came home. She'd get so excited that she'd just squat and pee – she couldn't help it. And when we'd be getting ready to come out to Long Island, she'd race around the apartment, barking furiously and knocking things over, just deliriously happy to be going to the country. She loved to ride in the car and would be like a perpetual motion machine, jumping from the back seat to the front and then back again, and barking incessantly to express her joy and excitement. At dinner, she'd always park herself under the table by my legs, expecting some secret handout, and if she didn't get enough, she'd nip me on my ankle to remind me that she was waiting. Poor Henry! Clara was jealous of his attentions to me and many a night she'd attack him in our bed."

Patti made a sympathetic gesture toward Henry who managed a small, clenched-teeth smile, more like a grimace, and a slight nod of his head.

"She was so precious," Patti gushed, a short sob punctuating her words. Turning to China, she said, "China, dear, would you like to share your memories of Clara with us"?

China dried her eyes and with remarkable composure for a child of ten, stepped forward and drew a piece of paper from the pocket of her skirt.

"This is a poem I wrote for Clara," she announced solemnly in a barely audible voice, as her audience pressed forward, straining to hear her.

Clara

Clara was my best friend
And we had lots of fun.
She played with me in the rain,
She played with me in the sun.
Sometimes she was bad
And I'd give her a good smack.
Then she'd get mad and bite me.
Then I'd bite her right back.
I love her and I miss her.
I wish that I could kiss her.
I think of her each day.
That's all I have to say.

As China stepped back and reached for Patti's hand, some people in the audience began to clap, but, uncertain of the protocol for this novel, unfolding ceremony, they quickly stopped when they sensed the unease among the other guests, trying to look appropriately somber.

"That was beautiful, dear," Patti said, hugging China before stepping forward again. "Estelle wanted to be here today…"

This new name threw me into confusion until I heard a woman behind me whisper to her male companion, "Henry's first wife," and in a bored, cynical tone he whispered back, "How civilized! How tedious! Are the maids and the bartender going to speak next? For Christ sake, it was a friggin dog, and a nasty one at that!" The woman said "Hush!" in too vehement a tone, causing several people in the immediate vicinity to focus on her momentarily before returning their leaden gaze to Patti.

"Unfortunately," Patti continued, "she was taken with a migraine this morning and called to express her regrets. So China read her beautiful poem to her mother over the phone and Estelle thought it was lovely. She loved Clara too."

The increasing body movements among the gathering suggested a growing restlessness. My drink, which I had been quietly imbibing throughout the proceedings, was empty, and I longed for a refill. A man immediately to my right was swaying noticeably and I saw that his eyes were closed. The trick of dozing in an upright position was something I had, regrettably, never mastered.

Patti now stepped to the very edge of the cleared corner until a large, blooming rose was practically nestled in her bosom, and she raised her arms.

"I know that many of you loved Clara and I wonder if anyone would like to share their memories of her."

An electric ripple swept through the crowd, as people felt the spotlight unexpectedly turning on them. It was one thing to be a passive audience, docile and indifferent; it was quite another thing to be asked to actively participate in the drama at hand.

"Please don't be shy." Patti said encouragingly. "We're all among friends, and we'd love to have you share your memories."

This last statement seemed like a great stretch to me since except for the bartender, the maid and maybe half a dozen people from the firm I recognized, everyone else was a complete stranger.

The silence was becoming embarrassing to all when it was finally broken by one of the senior partners from the firm, whose deep, stentorian voice reflected his many years of arguing cases at the bar.

"I remember those few occasions when Patti would bring Clara to the office and what a riotous time the dog would have, racing madly around Henry's office and barking at everyone who came in, and…" His voice trailed off but then was revived. "…and we all thought how cute she was!"

"Thank you, Douglas," Patti said, and looked expectantly at the crowd.

"And I remember…" a woman wearing a large sun hat spoke hurriedly, "one night at Patti's apartment when Jerry and I were invited for drinks, and I had placed my martini on a side table and got so busy chatting with another guest and when I went to reach for my drink, there was Clara licking the last drop. And a few minutes later she was rolling on the ground and just acting crazy."

Rolls of nervous laughter rippled across the crowd and the woman in the sun hat was beaming. I was hoping that these two testimonials would suffice so I could scurry back to the bar, but Patti seemed to feel that the mine was only barely tapped and was still surveying the crowd.

"Here's something I'll never forget," said an older man standing at the edge of the crowd who, from his tone and directness, indicated that, unlike me, he had made several successful trips to the bar. The crowd turned in his direction and must have assessed him as I had and watched nervously as he continued. "The first time I ever visited Henry and Patti, I hadn't sat down for more than two minutes when the damn dog came over to me, sniffed my pants and peed on my leg. We all went on to the theater and I sat there smelling of dog pee all night!"

The crowd took an audible, collective intake of breath, followed by some equally audible titters. Patti stood with a frozen smile on her face and Henry now stepped forward and, raising his arms, took command.

"Thank you for sharing those memories."

Patti started to say something but Henry placed an arm around her and easily drowned out her voice.

"My family appreciates your support in their grieving period, but there are other activities on the agenda this afternoon, and we must move on. Please return to the lawn where our barbecue will be served."

Spontaneous applause erupted as people seemed delighted to be released from the somber poses they had assumed throughout the memorial extravaganza. I joined the animated throng that beat a hasty exit through the hedge, around the pool and out to the lawn. We trudged, what seemed like the distance between New York and Philadelphia, across the vast lawn and then passed through another tall hedge to find a very large green and white striped tent covering the Hartrue tennis court. Round tables, covered with dark green tablecloths, plain white china, crystal water goblets, white linen napkins and tall floral centerpieces, were spaced generously under the tent, with eight white caneback chairs at each table. Running along the rear of the tent, the entire length of the tennis court, was a series of buffet tables manned by a throng of Latino men and women sporting black pants, white shirts with black bow ties and, in what evidently was intended to give the guests a down-home feeling, cowboy hats. The buffet tables were laden with an abundance of food suggesting nothing less than a six-course dinner. At the end of this line of tables stood the largest portable grill I had ever seen, all shining metal, knobs and compartments, supporting mounds of steaks and spareribs and supervised by an obese young man wearing a spotless apron and another cowboy hat.

"My god," exclaimed a woman in a stage whisper, "it's a barbecue cum hoedown. Where's the fiddler and square dance caller?"

Suddenly a mariachi trio came strolling through the hedge, all decked out in huge sombreros with lots of silver adorning their short, colorful jackets. I supposed it made sense that as long as we were pretending to be in Texas, we could take a quick hop across the border and be thematically multicultural.

People were seating themselves quickly, probably exhausted after the Clarathon, and the tables were filling up fast. I spotted a table with a vacancy and, after being told it was available, took my seat. The ritual of introductions among tablemates now took place, as names were stated, only to be mostly forgotten except, because I made an effort, for the two women on either side of me. The lady on my left was Edna, who was with her husband Robert (or Richard or Roland or Rupert or Ralph? – I knew it began with an R and wasn't Rhinehart). Edna's mother must have repeatedly told Edna when she was a child never to talk to strangers, for now, in advanced middle age, she could barely give three-word responses to any of my polite overtures. From her shy, timid, self-conscious answers, one would think I was asking her to tell me her net worth or to describe her sexual fantasies.

The young lady on my right was a polar opposite. Fat, jolly and loquacious, Helen, I quickly learned, lived in Wantagh, Long Island, was thirty-three, unmarried and worked as a veterinarian's assistant. The main focus and great love of her life, she told me, was breeding lhasa apsos. She proudly mentioned that she had bred Clara and Sherry, which, given the composite picture I had formed from the testimonials at the just completed service, didn't speak well for Helen's breeding skills. Helen was eager to sample the food and she and I chatted easily as we moved along the buffet line together.

The food was prodigious for both its abundance and its variety, and Helen's eyes glistened as she surveyed all the offerings. By the time we had finished with the hors d'oeuvres and salad sections, she had filled two plates and was looking perplexed as we approached the myriad warming trays offering assortments of vegetables, meats and pastas. I suggested that she deposit her two filled plates at our table and start anew, which she did, and another two plates were quickly filled. We returned to our table where our tablemates eyed Helen's booty with barely concealed disdain.

"What a wonderful selection!" she exclained happily. "Everything looks so good, I couldn't resist anything."

Smirks, disguised as smiles, from the rail-thin ladies at the table whose own plates were sparsely occupied, mostly with salad and a few shrimp, greeted Helen's remark, but, obliviously, she plunged on.

"I'm on a seafood diet. I eat all the food I see!" she said with a rush of laughter, mocking herself and undercutting the contempt of her silent accusers.

This was obviously not a crowd of hearty eaters nor, for that matter, could they be described as merry makers. Except for a brief exchange of comments on the traffic patterns they had encountered in coming here and the unusually warm weather for this time of year, conversation quickly lagged, and Helen was too busy devouring her food to engage in any further talk. A silence, awkward and pronounced, pervaded our table. I, too, concentrated on eating my food.

"Let's hit the desserts," Helen said enthusiastically, wiping the last of her food plates clean with a cheese role. I followed her back to the buffet tables, happy to have escaped the Siberian silence. Helen quickly selected a crème brule, a piece of Black Forest cake and a wedge of strawberry-rhubarb pie, plus an assortment of large, freshly baked cookies. When her two plates could accommodate nothing more, she reluctantly returned to our table. Again the other ladies stonily eyed her mounds of sweets while their plates displayed only some fresh strawberries and a cookie or two, nibbled on but not consumed. As though she was still ravenously hungry, Helen finished her desserts so quickly that they seemed to just disappear as part of a magic act.

"That Black Forest cake is so good, I think I'll have another piece," she announced, but before she could rise from her seat,

Patti's voice could be heard from the far side of the tent, and spoons were tapped against glasses in a signal for silence.

"I hope you all enjoyed the food that Suzanne, our wonderful caterer, prepared. I recently took a cooking course in the city but since I don't cook, I passed along some recipes to Suzanne who graciously made them for us today. I think she's marvelous; don't you?"

Patti pointed toward a stunning young blond standing by the dessert table and led the crowd in a round of applause. Suzanne smiled broadly and waved to everyone; then the audience turned its attention back to Patti who took a long drink of wine before continuing.

"This is a special day for our family, and we want to share our happiness with all our friends in welcoming the return of my stepson, Ralph."

Patti turned to face the sullen boy on her right.

"Your dad and I and your sister, China, are so pleased to have you back with us again, Ralph, and we know that this time you'll stay."

Ralph sat scrunched in his chair, his face a tomato red, radiating anger and embarrassment. His eyes were mere slits, shooting lethal darts at Patti, who turned again to the audience and continued.

The commandant at Ralph's ranch sent us a lovely note saying that after some false starts, Ralph had eventually seen the light and turned into a good cadet who accepted responsibility for his past actions and was resolved to lead a clean and sober life. So please join Henry and me in toasting our Ralph's return and offering him our love and support."

Turning again to face Ralph, Patti raised her wine glass.

"Your struggles will, no doubt, be many, but we love you and will be there for you, dear Ralph, every step of the way."

The assembled guests raised their glasses and a collective shout "To Ralph" echoed through the tent. Ralph's face had practically disappeared under the table. Patti continued.

"Ralph's off to a new boarding school next week but after Henry and I return from our trip to the Far East, we'll enjoy a two-week holiday reunion with Ralph and China before heading out for one of Henry's conventions in Aspen and a little skiing. And before you know it, it will be summer again and we'll be reunited right here for more glorious family fun."

As an afterthought Patti added: "Of course, Ralph will also spend some time with his mom over the holidays when her busy travel schedule permits."

People were quickly losing interest as indicated by the rising level of chatter in the tent. I turned to speak to Helen but she was gone. I glanced toward the dessert table but she was not there. Then we heard a large bell sounding from outside the tent and I recognized Helen's voice in full throttle.

"Special Delivery for the Davis family!" she hollered, as she appeared at the side of the tent, holding a large box with a big pink bow. Carefully, Helen made her way toward Patti's table while several waiters scurried about clearing the dishes and silverware so that when Helen arrived at the head table, she was able to set the box down on a clear space. Patti rose from her seat and with a huge grin untied the bow.

"Now, dear friends, we want you all to meet the newest member of our family," she shouted excitedly.

She reached into the box and removed a wriggling ball of fur.

"This is Sherry's new baby sister, Sonia."

Patti held the squealing puppy aloft and now I could see that it was another lhasa apso, evidently supplied once again from Helen's breeding stock. As if on cue, the puppy peed down the front of Patti's dress and everyone, including Patti, laughed uproariously. Barking was now heard outside the tent and then Sherry appeared, her fur flying as she raced toward Patti's table and jumped into her arms, while the puppy yelped in fright. Patti cradled each dog in one arm and after Sherry had stopped licking Patti's face and neck and collarbone, she turned her attention to Sonia and immediately started to growl, followed by a lunge toward the puppy with bared teeth. Clearly, Sherry was not well disposed to playing big sister.

"Sherry, now stop that!" Patti said with no severity in her tone. "You be nice to your new sister!"

Sherry, still growling, remained unrepentant. Patti placed the puppy back in its box and Helen left the tent with both dogs.

Henry now rose and in a peremptory voice thanked everyone for coming. The festivities were over and we were officially dismissed, but many people lingered at their tables, chatting over coffee or returning for one last dessert.

In leaving the tented area I somehow got confused and turned in the wrong direction. As I rounded another high hedge, I came upon a small, informal garden with a Victorian gazebo in the far, shaded corner. The sun was in my eyes and I was about to turn back when I dimly made out a silhouette in the gazebo. After focusing for a second more, the silhouette became discernible: the entwined bodies of a man and woman. They hadn't seen me and I was about to beat a hasty retreat when my brain, catching up with my eyes, registered the identities of the embracing couple: Henry and Suzanne, the caterer. Surreptitiously I slipped away, pondering the ways of the older, successful American male and vowing that my future would follow another trajectory. Off in the distance I could hear Sherry's barking and Patti's nasal rebuke, and I recognized that such scenes were bound to have limited runs, like trips to amusement parks or exotic vacations.

Ignoring my well-mannered impulse to say goodbye to my hostess, I hurried to the front courtyard with an urgent need to return to life of the ordinary. Helen was just getting into her station wagon and offered me a lift to the train station. She chatted all the way about what a wonderful couple Henry and Patti were and what an ideal life they led. The late afternoon sun tossed sharp etchings against the windshield, obscuring the trees and sky and houses, and we rolled along in a landscape of dreams.

In Transit

Summer of '65

She hadn't expected the drive to be so painful. For the first sixty miles or so, she was fine because Tom and she frequently traveled all the main roads radiating out from Manhattan, on visits to her in-laws in Connecticut, excursions to the Jersey shore or vacations on Cape Cod. As long as they were heading south, everything was usual, casual. It was only when they turned west that she started to focus on their destination and the purpose of this trip and she felt a tightness in her stomach and, soon, she had a mild tension headache.

The casual, relaxed conversation that flowed so easily between a couple married for five years, slowed to glancing remarks bridged with long periods of silence, equally understood and tolerated. By the time they crossed into northeastern Pennsylvania her headache was intense and her mood, sullen.

"I don't know why I decided to attend this tenth reunion," she suddenly said aloud, clearly annoyed with herself.

"Don't be silly, Patti," Tom said cheerfully. "It'll be fun. Besides, you get to see how all those high school kids turned out. And they get to see what a knockout I married."

His last remark plunged her into more conflicting thoughts as her mind raced between the past and the present. When she had gotten the reunion notice – How did they find her? How did they track her down? – she was instantly alarmed, as all the negative feelings, the images of awkward, alienating moments flooded over her like an emotional tsunami.

Even the name of the reunion chairperson at the bottom of the page, Barbara Sokolsky, evoked unhappy associations, and she had a vivid image of Barbara in all her blond seventeen-year-old lushness: clear skin, open face, jutting breasts and wide hips. And Barbara's kind, condescending smile toward her, Patricia Borden, the freak of the class, the chubby girl with severe acne who wore thick glasses and always had her nose in a book and didn't have any friends except for Jenny Pritchard (the girl who wore braces and was much fatter than Patti – another freak), and who didn't even have any family to speak of, except a wheelchair-bound mother, seldom seen, and who worked after school so she could afford private art lessons. She wanted to be an artist, which, in the eyes of her peers added to her peculiarity and made her a social outcast

Those memories of her former incarnation were too painful to revisit and she had tried to dismiss them. She had thrown the letter down on the console table in the foyer of her apartment but catching her image in the mirror above the table, enjoyed the contrast between the Patricia Borden of seventeen and the Patricia Borden-King of twenty-seven. The unhappy, insecure, lonely, longing-for-escape Patricia Borden of Cloverdale High School and the married, professionally successful – well, semi-successful – definitely attractive and confident Patricia Borden-King of Manhattan.

Her reflection was smiling at her. The body was slim and toned, the skin was smooth and shiny, the hair attractively styled, the glasses long ago replaced with contact lenses. She liked this Patricia and suddenly had an urge to show them what she had become, and, in showing them, prove something to herself. The teenager who had never been invited to parties or outings, who was not asked to the junior or senior prom, who never had a boyfriend, had metamorphosed into an attractive, poised young woman who had come to the big city, pursued an artistic career as a fashion illustrator and captured a handsome, successful husband. Cinderella would go to the ball with her prince in tow, she decided in one, quick, exultant moment.

"I'll go back!" she announced defiantly to her image in the mirror. "I'll go back to that worn, grubby little community with its faded clapboard houses and perennially muddy roads, and those country bumpkins who never thought of anything except sex and sports and local, limited futures. And those tiresome teachers who thought all learning consisted of memorization, except for Mrs. Smith. She alone encouraged me and made me feel special with my art."

She took a pen from her purse and checked the "Yes, I will attend" box and wrote her name, Patricia Borden-King, and in the space after "Accompanied by," she listed Thomas King, husband. She dropped the reply, sealed and stamped, in the mail chute in the hall of her apartment building and refused to reflect any further on her action, fearing she would waver in her decision. But as the date for the reunion drew near and she began the process of selecting an outfit for the cocktail reception, followed by a dinner-dance, old doubts rose up and she grew increasingly uneasy. Still, she was committed and she would go.

"Shouldn't be much longer," Tom said, interrupting her private reflections, and her eyes saw for the first time the landscape now surrounding them, pastoral and gritty.

Tom reached over and squeezed her hand, and with that one small gesture she knew that he realized how difficult this trip was for her. In their idyllic days of courtship, she had shared all her unhappy memories of growing up without a father or siblings in a town where she was an object of pity. Patti's mother, crippled first with Hodgkin's disease, followed by the sudden onset of Alzheimer's, was crippled, too, with bitterness and anger over the course her life had taken, and took her resentment out on the only person available, her daughter. Whether Patti was in school or at home, she felt belittled and scorned.

But she escaped. She escaped through her books and through her art: designs, sketches, drawings, paintings. She withdrew into herself, into her private worlds, into her dreams of rising far above her oppressive life and her provincial community.

The spring semester of her senior year in high school was a happy time, even though she did not go to the senior prom or any of the graduation parties, or attend the big game when the Cloverdale football team won the divisional championship and the town went wild. Four weeks before her graduation, her mother had been placed in a nursing home and the minister and his wife took her in, until she graduated. Still, she was happier than she could ever remember because, with Mrs. Smith's help and recommendation, she had won a full scholarship to the Rhode

Island School of Design, and she knew she was going to realize her dream of escaping from her suffocating environment, and her life would change.

After the graduation ceremony had ended – she had received an award in art – and the families gathered with the graduates on the lawn to take pictures and congratulate one another, she marched out into the glaring sunshine and said nothing to anyone, except Mrs. Smith, whom she warmly hugged. That evening she went to Jenny Pritchard's house for dinner and a tearful farewell. Jenny cried; she didn't. The next morning she left for Providence.

She had never returned to her home town before this high school reunion. When her mother died a year later, she arranged for a cremation and had the ashes sent to her. She still had them, packed away in a trunk at the back of her closet. The minister had written to her about a memorial service but she refused. Her only connection to her past was an occasional exchange of notes and cards with Mrs. Smith until the teacher retired and moved back to Wisconsin to be with her family.

"Did you remember to call the motel?" Tom asked. "There might be a rush on rooms with alumni coming from out of town."

Patti laughed.

"I doubt that too many people ever left this place," she said. "This is the kind of town where everybody is perfectly happy to stay put. You work on a farm or in a coal mine or at the local factory, following in the footsteps of your parents, having lots of babies and attending church socials."

"Sounds like a certifiable outpost of civilization to me," Tom said, looking toward Patti with mock solemnity.

"The backbone of America," she said scornfully. "The motel should be on the left at the next crossroad."

She observed her husband's profile as he studied the road ahead. She loved his profile: the straight nose and strong jaw; the high forehead, the thick brown eyebrow arching toward his temple and the auburn hair curling around his ear and at the nape of his neck. The first time she ever saw him, it was in profile, she recalled fondly. He was standing at the counter of a bakery on Thayer Street in Providence. It was a Sunday morning and she spotted him the minute she walked in. Tall and lean, he reminded her of the popular boys in high school for whom she had been invisible. But this was four years after high school, and her transformation had taken place and those popular high school boys would notice her now. She casually made her way to a spot next to him at the counter and he glanced at her and smiled; not a dazzling smile, really, because his teeth, while straight and even, were an off-white color. But it was a warm smile, enhanced by blue eyes that seemed to have their own lights – smiling Irish eyes, she thought. He leaned down and in a conspiratorial tone whispered in her ear, "Have you tried the sticky buns? They're great!" She felt his warm breath against her cheek, and she knew she was blushing.

For all the physical changes that she had maneuvered – the super slimness, the smooth skin and blond-streaked hair and contact lenses – the butterfly that was emerging was still partially cocooned in the shell of the shy, rejected girl. She gave him a tentative smile but said nothing. When one of the women behind the counter was free to serve her, she ordered a coffee and a sticky bun, hoping that her following his recommendation would suggest her receptivity.

By chance, they both paid for their orders and left the bakery at the same time. He held the door for her and followed her out into the bright sunshine of a warm April morning.

He said, "Mind if I walk with you?" and she was aware of the warm tones of his voice.

"Not as long as it isn't out of your way," she said, trying to be casual.

"Even if it were, it would be worth it," he replied with another big smile, and she noticed how tall he was as he kept in step beside her.

He asked the typically light, flirtatious questions of any self-assured young man displaying an interest in an attractive young woman. He talked freely, animatedly, and she struggled to sound breezy but paused before each response. Her reticence and shyness, he told her later, after they had slept together, was what he found so attractive that first Sunday morning. By the time they had walked three blocks along Thayer Street, she had learned that he was a senior at Brown, majoring in history, that his family lived in Connecticut, and that he'd like to see her again. She imparted only that she was a senior at RISD, and, after several requests, gave him her phone number, with the resignation of her former self that he would never call.

Two days later he called. The following Friday they went to see a foreign film which they both disliked, and on Saturday they drove down to Westerly in his dark green Mustang and strolled along the beach, talking excitedly about the future that each was planning after graduation in less than two months: she to New York to start a career in fashion and he, in jubilant coincidence, to Columbia Law School. By this time she was much more relaxed, feeling more like the new Patricia Borden under his warmly appraising eyes and encouraging compliments.

They had taken off their shoes and socks and rolled up their jeans and were wading in the frigid surf, racing back toward the beach to avoid oncoming surges and shouting exuberantly when they miscalculated and a wave snapped at their knees. Walking back to the car he took her hand. His hand was large and warm and she felt strangely peaceful and protected with her hand enveloped by his. He was telling her about some eccentric professor – he had a gift for mimicry, she thought – and she was laughing and squeezing his hand in encouragement, when he suddenly pulled her to him and gently kissed her.

She was startled for only a moment and then it seemed like the most natural action to come at this time, after this glorious day at the beach, with the pounding surf and the screaming gulls and the warm sunshine on their arms and necks and bare legs, and his tall, firm body leaning into hers. She reached up and put her arms around his neck and returned his kiss ardently.

The next day, Sunday – only a week since she had ordered the sticky bun, but so miraculously comfortable did she feel with him that it seemed much longer – they drove to Newport for brunch at a waterside restaurant he knew. Over the Bloody Marys, too many, really, and the eggs Benedict, they unfolded their pasts, holding hands across the table as painful memories were shared.

His father was a lawyer, his mother, a decorator, and he had lost his older brother, Jim, in an auto accident as Jim was returning from his high school prom, a passenger in the car that was going too fast. Jim was three years older than Tom, who, as the middle child – he had a younger sister, Michele – felt his role in the family change perceptibly as weighted expectations were shifted to him.

In questioning him for other details about his life and assessing his forthright responses, Patti concluded that, except for this one horrifically traumatic event that Tom had experienced at fifteen, the rest of his history revealed him to be a well adjusted and confident kid, a good student and capable athlete, raised in a loving, upper-middle-class home and cocooned in his attractiveness and popularity. The persistent dreariness, the isolation and near despair of her history was a sharp contrast to his, but under his warm gaze and supportive gestures she found herself talking freely and talking faster, as all the emotional havoc of her childhood came spilling out in one long regurgitating binge, and she, for the first time, fully unburdened herself of the hurt and pain and searing memories. He clutched both her hands as her tears flowed, and then he reached across the table and, with his napkin, brushed them from her cheeks and, without his eyes leaving her contorted face, peremptorily shooed the approaching waiter away.

When she had finished, he poured her another Bloody Mary from the pitcher he had ordered, and said simply, "I understand."

She didn't feel the depletion one would expect after such an emotional purge; rather, she felt uplifted, unburdened, even light-headed, to have finally shared the stark reality of her life with another human being who accepted it all and said supportively, "I understand."

She was giddy from his intimate acceptance, his undisturbed attraction for her, his unexpected depth of empathy, and she rose from her seat and stepped to his side of the table and kissed him on the lips.

They slept together that night in a motel between Newport and Providence. The awakening of her sexual being was so surprisingly natural that it seemed like there had been another person harbored within her body who finally revealed herself. Nothing was tainted; nothing was sinful. She expressed her passion like an explorer avidly advancing on newly discovered land.

He was startled by her boldness, her aggression; she was like some primordial woman, like Eve before the fall, who innocently responded to all urges and all suggestions with no self-consciousness, no shyness. Her spirited cooperation with all his initiated actions drove him to an uninhibited fervor he had never experienced with any girl before, as fantasies were acted out in the most natural, gleeful way. Their sexual romp continued through the night into the small hours of the morning. Before leaving the motel, they both had declared their love for each other.

"There it is!" Tom announced brightly, pointing ahead to a large sign announcing the motel, but she was still lost in her thoughts.

Tom King, the love of her life, her personal Prince Charming, the handsome, up-and-coming lawyer, the smiling, happy, even-tempered Tom King, who had taken her virginity and, even after five years of marriage, burned the bed sheets nearly every night with their inexhaustible appetite for each other, was, outside the bedroom, she was loathe to admit, a boring man. He was smart but not curious; dependable but always cautious; passionate but not romantic; comfortable but never spontaneous. His life had been mapped out for him, and now for her, too, by his parents: law school – corporate law like his father – eventually a partnership; a Manhattan co-op, the down payment, a gift from his father; vacations on the Cape at a compound that had been in his family for three generations; children – but not, she insisted, until they were both better established in their careers. She felt the pressure from both Tom and his parents who would indulge her for only a short time more.

Tom had accepted this predetermined life plan complacently, with no rebellious fixations, no yearnings, his only dreams being mere aspirations that would eventually become reality as part of the master plan. At twenty-nine his life – and her life – was set in amber for the next forty years, an endless cycle of work, dinners, sex and sleep, with periodic outings with friends and family get-togethers, and then children wedged in the interstices. What she admitted only to herself – it was too weird, almost un-American, certainly unnatural, to be shared with anyone – was that she had reservations about being a mother.

Most disheartening of all, she knew that Tom viewed her own career as a mere indulgence; something to occupy her days until she became a full-time mom; something similar to his own mother's work as a decorator before her children arrived. He recognized neither her talent nor her passion for her work, the only pursuit that had ever brought her recognition and validation. She bitterly resented his attitude.

The immutability of this planned life path frightened and distressed her. She thought of the classic Peggy Lee song, "Is That All There Is?" to which she, Patti, answered: Yes. She had settled for comfortable contentment and foregone happiness. A handsome, successful husband was proof to the world that she was a desirable female, a person worthy of love and admiration, a proud member of the universal club. Fulfilling her inner needs was another matter. She had caught the gold ring, but she knew it was only brass.

As they pulled into the motel, she thought she was gong to be sick.

* * * *

On Tom's arm she walked into the school library where the cocktail reception was being held. This was the one room in the school where she felt comfortable, remembering all the quiet hours she had spent here, reading and day-dreaming. But she was not feeling comfortable now and could feel beads of perspiration trickling down her sides.

She knew she looked good. She had chosen her black cocktail dress for its simple lines and elegant details, and a quick glance at the assembled group showed her that hardly any other woman was wearing black, which was just the effect she wanted. She had taken special care with her hair and makeup and she wore the good pearls that Tom's mother had given her as a wedding present. Her black pumps had the latest heel shape. Draped casually across her arm was a multi-colored cashmere shawl.

She thought Tom looked very handsome in his dark blue blazer, gray slacks, pin-stripe shirt and light blue tie. His broad smile reflected the ease with which he met the world.

She saw that most eyes had turned to them as they made their entrance, but under these stares she was momentarily transformed into the image of herself at seventeen, and she felt herself trembling. She clung more firmly to Tom's arm as they walked to the registration table, and the first person she recognized was Barbara Sokolsky.

"Welcome," Barbara said with a large smile. "Name, please."

Patti chose not to acknowledge Barbara by name, as if she had forgotten her. She could tell from the openly quizzical look on Barbara's face that she hadn't recognized her.

"Patricia Borden-King," she said in too loud a voice.

Barbara, who had been looking down at her list when Patti gave her name, held her pen in mid-air as her head bolted upward and her eyes searched Patti's face, clearly struggling to fit her longstanding image of Patricia Borden with the svelte, chic and very attractive Patricia Borden-King who appeared before her.

"Oh, my god, Patricia, how you've changed! I would never have recognized you."

Barbara put her pen down and rose from her seat. Patti saw how the curvaceous body of seventeen had quickly turned to a uniformly broad silhouette as Barbara came around the table and threw her arms around Patti as if she were greeting her long-lost best friend.

"You look terrific!" Barbara gushed. "I would never have believed it."

Patti's momentary delight in seeing the startling effect that her transformed appearance had on Barbara was now replaced with annoyance when this last comment evoked all the unhappy images of her former self. And why was Barbara greeting her so affectionately when she hardly spoke to Patti during their four years of high school?

"Thank you," said Patti, managing a half-smile. "This is my husband, Tom."

Barbara's eyes, which had been riveted on Patti's face – Patti wondered if Barbara thought she had had plastic surgery – flicked to Tom and her clear look of amazement remained frozen on her face.

"And what a handsome guy you snagged for yourself!" She said, extending a hand to Tom.

The buzz in the room was audible as people who had been standing near the reception table when Patti gave her name, now moved out among the crowd and spread the news. Patti could feel her skin turning red under her makeup, as most eyes were staring at her, scrutinizing, assessing.

"The bar's been set up at the check-out counter," Barbara said, pointing toward the old wood circular counter in the middle of the library that Patti knew so well. "We'll have dinner in the gym at seven-thirty. Some of our old teachers are joining us for dinner."

Patti knew that Mrs. Smith was not well and would not be among the teachers; she had no interest in seeing any of the others.

"Here's your name tag." Barbara continued. "Be sure to wear it please." Then she added, "If you don't, no one's going to believe it's you."

Barbara's emphasis on the amazing contrast served only to transport Patti involuntarily back to her former self again. She resolved to stay in the present, so she smiled, pinned the name tag carefully on her dress, and, still clutching Tom's arm, steered him toward the bar.

Their progress was slow, as men and women came forward to greet her – men and women who, as boys and girls, had largely ignored her or pretended she didn't even exist. She had little trouble recognizing most of them since she had secretly studied them in high school, observing their interactions from afar as though they were alien creatures, listening to their conversations as she sat alone in the cafeteria, since Amy Pritchard, her only friend, went home for lunch, or, again sitting alone on the school bus, staring fixedly out of the window, pretending to find the scenery endlessly interesting, while she monitored the joking and jostling and high spirits of the "in-crowd," gathered, in herding instinct, at the back of the bus. They were never nasty or mean to her, except for that one time in her senior year when Lois Rutledge was walking down the main corridor with her usual cohort of popular girls, and, spotting Patti at her locker, stopped, and, in a loud voice, said, "Hi Patricia. Who's your date for the prom?" Before she could even turn to face them, with absolutely no answer forming in her brain, the group had hurried on, their laughter trailing after them. But usually they just ignored her, reducing her to invisibility: a non-entity, like a piece of school furniture or the printed slogans on the school cafeteria's walls.

A chorus of "Hello Patricia" echoed around her as smiling faces blocked her progress toward the bar, and hands were extended in greeting – no hugs or kisses, just hands – and she saw the confused curiosity on their faces. Longing for a drink, she smiled back but there was little conversation. No wonder, she thought. They have no knowledge of me, no memories to draw on for any conversation except that I had existed in their midst and now suddenly reappear among them as a very different woman, escorted by a beaming and handsome man.

A sea of faces pressed around her, while she was repeatedly told that she looked terrific or great or wonderful or sensational, before the chorus of voices awkwardly retreated from her, with nothing more to say. Some of the women just scrutinized her from a distance, eyes narrowed, lips pursed, straining to recall her previous incarnation.

"Now that's what I'd call a grand entrance!" Tom said, after they finally reached the bar, and he ordered a gin and tonic for both of them.

She was enjoying her first sip when a large pair of arms encircled her from behind and a voice she instantly recognized said, "I didn't think you'd come."

She fumbled her drink, gave a little cry, and turned to embrace Amy Pritchard. Then Amy stood back and looked straight at Patti.

"My god, you're beautiful! What have you done to yourself?"

"It's the magic of makeup and a good hair stylist, and, most of all, a rigid diet and exercise program," Patti said, and then she regretted her words. Amy, who had always been fat, was now huge. But the broad smile never left Amy's face, and she said, "Well, whatever it is, it definitely works, and I want some. You're half the size you were in high school and…" placing her hands dramatically on her hips, continued, "I'm twice the size I was." She laughed, and Patti followed her lead.

Turning to Tom, Amy said, "And who's this handsome fella?"

"I'm the proud husband of this beautiful woman," Tom said, beaming, and extending his hand, but Amy pushed her huge bosom against him and gave him a peck on the cheek. Then she put her arm behind her and, as though she were producing a rabbit out of a hat, pulled forward a short, skinny man with a receding hairline who had been blocked by her enormous frame.

"And this is my husband, Walter," she said proudly.

Walter had the shy, nervous look of someone dressed in his Sunday best who feels uncomfortable. Patti noted his ill-fitting polyester jacket and out-of-style tie, but was taken with his warm, tentative smile. He shook hands with Tom, then with Patti, who made no motion to duplicate Amy's kiss. This formality over, he gladly retreated to Amy's side.

"Let's find a corner where we can catch up," Amy suggested, and they moved away from the bar, as Amy led the way to the least crowded area of the library. The tables had all been removed to accommodate the crowd, but chairs were lined up against the wall and they found four and settled into an intimate circle.

At first the conversation was animated between Amy and Patti, with their husbands smiling in the background. The general histories of their lives were quickly summarized. Amy had married a year out of high school and now had three children, all girls. Pictures were produced and appropriate praise rendered. Walter worked on his father's farm, which would someday be his, in the next county. They lived in the father's farmhouse with the father, a widower, and the youngest of Walter's brothers who was unmarried. Last year they had taken the kids to Disney World for a week, but otherwise they hadn't traveled, except to county fairs.

After a brief summary of Patti and Tom's history, Amy asked Patti a few questions about her work as a fashion illustrator, and then asked Tom about corporate law, but the absent look in her eyes suggested that fashion and law were worlds beyond her range of interests, so their replies were brief.

"What about children?" Amy asked with excitement, to which Patti tersely replied, "None."

"Oh, I'm sorry," said Amy, her face contorting in genuine commiseration.

"Oh, No," Patti added quickly. "We plan to have children, just not right now, when we're still struggling with our careers."

Amy offered a sad little smile and shook her head in an "I see" gesture. Patti could tell from the look on Amy's face that she might as well be speaking in Japanese, so foreign was the notion to Amy of pursuing any career before having children – a flagrant violation of the natural order of things – and Patti saw the great divide that now separated her from her only childhood friend.

In a short time they had exhausted their common links. Patti wasn't interested in crop rotation or the teething cycle of babies or the price of fertilizer; and Amy wasn't curious about life in the Big Apple, having already formed some vaguely threatening vision of New York, without ever having visited the city.

Then it occurred to Patti that her long-ago friendship with Amy was based on the exclusivity of their having been the class castoffs. It had not developed from common interests or similar personalities. Rather, their friendship was forged in loneliness, and confined to a mutual sympathy, an acknowledgment of their isolated status and the expediency of joining forces to serve as a modest bulwark against the dismissive world.

Amy rose from her seat.

"We're not staying for dinner," she announced. "I don't trust Walter's brother with the kids too long. He'll fall asleep in front of the TV and the kids will get into mischief." She paused. "Actually, I just came because I was hoping to see you."

Amy smiled, but Patti understood. They had met again after ten years and quickly exhausted their shared history and mutual interests. Amy gave Patti a warm hug, and Tom and Walter shook hands, but neither woman offered any suggestion about getting together or coming for a visit.

"It was good to see you," was all Amy said in a tone suggesting that seeing Patti for the first time as an adult brought recognition of the strangers they now were. Patti mumbled "Yes," and watched the huge woman and her skinny husband disappear into the crowd.

"How about another drink?" Tom asked.

Patti nodded, yes, and he was off. She sat quietly in the corner of the library, separated from the animated crowd, feeling like the old Patricia Borden, the isolate, the outsider. The people who had greeted her during her grand entrance and journey to the bar hadn't changed much since high school, except for receding hairlines on some of the men and thickening waists with most of the women. The snatches of conversation she overheard centered on children and family, deaths and jobs; not professions or college experiences or travels or adventures or politics or the arts. She noted how so many of them had paired up not too long after high school, content with the familiarity of shared boundaries and sense of place, and a perpetuation of life as lived by parents and grandparents, rendering time inconsequential.

Again she questioned herself on why she had come back, as anger started rising inside her. I wanted to show them how much I had changed and how far I had gone from this hick town. But I'm still the freak! Only now, instead of standing out for being the homely girl with strange interests, I'm a standout for my New York clothes, my work, my smart looking husband and our having no children. I couldn't be more different from these people if I were a Martian!

Then she had a disturbing thought as she watched the print dresses meld into a swirling kaleidoscope and recognized that the irreducible pattern of their lives, the daily routines of work, dinner, chores and sex, was not that different from hers, other than focus. And kids. Children were clearly at the center of any fulfillment they felt: their self-congratulatory, mutual admiration society; their proudest reason for being. Now, with a force that caused her to physically shudder, she recognized another glaring truth: She really didn't want children. Not with Tom; not with anyone. Not ever.

Something else to set me apart from others, she told herself angrily. I'm missing the most fundamental gene in all females: the maternal instinct. Her thoughts tumbled downward from that jarring recognition and she saw with equal clarity that her marriage to Tom was doomed.

She gazed out at the room with tearful eyes, wishing she could be more like these people who seemed to find a happy resolution to the big questions of life in this little pocket of the world, while she yearned and dreamed and searched and questioned and thought and thought and thought, a restless, driven soul who would probably always be a pariah, an outsider.

"Here we go," Tom said, holding two plastic cups, but seeing the frightened look on her face, asked, "Are you okay?"

She swam up from far below the surface and looked out at her husband.

"I have to leave!"

Tom looked confused.

"Are you sick?" he asked solicitously.

She didn't bother to answer, but rose from her chair and, looking neither right nor left – how well she had mastered the straight-ahead stare so many years ago in this building! – marched briskly though the crowd, with Tom following in her wake, and out the door.

Printed in the United States
100168LV00003B/251/A

9 781600 471650